Nora Roberts & J. D. Robb

REMEMBER WHEN

J. D. Robb

Anthologies

SILENT NIGHT
(with Susan Plunkett, Dee Holmes, and Claire Cross)

OUT OF THIS WORLD
(with Laurell K. Hamilton, Susan Krinard, and Maggie Shayne)

BUMP IN THE NIGHT
(with Mary Blayney, Ruth Ryan Langan, and Mary Kay McComas)

DEAD OF NIGHT
(with Mary Blayney, Ruth Ryan Langan, and Mary Kay McComas)

THREE IN DEATH

SUITE 606
(with Mary Blayney, Ruth Ryan Langan, and Mary Kay McComas)

IN DEATH

THE LOST
(with Patricia Gaffney, Mary Blayney, and Ruth Ryan Langan)

THE OTHER SIDE
*(with Mary Blayney, Patricia Gaffney, Ruth Ryan Langan,
and Mary Kay McComas)*

TIME OF DEATH

THE UNQUIET
*(with Mary Blayney, Patricia Gaffney, Ruth Ryan Langan,
and Mary Kay McComas)*

TIME OF
DEATH

J. D. ROBB

INCLUDES THREE FAVORITES

ETERNITY IN DEATH

RITUAL IN DEATH

MISSING IN DEATH

JOVE BOOKS, NEW YORK

THE BERKLEY PUBLISHING GROUP
Published by the Penguin Group
Penguin Group (USA) Inc.
375 Hudson Street, New York, New York 10014, USA
Penguin Group (Canada), 90 Eglinton Avenue East, Suite 700, Toronto, Ontario M4P 2Y3, Canada
(a division of Pearson Penguin Canada Inc.) • Penguin Books Ltd., 80 Strand, London WC2R 0RL,
England • Penguin Group Ireland, 25 St. Stephen's Green, Dublin 2, Ireland (a division of Penguin
Books Ltd.) • Penguin Group (Australia), 707 Collins Street, Melbourne, Victoria 3008, Australia
(a division of Pearson Australia Group Pty. Ltd.) • Penguin Books India Pvt. Ltd., 11 Community
Centre, Panchsheel Park, New Delhi—110 017, India • Penguin Group (NZ), 67 Apollo Drive,
Rosedale, Auckland 0632, New Zealand (a division of Pearson New Zealand Ltd.) • Penguin Books,
Rosebank Office Park, 181 Jan Smuts Avenue, Parktown North 2193, South Africa • Penguin China,
B7 Jaiming Center, 27 East Third Ring Road North, Chaoyang District, Beijing 100020, China

Penguin Books Ltd., Registered Offices: 80 Strand, London WC2R 0RL, England

This is a work of fiction. Names, characters, places, and incidents either are the product of the author's
imagination or are used fictitiously, and any resemblance to actual persons, living or dead, business
establishments, events, or locales is entirely coincidental. The publisher does not have control over
and does not have any responsibility for author or third-party websites or their content.

TIME OF DEATH

A Jove Book / published by arrangement with the author

PUBLISHING HISTORY
Berkley trade edition / July 2011
Jove mass-market edition / December 2012

Copyright © 2011 by Nora Roberts.
"Eternity in Death" by J. D. Robb copyright © 2007 by Nora Roberts;
previously published in *Dead of Night*.
"Ritual in Death" by J. D. Robb copyright © 2008 by Nora Roberts;
previously published in *Suite 606*.
"Missing in Death" by J. D. Robb copyright © 2009 by Nora Roberts;
previously published in *The Lost*.
Cover art: Badge copyright © by Dan Farrall / Getty Images; 3D caution tape copyright © by
Zentilla / Shutterstock; wall clock copyright © by Pchstudios / Shutterstock.
Cover design by Andrea Tsurumi.

ISBN: 978-0-515-15280-7

JOVE®
Jove Books are published by The Berkley Publishing Group,
a division of Penguin Group (USA) Inc.,
375 Hudson Street, New York, New York 10014.
JOVE® is a registered trademark of Penguin Group (USA) Inc.
The "J" design is a trademark of Penguin Group (USA) Inc.

PRINTED IN THE UNITED STATES OF AMERICA

10   9   8   7   6   5   4   3   2   1

ALWAYS LEARNING   **PEARSON**

CONTENTS

ETERNITY IN DEATH

The Sun's rim dips; the stars rush out,
At one stride comes the dark.

—COLERIDGE

Whence and what art thou, execrable shape?

—JOHN MILTON

PROLOGUE

Death was the end of the party. Worse than death, in Tiara's opinion, was what came before it. Age. The loss of youth, of beauty, of body and *celebrity* was the true horror. Who the hell wanted to screw an old, wrinkled woman? Who cared what some droopy bag of years wore to the hot new club, or what she didn't wear on the beach at the Côte d'Azur?

No-fucking-body, that's who.

So when he told her that death could be the beginning— the real beginning—she was fascinated. She was pumped. It made sense to her that immortality could be bought by those privileged enough to pay the price. All of her life everything she wanted, coveted, demanded had been bought, so eternal life wasn't any different, really, than her pied-à-terre in New York or her villa in France.

Immortality, unlike a penthouse or a pair of earrings, would never get boring.

She was twenty-three, and absolutely at her prime. Every-thing about her was tight and toned, which she assured herself of by examining her body in the mirror tube in her dressing room. She was perfect, she decided, giving her signature blond mane a carefully studied, and meticulously practiced, toss.

Now, thanks to him, she would always be perfect.

She stepped out, leaving the double mirrored doors open so that she could watch herself dress. She'd chosen form-fitting, nearly transparent red, with a hem of peacock eyes that shimmered and winked with every movement. Chandelier drops swung at her ears, in the same vibrant tones of sapphire and emerald as the accents on the hem of the short, snug gown. She added her blue diamond pendant, and wide pave cuffs on both wrists.

Her sharply defined lips were dyed to match the dress, and they curved now with smug pride.

Later, she thought, after it was done, she'd change into something fun, something for dancing, for celebrating.

Her only regret was that the awakening had to be done in private rather than at the club. But her lover had assured her all that nasty business about being buried, then having to climb out of some disgusting coffin was just the invention of tacky books and bad vids. The reality was so much more civilized.

One hour after the ritual—which was so frigging *sexy*— she'd wake up in her own bed, eternally young, eternally strong, eternally beautiful.

Her new birthday would be April 18, 2060.

All it would cost was her soul. As if she cared about that.

She strolled out of the dressing room into the bedroom she'd just had redecorated in her new favorite shades of blues and greens. In his bed—canopied to match his mistress's— Tiara's teacup bulldog snored.

She wished she could awaken Biddy as she was about to be awakened. He was the only thing in the world she truly loved almost as much as herself. But she'd given her little sweetie pie the sleeping drug, just as she'd been told. It wouldn't do to have her doggie interrupt the ritual.

Following instructions, she disengaged all security on her private elevator and entrance, then lit the thirteen white candles she'd been told to set around the room she'd chosen for the awakening.

When it was done, she poured the bottle of potion he'd given her into a crystal wineglass. She drank it all, every drop. Nearly time, she thought, as she carefully arranged herself on the bed. He'd slip in quietly, find her. Take her.

Already she felt hot and jittery with need.

He'd make her scream, he'd make her come. And when she was screaming, when she was coming, he would give her that final, ultimate kiss.

Tiara traced her fingers over her throat, already feeling the bite.

She'd die, she thought, running her hands over her breasts and belly in anticipation of him. Wasn't that wild? She'd die, then she'd awaken. And she'd live forever.

CHAPTER

ONE

The room smelled of candle wax and death. In their fat, jewel-toned holders, the candles had pooled into dripping puddles. The body lay in a lake-sized bed canopied with silk, mounded with a multitude of pillows, and stained with blood.

She was young, blond, with a bright red dress rucked up to her waist. Her eyes, a crystal green, were open and staring.

As she studied the body of Tiara Kent, Lieutenant Eve Dallas wondered if the dead blonde had looked into her killer's eyes as she died.

She'd known him, in any case, almost certainly she'd known him. There was no sign of forced entry, and in fact, the security system had been shut down from the inside, by the victim. There was no sign of struggle. And though Eve was certain they'd find the victim had engaged in sexual intercourse, she didn't believe it would prove to be rape.

She hadn't fought him, Eve thought as she bent over the

body. Even when he'd drained the blood out of her, she hadn't fought him.

"Two puncture wounds, left side of the throat," Eve stated for the record. "The only visible injury." She lifted one of Tiara's hands, examined the perfectly shaped, fussily painted nails. "Bag the hands," she told her partner. "Maybe she scratched him."

"Not as much blood as you'd think there should be." Detective Peabody cleared her throat. "Not nearly enough. You know what they look like, on her neck there? Bite marks. Like, ah, fangs."

Eve spared Peabody a glance. "You think that ugly little dog the maid's got in the kitchen bit her on the neck?"

"No." Peabody angled her head, leaned down with her dark eyes wide and bright. "Come on, Dallas, you *know* what it looks like."

"It looks like a DB. It looks like the vic had a date that went over the top. There's going to be illegals in her system, something that dulled her down or hyped her up enough for her killer to jab something into her throat, or, yeah, sink his teeth into it if he had the incisors filed to points or was wearing an appliance. Then he bled her out, and she lay there and let him."

"I'm just saying it looks like your classic vampire bite."

"We'll put out an APB on Dracula. Meanwhile, let's find out if she was—just possibly—seeing someone with a heartbeat."

"Just saying," Peabody repeated, this time in a mumble.

Eve did another scan of the bedroom before stepping out and into the enormous dressing room area.

Bigger than a lot of apartments, she mused, and outfitted with a security screen, entertainment screen, full round of mirrors. The closet itself was a small department store, ruthlessly organized into categories.

For a moment, Eve stood with her hands on her hips and

simply stared. One person, she thought, with enough clothes to outfit the Upper West Side, and more than enough shoes to shod every man, woman, and child in that sector. Even Roarke—and Eve knew her husband's wardrobe was awesome—didn't rate this high on the clothes-hog scale.

Then she just shook her head and focused on the job at hand.

Dressed for him, Eve thought. Slutty dress, fuck-me heels. So where was the jewelry? If a woman was going to deck herself out for a booty call, down to shoes, wouldn't she drape on some glitters?

If she had, her killer had helped himself there.

She studied the drawers, the cabinets that ran below the rungs and carousels and protective domes. All locked, she noted, all passcoded, which meant valuables housed inside. There was no sign that she could see of any attempt to break in.

There were plenty of expensive bits and pieces sitting around in the penthouse: statuary, paintings, electronics. She'd seen nothing on her once-over of both levels that indicated anything had been disturbed.

If he was a thief, he was a lazy one, or a very picky one.

She stood for a moment, evaluating. Eve was a tall woman, slim in boots and trousers, with a short leather jacket over a white shirt. Her hair was short and brown, chopped around a lean face dominated by deep brown eyes. The eyes, as they studied, were all cop.

She didn't turn at Peabody's low whistle behind her. "Wow! This is like something out of a vid. I think she had all the clothes in all the land. And the *shoes*. Oooh, the shoes."

"A few hundred pair of shoes," Eve commented. "And she had the requisite two feet. People are screwy. Take head of building security, see if he's got any knowledge or documentation of who she's been seeing or entertaining in the last few weeks. I'll take the maid."

She moved through the apartment, down a level. The place was full of cops and crime-scene techs, of noise, of equipment. The busy business of murder.

In what she was told was the breakfast room, she found the maid with her red-rimmed eyes, clutching the small, ugly dog. Eve eyed the dog warily, then gestured for the uniforms to step out of the room.

"Ms. Cruz?"

At the mention of her name, the woman burst into fresh sobs. This time Eve and the dog exchanged looks of mild annoyance.

Eve sat so she and the maid were on the same level, then said, firmly, "Stop it."

Obviously used to following orders, the maid instantly snuffled back the sobs. "I'm so upset," she told Eve. "Miss Tiara, poor Miss Tiara."

"Yes, I'm very sorry. You've worked for her for a while?"

"Five years."

"I know this is hard, but I need you to answer some questions now. To help me find who did this to Miss Tiara."

"Yes." The maid pressed a hand to her heart. "Anything. Anything."

"You have keys and passcodes to the apartment?"

"Oh, yes. I come in every day to do for Miss Tiara when she's in residence. And three times a week when she's away."

"Who else has access to the apartment?"

"No one. Well, maybe Miss Daffy. I'm not sure."

"Miss Daffy."

"Miss Tiara's friend, Daffodil Wheats. Her very best friend, except when they're fighting, then Miss Caramel is her best friend."

"Are you putting me on with these names?"

The maid blinked her swollen, bloodshot eyes. "No, ma'am."

"Lieutenant," Eve corrected. "All right, this Daffodil and

Caramel were friends of Miss Kent's. What about men? What men was she seeing?"

"She saw a lot of men. She was so beautiful, so young, and so vibrant that—"

"Intimately, Ms. Cruz," Eve interrupted to stop both the eulogy and the fresh tears. "And most recently."

"Please call me Estella. She enjoyed men. She was young and vibrant, as I said. I don't know them all—some were just a moment, others longer. But in the past week or two, I think there was just one."

"Who would that be?"

"I don't know. I never saw him. But I could tell she was in love again—she laughed more, and danced around the apartment, and . . ." Estella seemed to struggle for a moment with her own code of discretion.

"Everything you tell me may help in the investigation," Eve prompted.

"Yes. Well . . . when you take care of someone, you know when they've had a . . . an intimacy. She had a lover in her bed every night for a week or more."

"But you never saw him."

"Never. I come at eight every morning, and leave at six, unless she needs me to stay longer. He was never here when I was here."

"Was it her habit to turn off her security system from in-house?"

"Never, never." Dry-eyed now, Estella shook her head decisively from side to side. "It was never to be disengaged. I don't understand why she would have done that. I saw it was off when I came in this morning. I thought there must be a glitch in the system, and Miss Tiara would be angry. I called downstairs to report it even before I went up to the bedroom."

"All right. You came in at eight, noted the security was off, reported it, then went upstairs. Is that your usual routine, to come in, go up to her bedroom?"

"Yes, to get Biddy." Estella bent her head to nuzzle the

dog. "To take him for his morning walk, then to feed him. Miss Tiara usually sleeps until about eleven."

Estella's brow creased. "Later these last days, since—the new lover. Sometimes she didn't come downstairs until into the afternoon, and she ordered all the windows draped when she did. She said she only wanted the night. It worried me because she looked so pale, and wouldn't eat. But I thought, well, she's in love, that's all."

After a long, long sigh, Estella continued. "Then this morning, Biddy wasn't waiting by the bedroom door. He always waits there for me in the morning. I went in, very quietly. He was coming to the door, but he wasn't walking right."

Eve frowned at the dog. "What do you mean?"

"It was . . . I thought: Biddy looks drunk, and I had to hold back a laugh because he looked so funny. I went in more, and I smelled . . . it was the candles at first. I could smell the candles, so I thought she'd had her lover in the night. But then there was another smell, a hard smell. It was the blood, I think," she said as her eyes welled again. "It must have been the blood and . . . her, I smelled her, and when I looked over at the bed, I saw her there. I saw my poor little girl there."

"Did you touch anything, Estella? Anything in the room?"

"No, no. Yes. Biddy. I grabbed Biddy. I don't know why exactly, I just grabbed little Biddy and I ran out. She was dead—the blood, her face, her eyes, everything. She couldn't be anything but dead. I ran out screaming, and I called security. Mr. Tripps came right up. Right away, and he went upstairs. He was only a minute, then he came down to contact the police."

"Could you tell if anything's missing?"

"I know her things. I didn't notice . . ." Distressed again, she glanced around the room. "I didn't look."

"I'm going to have you look through her jewelry first. You know her jewelry?"

"I do. Every piece. I clean it for Miss Tiara because she doesn't trust—"

"Okay. We'll start there."

She sent Estella to the dressing area with two cops and a recorder. She was scribbling a few notes, adding time lines when Peabody tracked her down.

"Tripps reports that the maid contacted Security at eight-oh-two to report the system was down. She contacted them again at eight-oh-nine, hysterical. He came up personally, went upstairs, verified the death, contacted the police. Times jibe."

"Yeah, they do. What did he say about the system being down?"

"He said—and documented—that Kent told him she would be shutting it down internally near midnight, and would re-engage it when she wanted. He advised against, she told him to mind his own. She did the same every night for the last eight days, though the time of shutdown varied. She'd re-engage before dawn."

Thoughtfully, Eve tapped her fingers on her own notes. "So the boyfriend didn't want to be on the security tapes. Got her to shut it down, came in her private entrance, left the same way. She must've been monumentally stupid."

"Well, she wasn't known for her brains."

Eve slanted Peabody a look. If it was gossip or popular culture, Peabody usually had her finger on the pulse. "What was she known for?"

"Clubbing, shuttle-hopping, shopping, scandals. The usual, I guess, for a fourth-generation—I think it's fourth—megarich kid. She got engaged a lot, broke up a lot—usually publicly and with a lot of passion. Went to premieres, shuttled off to wherever the current hot spot might be. Hobbed and nobbed. Usually something on her in the tabs or one of the gossip or society channels every day."

"Who was she running with these days, and why did I

feel I had to interview the maid about her lifestyle when I've got you?"

"Well, she's tight with Daffy Wheats, and Caramel Lipton, recently disengaged to Roman Gramaldi, of Zurich. But she hangs with the sparkles of the young, rich, and looking-for-trouble club."

"Trouble she found," Eve commented, then glanced up when Estella came rushing in.

"Her pendant, her blue diamond pendant, and the cuffs, her peacock earrings. Gone, all gone." Her voice pitched up sharply enough to cut glass. "He robbed my poor little girl, robbed her and killed her."

Eve held up a finger to stop the tirade. "Do you have photo documentation of the missing items?"

"Of course, of course. Insurance—"

"I'll need those. You get me the insurance information of whatever's missing. Go ahead." She waited until Estella hurried out again, smiled grimly. "That was a mistake. Sooner or later some big, fat blue diamond's going to show up. We'll get the details, then inform next of kin. After that, I want to have a chat with Daffy."

TWO

As Tiara's mother was living with her fourth husband in Rome, and her father was currently vacationing on the Olympus Resort with his newest fiancée, notification was done via 'link.

Eve left the sweepers to finish processing the scene, and headed out with Peabody to interview Daffodil Wheats.

Another penthouse, Eve thought, another absurdly rich, young blonde. She badged and bullied her way past the doorman, past security, and finally past the housekeeper who might have been a clone of Estella Cruz. It turned out to be her sister.

The apartment was slightly smaller than Tiara's, a bit more tastefully furnished. They waited in a living area done in bold, vibrant colors while Martine Cruz went upstairs to wake her mistress and inform her the police wished to speak with her.

"What's the dish on this one, Peabody?"

"Um, third-generation rich, I think. Not as mega as the vic, but not worried about the grocery bill either. I think the fam made it big in textiles or something back in the day. Anyhow, she's another party girl and gossip channel regular."

"Who'd want to live like that?" Eve wondered.

"They do." Peabody gave a shrug. "You've got as much ready as they do, you can buy some privacy if you want it."

Eve thought back to the acres of mirrors and reflective surfaces at the crime scene. "The type who like to see themselves."

"Yeah, and unless Daffy and the vic were having one of their periodic fallings-out, they were pretty much joined at the hip. Played together, traveled together, and rumor has it shared some of the same men, maybe at the same time. Been tight since they were kids. Vic's father was married to Daffy's mother—or cohabbed, can't remember—for a couple of years."

"Small, incestuous little world."

Eve glanced up. Daffodil Wheats had a short, streaky crop of blond hair, sleepy blue eyes, and a sulky mouth. She wore a black silk robe that hit her midthigh and gaped open at the breasts so the full white mounds of them played peek-a-boo as she walked down the swirl of silver steps.

"What's the deal?" she said in a blurry voice, then plopped down on the bright red sofa and yawned.

"Daffodil Wheats?" Eve demanded.

"Yeah, yeah. God, it's barely dawn. Martine! I'm desperado for that mocha! I was out till four," she explained with a long, feline stretch. "I didn't do anything illegal, so what's what with the badges?"

"You know Tiara Kent?"

"Hell, what's Tee done now?" She slumped, obviously already bored. "Look, I'll bail her, even if she has been a bitch lately. But I have to have my fix first. Mocha, mocha, mocha!" she shouted like an Arena Ball cheer.

"I'm sorry to tell you that Tiara Kent is dead."

The sleepy eyes narrowed a little, then rolled dramatically. "Oh, get off. You tell Princess Bitch that dragging me out of bed to lay it on didn't get a chuckle. Thank God! Thanks, Martine. Life saved." She made kissy noises at the maid as she grabbed the tall white cup of steaming liquid.

"Listen up, *Daffy*." Eve's tone had the blue eyes blinking in surprise. "Your pal was murdered last night, in her bed. So you're going to want to straighten your ass up—and cover your tits, for God's sake—or we're going to take the rest of this downtown."

"That's not funny." Slowly now, Daffy lowered the cup. "That's seriously un." The hand holding the cup shook as Daffy reached out for Martine with the other. "Martine, call Estella. Call her right now and have her put Tiara on the 'link."

"She can't come to the 'link." Peabody spoke now, more gently. "Ms. Kent was killed last night in her apartment."

"My sister," Martine said even as she gripped Daffy's hand.

"Your sister's fine," Peabody told her. "You can go ahead and contact her."

"Miss Daffy."

"Go on," Daffy said stiffly, and the bored young party girl was gone. In her place was a stunned young woman clutching her robe together at her throat with a trembling hand. "Go on, go on. This isn't a joke, this isn't Tee taking a slap at me? She's dead?"

"Yes."

"But . . . I don't see how that can be. She's only twenty-three. You're not supposed to be dead at twenty-three, and we're fighting. We can't be fighting when she's dead. How . . . Killed? Did you say somebody killed Tee?"

Now Eve sat, choosing the glossy white table in front of the sofa so she and Daffy were on a level. "She's been see-ing someone recently."

"What? Yeah. But . . ." Daffy looked around blankly. "What?"

Reaching out, Eve took the cup of mocha from Daffy's limp fingers, set it aside. "Do you know the name of the man she's been seeing recently?"

"I . . . She called him her prince. Lots of times she had names for her men. This one was Prince. Dark Prince, sometimes." Daffy pressed her hands to her eyes, then dragged them up over her face, through her hair. "She's only been into him for a week or so. Maybe two. I can't think." She put her hand to her head, rubbed her temple as if she couldn't keep her fingers still. "I can't think."

"Can you describe him?"

"I never met him. I was supposed to, but I didn't. We've been fighting," she repeated as tears spilled down her cheeks.

"Tell me what you know about him."

"Did he hurt her?" Her voice broke on the question as the tears started to gush. "Did he kill Tee?"

"We're going to want to talk to him. Tell me what you know about him."

"She . . . she met him at some underground club. I was supposed to go, but I got hung up, and I forgot. I was supposed to meet her there."

"Where?" Eve prompted.

"Um . . . a cult club, underground, near Times Square, I think. I can't remember. There are so many." When Peabody offered tissues, Daffy sent her a pathetically grateful look. "Thanks. Thanks. She—Tee, she tagged me about eleven when I didn't show, and we got into it because I'd forgotten, and this guy I hooked up with and I decided to zip down to South Beach for the night. I was already down there when she tagged me."

On a long breath, she bent forward to retrieve the cup of mocha, and now sipped slowly. "Okay. Okay." She breathed in and out. "It was my screwup, about the club, so I mea culpa'd the next day. She was all about this guy, this Prince. But she looked out of it, so I knew she'd been using."

Daffy pressed her lips together. "I'm clean, and I've got to stay clean. My father still holds some of the purse strings on me, you know? If I get in any trouble like that again, he said he'd cut me off. He means it, so . . . Shit, you're cops. I'm not going to impress you, so the straight deal is this: Besides the edict from my dad, I've had enough of chems."

"But Tiara hadn't," Eve said.

"Tee's always going to go over the top, it's just her way. Always going to push the limits, then look for the next big thing." As Daffy mopped tears, she managed a wan smile. "But she knows I've got to stay clean. She'd been using, and she'd sworn off six months ago, like a solidarity deal? We took an oath, so I was pissed."

"What was she on?" Eve asked.

"I don't know, but she was strung. We scratched at each other about that, but it was mostly her telling me how I had to go with her to this club, meet this guy and his friends. She said he was complete, the absolute. That they'd banged all night, and it was the best she'd ever had. She nagged me brainless about it until I said I'd go."

Shaking her head, Daffy drank again. "Then later I started thinking how even if I didn't use, she would, and I'd get busted. So I tagged her back and told her I wasn't going, and why didn't we hook up with this guy somewhere else. No go. His club or nowhere."

"His club?"

"Not like he owned it. Or maybe he does. She never said; I never asked. But she got stewed because I wouldn't go, and Carm's in New L.A. until next month, so she couldn't pull her instead of me."

Eve waited while Daffy brooded into the mocha she'd so desperately wanted. "Do you know if anyone else went with her to this club? Any of your other mutual friends?"

"I don't think so. I never heard any buzz about it, not from anyone but Tee. Anyway, we didn't talk for a couple days, then yesterday she came by here, earlier than this even.

Like just after sunrise. She looked bottomed. Pale and glassy-eyed. Using again, and she hadn't been using before this run for that whole six months. She was still hyped, talking wild. Going to live forever, that's what she said. Laughing and busting around. She and her prince were going to live forever, and screw me for flipping her off. I tried to get her to stay, but she wouldn't, just told me I'd be sorry, I'd had my chance. Now he was only taking her."

"Taking her where?" Eve asked.

"I don't know. She wasn't making any sense. I'm telling you, she was over. I got pissy right back at her, and we yelled at each other, then she stormed out. And now she's dead."

"That's the last time you saw or spoke with her?"

"Yeah. Did he hurt her? I mean . . . you didn't say how she, she died. Did he hurt her?"

"I can't tell you that yet, I'm sorry."

"She's such a baby about pain." Daffy swiped the back of her hand over her cheek. "I hope he didn't hurt her. I should've gone to the club that night. If I'd gone to the club instead of South Beach, maybe . . . Is it my fault? I should've looked after her better. She got sucked into stuff so easy. Is it my fault?"

"No, it's not your fault."

"She was almost a year older, but I was the one who looked after her—mostly. I could pull her back from the edge when she went too far. But I didn't, you know? I just told her she was being an idiot or whatever. Only Tee would actually believe in vampires."

"Vampires?" Eve repeated as Peabody sucked in her breath.

"Yeah. The prince deal? The Dark Prince. Living forever. Get it?" Daffy gave a harsh laugh that choked on a sob. "She thought this guy was a frigging vampire, like for real, and he was going to make her one so she'd be immortal. That's what the club was—a wannabe vampire club. Bloodbath! I remember now. It's called Bloodbath. Who the hell wants to go to some club with a name like that?" She swiped at tears again. "Only Tee."

"Didn't I say vampire? I said vampire right off." Peabody gave a smug nod as they exited the building.

"And our vic's going to be deeply disappointed when she just stays dead. Track down this club. I'd love a little chat with the Dark Prince."

"It's not like I believe in the undead or anything." Peabody slid into the passenger seat. "But it wouldn't hurt, once we find this guy, to interview him during the day. In a room with good natural lighting."

"Sure. And requisition some garlic and some wooden stakes while you're at it."

"Really?"

"No." Eve swung out into traffic. "Reach down inside yourself, Peabody, and get a grip on reality, however slippery. Find the club. Right now we're going to visit somebody who knows all about what's dead."

Chief Medical Examiner Morris sent Eve an easy smile as he stood over the naked body of Tiara Kent. He wore a snappy suit the color of good claret with a matching tie thin as straw. His dark hair was intricately braided, and curled into a loop at the nape of his neck.

Eve often thought Morris's sharp fashion sense was wasted on his clientele.

"Running a bit behind today," he told them. "Sent off for tox as you'd flagged that. Shouldn't take long."

She glanced down at the body. Morris hadn't yet made his Y cut. "What can you tell me just from the visual?"

"Lieutenant, this woman is dead."

"Peabody, note that down. We've got a dead woman."

"With excellent breast work," Morris added. "And some very first-class sculpting, belly and butt."

"Jesus, she was twenty-three. Who needs sculpting and new tits at twenty-three?"

Peabody raised her hand, and got a bland look from Eve.

"You're not twenty-three."

"Okay, I've got a couple years on her, but if they're handing out butt sculpting, I'm first in line."

"You have a very nice butt, Detective," Morris assured her, and made Peabody beam.

"Aw, thanks."

"And now, back to our regularly scheduled program?" Eve suggested. "The dead woman on the slab."

"Tiara Kent, party princess. Live fast, die young." Morris tapped his comp screen to magnify the neck wounds. "These are the only injuries or insults to the body. The victim was exsanguinated through these two punctures in the carotid. No visible signs of physical restraint or struggle. Apparently, she lay there and let him suck her dry."

"Suck." Peabody drew a righteous breath through her nose. "See? Vampire bite."

Morris's smile spread to a grin. "Impossible not to have a little play with that, isn't it? The beautiful young blonde, seduced by the Prince of Darkness—or one of his minions— drained of her life's blood while in his thrall. Cue fog and shadows."

"Don't forget the creepy music," Eve added.

"Of course. Mostly, however, I suspect she was drugged to the eyeballs, and was punctured by an appliance during sex."

He lifted his eyebrows as he looked down at Tiara. "Of course, I could be wrong, and she'll pop up shortly after sundown and terrify the night staff."

"Let's go with number one," Eve decided. "If he actually

bit her, appliance or not, there's going to be saliva. Same if he didn't use a cloak for sex. I bet even vampires have DNA."

"I'll send samples to the lab."

"Guy had her convinced he could give her eternity." Eve took one last look at Tiara Kent. "Now she gets a steel box in a cold room."

THREE

"Got the club." Peabody studied the readout on her PPC as they drove toward Cop Central. "Daffy had it right about Times Square, it's under Broadway. Got the hours, too. Sunset to sunrise." Peabody tracked her eyes toward Eve's profile. "Vampire hours."

"Owner?"

"Eternity Corporation, no owner or manager listed in this data."

"Dig," Eve suggested.

"Digging. Are we going by the club now?"

"If the guy frequents the place, works in the place, or owns the place, he's not going to be there when the joint's closed. We'll go after dark."

"I knew you were going to say that. Aren't you just a little bit creeped? I mean, at the very least this guy slurps blood."

"Maybe he does, maybe he doesn't." Eve stopped at a light, and watched the throng bull, shuffle, and clip its way along the crosswalk. She saw a pair of transvestites in span-

gled skin-suits, a tourist approaching three hundred and
fifty pounds in his baggy shorts—carrying a variety of cams
and vids that had to weigh nearly what he did—a kid in a
red cape and skullcap streaking through bodies on an air-
board, and a mime.

Whatever weirdos existed, New York made them welcome. A self-proclaimed vampire would fit right in.

"She didn't leave a full pint on the sheets," Eve continued
as the light changed. "I don't care how hungry some pseudo-
vampire is, no way he's going to guzzle down more than
eight pints of blood in a sitting."

"Right. Right. Well, then what . . ."

"He took it with him."

"I have to say eeuuw."

"Bottled it up, bagged it up. Maybe he sells it, maybe he
stores it, maybe he takes a fucking bath in it. But he came
prepped for it." She turned into the garage at Central. "So
we work that. What's a guy do with several pints of human
blood? Let's see if there's a call for it on the black market.
And we have the list and description of the jewelry missing
from the scene. We've got the club."

She pulled into her slot, climbed out. "We'll see what the
sweepers got for us, see if the lab can pull DNA. We'll check
like crimes, see if we got anything like this before."

Once inside the elevator, Eve leaned back. The car
smelled like cop—coffee and sweat. "Somebody saw her
with this guy. She hooked up with him at the club, and
somebody saw them together. She goes for thrills, gets
drawn in. Starts letting him into her place, fun and games.
The way it looks, he could've killed her any time he wanted,
robbed her freaking blind. But he waited, and he only took
what she either had on or had out.

"He's picky, and he likes the ritual, likes the seduction."

Eve stepped off the car to switch to the glides before the
elevator got crowded. "Go ahead and write up what we've
got, keep looking for a name to go with the club. I'm going

to try to get a session in with Mira, get a better idea of what we'll be dealing with when we take ourselves a Bloodbath."

"I'll bring the rubber ducky."

Eve peeled off in the bullpen, headed for her office. As she expected, her 'link was loaded with calls from the media. A paparazzi darling ends up dead, it's a ratings bonanza, she thought, and ruthlessly forwarded all of the calls to the media liaison.

She tried for Mira first and ran headfirst into Mira's admin—the guardian at the doctor's gate. "Okay, okay. Jesus. Just tell her I'd like five whenever she can spare it. Here, there, in adjoining stalls in the john. Just five."

Eve disconnected, got coffee from her AutoChef. She set up her murder board, wrote up her notes, studied the time line.

Walked right in, that's what he did. She practically showered his path with rose petals. More money than brains.

Did he mark her first, or was it just chance she walked into the club one night? A recognizable face that liked to dance on the wild side. Known more for her exploits than her smarts.

A pathetically easy mark.

But if it had been just for the score, why kill her at all, much less in the chosen method? Because the score was secondary, she decided. The killing was the prize.

Eve glanced toward her tiny window, into the light of a sunny spring day, and calculated the time until sundown.

Thinking of that, she winced, engaged her 'link again. She wasn't just a cop, she reminded herself, but a wife. There were rules in both jobs.

She tried Roarke's private line, intending to leave a voice mail telling him she'd be late, see you when, but he picked up on the first beep. And that face, the heat-in-the-belly sexuality of that face, filled her view screen.

Dark hair framed it. Eyes of wild Irish blue gave her heart

just a quick flutter that even after two years of having them look at her, just that way, was a surprise. Those perfectly sculpted lips curved as he said, "Lieutenant," with the wisp of his homeland in the word.

"How come you're not busy buying Australia?"

"I'm just between buying continents at the moment. I believe Asia's up next. And how are you?"

"Okay. I know we had sort of a thing on for tonight—"

"Dinner, I believe it was, followed by naked poker."

"That was strip poker, as I recall."

"You'd be naked soon enough. But I'm thinking that competition's been postponed. You have Tiara Kent, I take it."

"Heard about her already?"

"Multimillionaire bad girl murdered in her luxury penthouse?" His eyebrows lifted. "Word travels. How did she die?"

"Vampire bite."

"That again?" he said and made her laugh.

"She was into some kind of vampire cult crap, and it came back to, well, bite her. I've got to check out this club where she likely met her killer. It doesn't open until sunset, so I'm going to run late."

"Almost as interesting as naked poker. I'll meet you at Central by six. Darling Eve," he continued before she could speak, "you can't expect me to pass up the opportunity to accompany my wife into the den of the undead."

She considered a moment. He'd be useful; he always was. And another pair of eyes, another set of reflexes would come in handy underground.

"Don't be late."

"I'll leave in plenty of time. Should I pick up some garlic and crosses on the way?"

"I think Peabody's on that. Later," she said, and clicked off.

While she was at her desk, she contacted the lab to give them a not-so-gentle push, then began to research vampire lore. She broke off when Peabody poked her head in.

"Did you know there are dozens of websites on vampirism, and any number of them have instructions on how to drink from a victim?"

Peabody cocked her head. "This surprises you because?"

"I know I say people suck, but I didn't mean it literally. And it's not just kids in their I'm-so-bored twenties into this."

"I've got a couple of names we might want to look at, but meanwhile, Tiara Kent's mother just came in. I had one of the uniforms take her to the lounge."

"Okay, I'll take her, you keep digging." Eve pushed back from her desk. "Roarke's going to tag along tonight."

"Yeah?" Relief showed on Peabody's face before she controlled it. "It doesn't hurt to have more of us when we head down."

"He's an observer," Eve reminded her. "I'm waiting for a callback from Mira. That comes through, tag me."

Eve made Iris Francine the minute she stepped into the lounge with its lines of vending machines and little tables, and chairs designed to numb the ass after a five-minute sit-down.

Her daughter had favored her, taking the blond hair, the green eyes, the delicate bone structure from her mother.

Iris sat with her hand clutched by a man Eve imagined was husband number four, Georgio Francine. Younger than his wife by a few years, Eve judged, and dark and sultry where she was light and elegant.

But they sat like a unit—she recognized that. Like two parts of a whole.

"Ms. Francine, I'm Lieutenant Dallas."

Iris's eyes looked exhausted as they lifted to Eve's, a combination Eve also recognized as grief, guilt, and simple fatigue.

"You're the one in charge of . . . in charge of what happened to Tiara."

"That's right." Eve pulled up a chair. "I'm very sorry for your loss."

"Thank you. Will I be able to see her?"

"I'll arrange that for you."

"Can you tell me how she . . . what happened to her?" Iris's breath hitched, and she took two slow ones to smooth it out. "They won't tell me anything, really. It's worse not knowing."

"She was killed last night, in her apartment. We believe she knew her killer, and let him in herself. Some pieces of her jewelry are missing."

"Was she raped?"

They would always ask, Eve knew. For a daughter, they would always ask, and with their eyes pleading for the answer to be no. "She'd had sexual relations, but we don't believe there was rape."

"An accident?" There was another plea in Iris's voice now, as if death wouldn't be as horrible somehow if it were accidental. "Something that got out of hand?"

"No, I'm sorry. We don't believe it was an accident. What do you know about your daughter's activities recently, her companions? The men in her life?"

"Next to nothing." Iris closed her eyes. "We didn't communicate much, or often. I wasn't a good mother."

"Cara."

"I wasn't." She shook her head at her husband's quiet protest. "I was only twenty when she was born, and I wasn't a good mother. I wasn't a good anything." The words were bitter with regret. "It was all parties and fun and where can we go next. When Tiara's father had an affair, I had one to pay him back. And on and on, until we loathed each other and used her as a weapon."

She turned her shimmering eyes to her husband as he lifted their joined hands, pressed his lips to her fingers. "Long ago," he said softly. "That was long ago."

"She never forgave me. Why should she? When we divorced, Tee's father and I, I married again like that." Iris snapped her fingers. "Just to show him he didn't matter. I paid for that mistake six months later, but I didn't learn. When I finally grew up, it was too late. She preferred her father, who'd let her do whatever she liked, with whomever she liked."

"You made mistakes," Georgio told her. "You tried to fix them."

"Not hard enough, not soon enough. We have an eight-year-old daughter," she told Eve. "I'm a good mother to her. But I lost Tiara long ago. Now I can never get her back. The last time we spoke, more than a month ago, we argued. I can never get that back either."

"What did you argue about?"

"Her lifestyle, primarily. I hated that she was wasting herself the way I did. She was pushing, pushing the boundaries more all the time. Her father's engaged again, and this one's younger than Tee. It enraged her, had her obsessing about getting older, losing her looks. Can you imagine, worried about such things at twenty-three?"

"No." Eve thought of the mirrors again, the clothes, the bodywork Tiara had done. Obviously, this was a young woman who obsessed about anything that had to do with herself. "Did she have any particular interest in the occult?"

"The occult? I can't say. She went through a period several years ago where she paid psychics great gobs of money. She dabbled in Wicca when she was a teenager—so many girls do—but she said there were too many rules. She was always looking for the easy way, for some magic potion to make everything perfect. Will you find who killed her?"

"I'll find him."

Even as Eve made arrangements to have the Francines transported to the morgue, she saw Mira come in. After an acknowledging nod, Mira wandered to a vending machine.

She'd cut her hair again, Eve noted, so it was short and springy at the nape of her neck, and she'd done something to that soft sable color so that little wisps of it around her face were a paler tone. She sat, trim and pretty in her bluebonnet-colored suit, with two tubes of Diet Pepsi.

"Iris Francine," Mira stated when Eve came over. "I recognized her. Her face was everywhere a generation ago. I always thought her daughter was hell-bent on outdoing her mother's youthful exploits. It seems she succeeded in the hardest possible way."

"Yeah, dying will get you considerable face time, for a while."

"Quite a while, I'll wager in this case. Vampirism. I had a meeting one level up," Mira explained, "and thought to catch you in your office. Peabody gave me the basics. Murder by vampire proponents is very rare. For the most part, it's the danger, the thrill, the eroticism that draws people— primarily young people. There is a condition—"

"Renfield Syndrome. I've been reading up. What I'm getting from the people who knew the vic was a predilection to walk the edge, a desperation for fame, attention, a serious need to be and stay young and beautiful. She'd already had bodywork. And you have to add in sheer stupidity. I get her. She's not unusual, she just had more money than most so she could indulge her every idiocy."

Eve paused as she broke the seal on the Pepsi tube. "It's him. The method of killing was very specific, planned out, and there was no attempt to disguise it. He took jewelry, but that was more of the moment than motive. He went there to do exactly what he did, in exactly the way he did it."

"The compulsion may be his," Mira considered. "A craving for the taste of blood, one that escalated to the need to drain his victim. Have you gotten the autopsy results as yet?"

"No."

"I wonder if they'll find she drank blood as well. If so, you may be dealing with a killer who believes he's a vampire, and who sought to turn her into one by taking her blood and sharing his own with her."

"And if at first you don't succeed?"

"Yes." Mira's eyes, a softer blue than her suit, met Eve's. "He may very well try again. The rush, the power—particularly when coupled with scx and drugs—would be a strong pull. And she made it so easy for him, even profitable."

"How could he resist?"

"And why should he?" Mira concurred. "He was able to enter her highly secured building undetected. More power, and again cementing the illusion of a supernatural being. She gave herself to him, through sex, through blood, through death. Held in thrall—whether by his will or chemicals—another element. He removed her blood from the scene. A souvenir perhaps, a trophy, or yet another element of his power. His need for blood, and his ability to take it. You believe she was drugged?"

"I haven't had that confirmed, but yeah. Her closest pal states she'd been using, and heavily, the last week or so."

"If he drank any of her blood, he'd have shared the drug." Seeing Eve had already considered that, Mira nodded. "More power, or the illusion of it. From what you know, they'd only met a week or two earlier. It wasn't eternal love, which is one way of romanticizing vampirism."

"I don't get that." Interrupting, Eve gestured with her drink. "The romantic part."

Mira's lips curved. "Because you're a pragmatic soul. But for some, for many, the idea of eternity, that seeking a mate throughout it, coupled with the living by night, the lack of human boundaries is extremely romantic."

"Takes all kinds."

"It does. However, the way he left the body wasn't romantic, or even respectful. It was careless, cold. Whether or not he believes he could sire a vampire through her, she was no more than a vessel to him, a means to an end.

"He'll be young," Mira continued. "No more than forty. Most likely attractive in appearance and in good health.

Who would want eternal life if they were homely and physically disadvantaged?"

"This vic wouldn't have gone for anyone who wasn't pretty anyway. Too vain. Her place was loaded with mirrors."

"Hmm. I wonder how she resigned herself to the lore that she'd have no reflection as a vampire."

"Could be she only bought what she wanted to buy."

"Perhaps. He'll be precise, erudite, clever. Sensual. He may be bisexual, or believe himself to be, as in lore, vampires will bed and bite either sex. He will, at least for the moment, feel invulnerable. And that will make him very dangerous."

Eve drank some of her soft drink, smiled. "Knowing I'm mortal makes me very dangerous."

CHAPTER

FOUR

Eve grabbed the tox report the second it came through. Then she stared at the results. She engaged her interoffice 'link, said only, "Peabody," then went back to studying the lab's findings.

"Yo," Peabody said a moment later at Eve's office doorway.

"Tox report. Take a look." Eve passed her a printout while she continued to read her computer screen.

"Holy crap. It's not what she took," Peabody decided, "it's more what didn't she take."

"Hallucinogens, date-rape drugs, sexual enhancers, paralytic, human blood, tranq, all mixed in wine. Hell of a cocktail."

"I've never seen anything like this." Peabody glanced over the printout. "You?"

"Not with so many variables and with this potency. It's new to me, but let's run it by Illegals and see if it's new to them. According to the results, and the time line, she downed this herself, before she disengaged the alarm, or just after. Maybe she knew what was in it, maybe she didn't. But she drank it down, on her own."

"Hard to say, seeing she's dead, but she pretty much wins the stupid prize."

"All-time champ." Eve paused as her machine signaled another incoming. "And we may have a runner-up. We've got DNA." She scanned the data quickly. "Semen, saliva, and the blood she ingested. All the same donor."

"Pretty damn careless of him," Peabody commented.

"Yeah." Eve frowned at the screen. "It is, isn't it?"

"Another conclusion is he just didn't care—being a vampire." Peabody shrugged as Eve glanced back at her. "He doesn't care if we match his DNA because he'll just, I don't know, turn into a bat and fly off, or poof into smoke. Whatever."

"Right. A whole new scope on going into the wind."

"I'm not saying it's what I think, but maybe what he thinks."

"We'll be sure to ask him when we find him. Meanwhile, go ahead and run the cocktail by Illegals. I'll do a standard search for the DNA match. Maybe he's in the system."

But she didn't think so. He wasn't careless, Eve thought. He was fucking arrogant. It didn't surprise her when her search turned up negative.

"Lieutenant."

She glanced over, experienced that quick heart punch when her eyes met Roarke's. He was dressed in the dark suit he'd put on in their bedroom that morning, one of the countless he owned tailored to fit his long, rangy frame.

"Right on time," she said.

"We aim to please." He stepped in, eased a hip onto the corner of her desk. "How goes the vampire hunting?"

"I don't think we'll have to call in Van Helsing." When he lifted his brows and grinned, she shrugged. "I do my research. Plus I've sat through some of those old vids you like so much."

"And so armed, we'll venture into the den of the children of the night. Never a dull moment," he added and flicked his fingers at the choppy ends of her hair. "Your case is all over the media."

"Yeah. Bound to be."

"I noticed the primary hasn't given a statement."

"I'm not going to play the game on this one, or give this asshole the satisfaction. She drugged her own brains out prior—mix of Zeus, Erotica, Whore, Rabbit, Stunner, Bliss, Boost, along with a few other goodies, including her killer's blood."

"There's an ugly recipe."

"And my money says he provided the brew, pushed on her vanity and stupid buttons, got his rocks off, then drained her like a faulty motor."

"For what purpose?" Roarke wondered.

"Best I can tell, he wound her up because he could. And he killed her because he could. He'll want to do it again, real soon."

"Foolish of him, don't you think, to have chosen such a high-profile victim?"

She'd considered that, and had to appreciate being married to a man who could think like a cop. "Yeah, smarter, safer to bite a vagrant off the street. But this was more fun, more exciting. Why snack on street whores or sidewalk sleepers, the nobodies, when you can gorge yourself on the prime? Plus, it was profitable. A street level LC isn't going to be sporting blue diamonds. He's stoked, believe it, watching all the media coverage."

"Unless he's spent the day napping in his coffin."

"Ha-ha." She pushed up, instinctively brushed a hand over the weapon at her side. "Almost sundown. Let's go clubbing."

Peabody was lying in wait, along with her cohab, E-Division Detective McNab. He wasn't just a fashion plate, but an entire place setting, and was decked out in pants of neon blue that appeared to be made up almost entirely of pockets. He'd matched it with a bright green jacket with streaks of yellow jagged across it and some sort of skinny tank that melded all the colors of the spectrum in a kind of eye-searing cloudburst.

"I thought we could use another pair of eyes," Peabody began even as Eve's eyes narrowed. "You know, strength in numbers."

"I did a rotation in Illegals when I was still in uniform." McNab grinned out of his pretty, narrow face. "And when I worked Vice, we ran into all kinds of freaky shit."

"You don't want to miss a chance to cruise a vampire club."

His smile turned winsome. "Who would?"

She could use him, Eve thought, but she gave him the hard-eye first, just for form. "This isn't a damn double date."

"No, sir." So he waited until Eve turned her back to walk to the elevator before hooking pinkies with Peabody.

"Illegals hasn't worked the combo," Peabody began once they'd shoehorned into the elevator. "They don't even have Bloodbath on their list of watch points. But they have worked a combination of Erotica, Bliss, Rabbit, with traces of blood—usually animal blood—in cases of vampire fetishism. They call it Vamp, and the use generally skews young. They haven't had any homicides as a result of."

"Our guy upped the stakes, considerably. Have to wonder why the club hasn't made their list."

"It's new," Peabody told her. "Way underground. Hadn't hit their radar until I contacted them regarding our investigation."

"Underground clubs pop up faster than weeds," McNab put in. "Live or die on word of mouth. Since it's more than urban legend that people tend to go down and not come back up, they don't get heavy tourist traffic."

"Tiara Kent found out about it somewhere." Eve strode off the elevator and into the garage.

"Crowd she runs with." Peabody jerked a shoulder. "New place with a jagged edge? It would be right up her alley."

"And in less than two weeks from the first time she goes down, she's guzzling a new, exciting illegals cocktail, and dies from a neck wound." Eve slid behind the wheel of her vehicle. "That's fast work, smooth work when you consider the security in her building never made him." She glanced over at Roarke. "How much would a few pints of human blood net on the black market?"

"A few hundred."

"What about famous human blood?"

"Ah." He nodded as she drove out of the garage. "Yes, that might drive up the price to the right buyer. Are you thinking she was specifically targeted?"

"It's an angle. She's known, and she's known to take risks, to slut around, to live wild. Her best friend hadn't heard of the club before Kent clued her in. So maybe the idea or an invitation got passed straight onto the vic. In any case, she hooked up with her killer there, so someone saw them together. Someone knows him."

"You know," McNab speculated, "if you factor out the blood-sucking, soulless demon angle, this should be a slam dunk."

"Good thing none of us believe in blood-sucking, soulless demons." But Peabody's hand crept over and found McNab's.

Eve caught the gesture in the rearview, just as she caught the way the fingers of Peabody's free hand snuck between the buttons of her shirt to close over something.

"Peabody, are you wearing a cross?"

"What? Me?" The hand dropped like a stone into her lap. Her cheeks went pink as she cleared her throat. "It just happened that I know Mariella in Records, who just happened to have one, and I happened to borrow it. Just for backup."

"I see. And would you also be carrying a pointy stick?"

"Not unless you mean McNab."

McNab smiled easily as Eve stopped at a light, turned around in her seat. "Repeat after me: Vampires do not exist."

"Vampires do not exist," Peabody recited.

With a nod, Eve turned back, then narrowed her eyes at Roarke. "What's that look on your face?"

"Speculation. Most legends, after all, have some basis in fact. From Vlad the Impaler to Dracula of lore. It's interesting, don't you think?"

"It's interesting that I'm in this vehicle with a trio of lamebrains."

"Lamebrained to some," Roarke replied equably, "open-minded to others."

"Huh. Maybe we should stop off at a market on the way, pick up a few pounds of garlic, just to ease those open minds."

"Really?" Peabody said from the back, then hunched her shoulders as Eve sent her a stony stare in the rearview mirror. "That means no," Peabody muttered to McNab.

"I translated already."

Eve had to settle for a second-level street slot five blocks from the underground entrance. The sun had set, and the balmy April day had gone to chill with a wind that had risen up to kick through the urban canyons.

They moved through the packs of pedestrians—heading home, heading to dinner, heading to entertainment. At the mouth of the underground entrance, Eve paused.

"Stick together through the tunnels," she ordered. "We can work in pairs once we get to the club, but even then, let's keep visual contact at all times."

She didn't believe in the demons of lore, but she knew the human variety existed. And many of them lived, played, or worked in the bowels of the city.

They moved down, out of the noise, out of the wind, into the dank dimness of the tunnels. The clubs and haunts and dives that existed there catered to a clientele that would make most convicted felons sprint in the opposite direction.

Offerings underground included sex clubs that specialized in S&M, in torture dealt out for a fee by human, droid, or machine, or any miserable combination thereof. In the bars, the drinks were next to lethal and a man's life was worth less than the price of a shot. The violent and the mad might wander there, sliding off into the shadows to do what could only be done in the dark, where blood and death bloomed like fetid mushrooms.

She could hear weeping, raw and wild, echoing down one of the tunnels, and laughter that was somehow worse. She saw one of the lost addicts, pale as a ghost, huddled on the filthy floor, panting, pushing a syringe against his arm, giving himself a fix of what would eventually kill him.

She turned away from it, passed a sex club where the lights were hard and red and reminded her of the room in Dallas where she'd killed her father.

It was cold underground, as it had been cold in that room. The kind of cold that sank its teeth into the bone like an animal.

She heard something scuttling to the left, and saw the gleam of eyes. She stared into them until they blinked, and they vanished.

"I should've given you my clutch piece," she said under her breath to Roarke.

"Not to worry. I have my own."

She spared him a glance. He looked, she realized, every bit as deadly as anything that roamed the tunnels. "Try not to use it."

They turned down an angle beyond a vid parlor where someone screamed in a hideous combination of pain and delight.

She smelled piss and vomit as they descended the next level. When a man with bulging muscles stepped out of the dark, turned the knife he held into the slant of light so it gleamed, Eve simply drew her weapon.

"Wanna bet who wins?" she asked him, and he melted away again.

From there, she followed the strong vibration of bass, the scent of heavy perfume, and the ocean surf roar of voices.

The lights here were red as well, with some smoke blue, fog gray shimmered in. Mists curled and crawled over the floor. The doorway was an arch, to represent the mouth of a cave. Over the arch the word BLOODBATH throbbed in bloody red.

Two bouncers, one black, one white, both built like tanker jets, flanked the arch, then stepped together to form a wall of oiled muscle.

"Invitation or passcode," they said in unison.

"This is both." Eve pulled out her badge, and got twin smirks.

"That doesn't mean jack down here," the one on the left told her. "Private club."

Before she could speak again, Roarke simply pulled out several bills. "I believe this is the passcode."

After the money passed, the bouncers separated to make an opening. As they walked through, Eve shot Roarke an annoyed look. "I don't have to bribe my way in."

"No, but you were going to hurt them, and that's a lot messier. In any case, it was worth the fee as you take me to the most interesting places."

The club was three open levels, dark and smoky, with the pentagram bar as the center. A stage jutted out on the second level where a band played the kind of music that bashed into the chest like hurled stones. Fog crept over it like writhing snakes. Patrons sat at the bar, at metal tables, lurked in corners or danced on platforms. Nearly all wore black, and nearly all were well under thirty.

There were some privacy booths and some were already occupied with couples or small groups smoking what was likely illegal substances inside the domes, or groping each other. Eve's gaze tracked up to note there were private rooms on the third level. The club had a live sex license, and no doubt all manner of acts transpired behind the doors.

She approached the bar where a man or woman worked at every point of the pentagram. Eve chose a woman with straight black hair parted in the center to frame a pale, pale face. Her lips were heavy and full and dyed deep, dark red.

"What can I get you?" the woman asked.

"Whoever's in charge." Eve set her badge on the slick black metal of the bar.

"There a problem?"

"There will be if you don't get me whoever runs this place."

"Sure." The bartender drew a headset out of her pocket. "Dorian? Allesseria. I've got a cop at station three asking for the manager. Sure thing."

She put the headset away again. "He'll be right down. Said I should offer you a drink, on the house."

"No, thanks. Have you seen this woman in here, Allesseria?" Eve drew out Tiara's ID photo.

She saw recognition immediately, then the quick wariness. And then the lie. "Can't say I have. We get slammed in here by midnight. Hard to pick out faces in the crowd, and with this lighting."

"Right. You got anything on tap here but beer and brew?"

Once again, Eve saw the lie. "I don't know what you mean. I just run the stick at this station. That's it, that's all. I got customers."

"She's not only a poor liar," Roarke observed. "She's a frightened one."

"Yeah, she is." Eve scanned the crowd again. She saw a man barely old enough to make legal limit actually wearing a cape, and a woman, nearly a decade older, all but bursting out of a long, tight black dress, who was wrapping herself around him like a snake on one of the dance platforms.

Another woman in sharp red sat alone in a privacy booth and looked mildly bored. When a man wearing mostly tattoos glided up to the bar, ordered, Allesseria poured something into a tall glass that bubbled and smoked. He downed it where he stood, throat rippling, then set the glass down with a snarling grin that flashed pointed incisors.

Eve literally felt Peabody shudder beside her. "Jesus, this place is creepy."

"It's a bunch of show and theater."

Then Eve saw him coming down the corkscrew of steps from the top level. He was dressed in black, as would be expected. His hair, black as well, rained past his shoulders, a sharp contrast to the white skin of his face. And that face had a hard and sensual beauty that compelled the eye.

He moved gracefully, a lithe black cat. As he reached the second level, a blonde rushed toward him, gripped his hand. There was a pathetic desperation about her as she leaned into him. He simply trailed his fingers down her cheek, shook his head. Then he bent to capture her mouth in a deep kiss as his hands slid under her short skirt to rub naked, exposed flesh. She clung to him afterward so that he had to set her aside, which he did by lifting her a foot off the ground in a show of careless strength.

Eve could see her mouth move, knew the woman called to him, though the music and voices drowned out the sound.

He crossed the main level, and his eyes locked with Eve's. She felt the jolt—she could admit it. His eyes were like ink, deep and dark and hooded. As he walked to her, his lips curved in a smile that was both knowing and confident.

And in the smile she saw something that didn't cause that quick, physical jolt, but a deep and churning physical dread.

"Good evening," he said in a voice that carried a trace of some Eastern European accent. "I'm Dorian Vadim, and this is my place."

Though her throat had gone dry, Eve gave him an acknowledging nod. "Lieutenant Dallas." She drew out her badge yet again. "Detectives Peabody and McNab. And . . ."

"No introduction necessary." There was another quality to him now, what seemed to be a prickly combination of admiration and envy. "I'm aware of Roarke, and of you, Lieutenant. Welcome to Bloodbath."

CHAPTER

FIVE

She knew what she saw when she looked at him. She saw in those pitch-dark eyes her greatest single fear: She saw her father.

There was no physical resemblance between the man before her and the one who had tormented and abused her for the first eight years of her life. It went, she understood, deeper than physical. Its surface was a calculated charm thinly coated over an indifferent cruelty.

Under it all was utter disregard for anything approaching the human code.

The monster that had lived in her father looked at her now out of Dorian Vadim's eyes.

And he smiled almost as if he knew it. "It's an honor to have you here. What can I get you to drink?"

"We're not drinking," Eve told him, though she would have paid any price but pride for a sip of water to cool the burning in her throat. "This isn't a social call."

"No, of course not. Well then, what can I do for you?"

Eve slid the photo of Tiara across the bar. Dorian lifted

it, glanced at it briefly. "Tiara Kent. I heard she was killed this morning. Tragic." He tossed it down again without another glance. "So young, so lovely."

"She's been in here."

"Yes." He affirmed without an instant's hesitation. "A week or two ago. Twice, I believe. I greeted her myself when I was told she'd come in. Good for business."

"How did she get the invitation?" Eve demanded.

"One may have been sent to her. A selection of the young, high-profile clubbers is sent invitations periodically. We've only been open a few weeks. But as you can see . . ." He turned, gestured to the crowd that screamed over the blasting music. "Business is good."

"She came alone."

"I believe she did, now that you mention it." He turned back, angling just a little closer to Eve, until the hairs on the back of her neck prickled. "As I recall, she was to meet a friend, or friends. I don't believe she did. I'd hoped she'd come back, with some of her crowd. They spend lavishly, and can make a club such as this."

"Underground clubs aren't made that way."

"Things change." He picked up the drink Allesseria had set on the bar, watching Eve over the rim as he sipped. "As do times."

"And how much time did you spend with Kent?"

"Quite a bit on her initial visit. I gave her a tour of the place, bought her a few drinks." He sipped again, slowly. "Danced with her."

Her father had smelled of candy from the mints he chewed to cover the liquor. Dorian smelled of musk, yet she scented the hard sweetness of candy and whiskey. "Went home with her?"

He smiled, and when he set down his glass his knuckles lightly brushed Eve's hand. "If you want to know if I fucked her, you've only to ask. I didn't, though it was tempting. But bad for business. Wouldn't you agree?" he said to Roarke. "Sex with clients is a tricky business."

"It would depend on the client, and the business." Roarke's voice was a silky purr, a tone Eve knew was dangerous. "Other things are bad for business as well."

As if acknowledging some unspoken warning, Dorian angled his head in a slight nod, shifted his body away from Eve's.

"Did you tell her you were a vampire?" Eve demanded. "That you could turn her?"

Dorian slid on a stool and laughed. "Yes, to the first. It's part of the atmosphere, as you can clearly see. The core clientele come here for the thrill, the eroticism of the cult, the thrill of possibility. Certainly part of the draw is the fear and the allure of the undead, along with the dark promise of eternal youth and power."

"So you sell it, but you don't buy it."

"We'll just say I very much enjoy my work."

"Tiara Kent was exsanguinated, through a two-pronged wound through the carotid artery."

He lifted one arched black brow. "Really? Fascinating. Do you believe in vampires, Lieutenant Dallas? In those who prey on the human, and thirst for their blood?"

"I believe in the susceptible, in the foolish, and in those who exploit them. She was drugged first." Eve took a careless glance around and hated, *hated* that her chest felt tight. "I wonder how many illegals I'd net if I ordered a sweep of this place?"

"I couldn't say. We both know such things aren't as . . . regulated underground." He stared deeply into her eyes. "Just as we both know that's not what you're here for."

"One leads to another. Her killer left his DNA behind."

"Ah, well. We can, at least, settle that one particular element." Watching her still, he rolled up his sleeve. "Allesseria, I'll need a syringe with a vial. Unopened."

"You keep needles behind the bar?" Eve snapped out.

"Part of the show. We serve several drinks that contain a dram or two of pig's blood, and it's added with a syringe for flourish." He took the needle from the bartender. "Should you do the honors," he asked Eve, "or I?"

"A swab of your spit would be easier."

"But not nearly as interesting." He pumped his fist until a vein rose, then slid the needle neatly—expertly, Eve thought—into it. Depressed the plunger. "Allesseria, you'll witness I'm providing the lieutenant with my blood voluntarily."

When the bartender didn't speak, Dorian turned his head toward her slowly, stared.

"Yes. Yes, I will."

"That should be enough." He flashed a hard smile at Eve, then removed the needle, capped off the vial. "Thank you, Allesseria." Flipping the syringe agilely, he held it out, plunger first. "Dispose of that properly," he ordered, then handed the vial to Eve. "You'll mark and seal that in our presence?"

As she did, Dorian swiped his fingertip over the drop of blood on the tiny puncture in his flesh, then laid it on his tongue. "Is there anything else?"

"Did you see Miss Kent with anyone in particular, see her leaving with anyone?"

"I can't say I did. I believe she danced with any number of people. Feel free to ask any of the staff, and I'll be happy to ask myself."

"You do that. We'll need an address, Mr. Vadim."

"Dorian, please. I'm known as Dorian. I can be reached here. I'm living upstairs at the moment. Let me give you a card." He waved his fingers, flicked them, and a glossy black card appeared between the index and middle finger. As he passed it to Eve, his fingers brushed down her palm, lingered for just an instant too long. Then he smiled. "I tend to sleep days."

"I bet. One more thing. Can you verify your whereabouts from midnight to three this morning?"

"I would have been here. As I said, I'm most often here."

"Anybody vouch for that?"

His lips quirked again, in a kind of smug amusement that put her back up. "I imagine so. You might ask any of the staff or the regulars. Allesseria?" He turned his black gaze from Eve's face to the bartender. "You were on last night. Didn't we speak some time after midnight?"

"I was on until two." Allesseria kept her eyes locked on Dorian's. "You were, ah, working the floor before I left, came by the bar for a spring water just before I clocked out. At two."

"There you are. Lieutenant, it's been a pleasure." He took her hand, held it firmly. "But I really need to get back to work. Roarke. I hope you'll both come back, for the entertainment."

Through the fog that shimmered and curled, he glided off again, easing his way through the crowd. Eve shifted her body, stared hard at the bartender. "You want to tell me why you lied for him?"

"I don't know what you're talking about." Busily now, Allesseria wiped the bar.

"You don't see a woman whose face is all over the screen and mags, and she comes in at least twice, hangs with your boss. You don't make her." Some of the anger she felt for herself snapped out in her voice. "But you remember Dorian got a spring water at two in the morning."

"That's right."

"I need your full name."

"You're going to cost me my job if you don't back off."

"Full name," Eve repeated.

"Allesseria Carter. If you have any more questions, I'm calling a lawyer."

"That'll do it for now. You *remember* anything, get in touch." Eve laid one of her cards on the bar before she stepped away. "If that wasn't Kent's Prince of frigging Darkness pigs are currently dive-bombing Fifth Avenue."

"Blood will tell," Roarke said quietly.

"Bet your fine ass."

Once they were out on the street, Peabody's sigh was long and heartfelt. "Man. Creepshow—even if the Lord of the Undead is intensely sexy."

"Looked like another freak to me," McNab muttered.

"You're a guy who likes women. If you were a woman who liked men, we'd still be rolling your tongue back into your mouth. He completely smoked, right, Dallas?"

Women had found her father attractive, Eve thought. No matter what he'd done to them.

"I'm sure Tiara Kent thought the same even as he was draining the life out of her. I'm going to call a black-and-white for you. I want you to take the blood sample directly to the lab, wait while it's logged in."

"Got it." Peabody took the sample, stowed it in her bag.

"I'll run our host, and the bartender. This isn't his first time around the block—and she was lying about seeing him this morning. Lab comes through quickly enough, we'll be giving Vadim a very unpleasant wake-up call."

They separated, and as she walked Eve gave Roarke a quick hip bump. Now that she was on the street, away from Vadim, away from those pulsing lights, she felt herself again. "You're quiet."

"Contemplating. He was scoping you, you know. Subtle but quite deliberate." When she started to jam her hands into her pockets, Roarke took one, brought it casually to his lips. "He wanted to see your reaction—and mine."

"Must be disappointed we didn't give him one. Or much of one on your part."

"More puzzled, I'd think."

"Okay, why didn't you slap him back?"

"It was tempting, but more satisfying to let him wonder. In any case, he's not your type."

She snorted. "Nah. I don't go for the tall, dark, gorgeous types who exude sexuality like breath."

"You don't go for sociopaths."

She glanced up at him. He'd seen it, too, she realized. He'd seen at least that much, too. "You got that right."

"Besides, I'm taller."

Now she laughed, and because really, what did it hurt, she turned as she climbed the platform to the car, feigned judging his height as she laid her hands on his shoulders. She pressed her lips to his, warm, ripe, real, then eased back. "Yeah, I'd say you're exactly tall enough to fit my requirements. You drive, ace. I want to start the runs on the way home."

She used her PPC, and though it was limited to a mini-screen, Dorian Vadim's ID photo still had punch. His hair had been shorter when it was taken, but it still brushed past his shoulders. It listed his age at thirty-eight, his birthplace as Budapest, where according to his data, he still had a mother.

It also listed a very impressive sheet.

"Grifting's a specialty of our suave Mister V," Eve related. "Lotsa pops there, starting with a juvie record that was never sealed. Bounced around Europe and came to the States, it seems, in his early twenties. Arrests for smuggling—no convictions on that. Illegals, some pops, some questioned and released. Worked as an entertainer—mesmerist and magician. Hmmm. A lot of dropped charges, heavy on the female vics. Was questioned about the disappearance of two women he reputedly bilked. Not enough evidence to arrest, and no DNA in his records.

"Slithered through the system like a snake," she muttered. "No violence on record, but wits recant or poof with regularity." She frowned over at Roarke. "You buy into that mesmo stuff?"

"Hypnotism is a proven art, you know Mira uses it in therapy."

"Yeah, but mostly I think it's bull." Still, she remembered

the odd sensation she'd felt when Dorian had stared into her eyes. Her problem, she told herself. Her personal demons.

"Anyway, the man's bad news. And he's got a pattern of victimizing women, wealthy ones particularly."

She did a quick run on the bartender and found no criminal on Allesseria. "Bartender's clean. Divorced, with a kid just turning three." Eve pursed her lips as Roarke drove through the open gates toward home. "I get her in the box, even alone at her own place, I can break her. She's lying about seeing Dorian. I could snap her statement in five minutes without him around. He scares her."

"He's a killer."

"Yeah, no question."

"I mean she knows it, or believes it. You're capable of snapping her statement, and he's equally capable of snapping her neck—and with a great deal less passion."

"Wouldn't disagree. I just wonder why you'd say that after one conversation with him."

"I would have said it after one look at him. His eyes. He's a vampire."

Her mouth dropped open as he stopped the car. She hadn't managed to get words working with her thoughts until she'd pushed out of the car, rounded the hood to meet him. "You said what?"

"I mean it literally. His type sucks the life out of people, and does it for momentary pleasure, just as effectively as any fictional vampire. And he's just, darling Eve, as soulless."

Like her father, Eve thought. Yes, Roarke had seen it, too. He'd seen all of it. There was nothing strange or frightening about recognizing a monster.

It only meant she understood her quarry.

Eve stepped in, pulled off her jacket. She gestured toward Summerset, Roarke's majordomo, who—as he inevitably did—stood waiting in the foyer in his funereal black suit. "I always figured vampires looked like that. Pale, bony, dour, and dead." She tossed the jacket on the newel and started up the stairs.

"Will you be having dinner in the dining room like normal human beings this evening?" Summerset asked.

"Got work, and nobody who looks like you should toss around words like 'normal.'"

"We'll get something upstairs," Roarke said placidly.

He strolled with Eve into her office, then immediately whipped around and boxed her against the wall. "I think I'll start with an appetizer," he said, then crushed his lips to hers.

Her blood went to instant sizzle. She could all but feel her brains leaking out of her ears as his mouth ravaged hers with a kind of feral impatience that thrilled. Even as she gripped his hips, he was doing torturous things to her body with those quick and clever hands.

She gulped in air, and simply gave herself to the wild and wanton moment. And to him.

She would always give. He knew no matter how much he wanted, she would always be there to give, or take, to meet those endless, urgent needs with her own. Her mouth was a fever on his. A moan poured from her as he tugged her shirt apart, then found that warm, trembling flesh with his lips, his teeth.

The taste of her incited a fresh and mammoth wave of hunger.

Her hands yanked at the hook of his trousers as his yanked at hers. And she pressed erotically against him, core to core.

Her eyes were dark when he looked into them and, for one brilliant moment, went blind when he plunged inside her.

She matched him, beat for frantic beat, riding and racing the violent pleasure as he dragged her arms over her head, as he pinned them there. As he battered them both over the last turbulent crest.

Her breath whistled in and out; he rested his cheek on her hair as he caught his own. And in sweet opposition to the force of their mating, he brushed his lips at her temple, soft as gossamer wings.

"I believe I was a bit more than mildly annoyed by having some poster boy for Dracula hit on my wife in front of my face."

"Worked for me." Grateful for the wall behind her, Eve leaned back, managed to focus on Roarke's eyes. "Feel better?"

"Considerably, thanks."

"Anytime. You know what, I feel like a big, fat hunk of red meat. How about you?"

He smiled, touched his lips to hers. "I could eat."

CHAPTER
SIX

She had an enormous hamburger while she backtracked through Dorian Vadim's criminal record. She burned up the 'link as she ate, as Dorian hadn't just slithered through the system, but had wound his way around the country and in and out of Europe while he did so. She spoke to detectives and investigators in Chicago, Boston, Miami, New L.A., East Washington, and several European cities.

She took copious notes, requested files, and made promises to keep other cops in other cities in the loop.

At some point during the process, Roarke wandered out. She'd set up another murder board, typed up her notes, and was talking to the head of security at Tiara Kent's building when Roarke wandered back in again.

She held up a finger.

"Go back as far as you can. If you see this guy on any of your discs, at any point, I want to know. Yeah, day or night. Thanks."

She disconnected. "Gist from the cops I've talked to across the frigging globe is Vadim is a smart grifter with the conscience and agility of a snake, an ego as big as . . . how big is Idaho?"

"There are bigger," Roarke considered, "but I'd say that's big enough."

"Okay, we'll go with Idaho, and an appetite for rich females and illegal substances. I'm damned if he'll slip through my fingers. Going to wrap him up quick, going to wrap him up tight," she told Roarke. "If we get him on any of the building's security discs, it's one more—ha-ha—nail in his coffin."

"Then you might be interested in what I ferreted out, regarding his financials."

Her expression went from intent to annoyed. "I don't have authorization to ferret in his financials, as yet."

"Which is why I used the unregistered. I don't like him," Roarke said very clearly before Eve could complain.

"Yeah, loud and clear on that. But I don't need his financial data at this point, and I can't use anything you found by illegal means, so—"

"So don't use it. And if you're not as curious as I was, I'll keep the information to myself."

He walked over, opened a wall panel, and got out the brandy. She lasted until he'd poured himself a snifter.

"Damn it. What did you find?"

"He's not officially listed as the owner of the club, but he owns it—such as it is. He's built several fronts, and is registered as its manager."

"Shady," she commented, "but not strictly illegal."

"He's also sunk quite a bit into the club—more, in my opinion, than makes good business sense on an underground establishment. I'd say Idaho might be lacking in square miles, after all. His overhead's considerably more than his take, particularly considering his payroll."

"You hacked into his books for Bloodbath?"

"It wasn't any trouble." He swirled, then sipped brandy. "Not much of a challenge. He's losing money on it, every week. Yet his personal finances don't reflect that. Instead there's a nice steady build. Nothing that would wave flags, which tells me he's very likely tucked away other accounts. I only scraped off a few layers on this run."

"What's his other income?" Eve wondered, and Roarke smiled.

"That's a question."

"Illegals are likely one chute. Bilking, blackmail, extortion. Once a grifter . . . He could've been milking Kent, but if it was just about money, why kill the really rich cow before she runs dry? It's not just about money," she said before Roarke could. "That's a shiny side benefit."

"Agreed. And I'm going to wager very shiny. I can take a hard look at Kent's finances, but I suspect she was the type who flung money about like confetti on New Year's Eve."

"Yeah, she had hundreds of shoes."

"I don't see the correlation, however," he continued as she rolled her eyes. "With enough time, I could find his hidey-holes, and jibe any unusual income with the same outlay from Kent's."

"Given enough time," Eve repeated. "Hours or days?"

"From the subjects in question, it could take a few days."

"Crap. Poking there won't hurt. But that's not what's going to get him."

"Again, we agree." He strolled over, sat on her desk. He liked it there, where he could look down into those whiskey-toned eyes. Those cop's eyes. "It may be weight, but it won't be your hammer. And as for the club, he's certainly got a second set of books on that, one that includes any exorbitant, and likely illegal membership fees, illegals transactions, and the like. Which I'll find for you, in time, as well."

"You're really handy to have around." She tapped his knee with her finger. "And not just for the sex."

"Darling, how sweet. I'll say the same of you." He bent down to kiss her lightly—another reason he liked sitting in just that spot. "On Vadim, if he were smarter, he'd be keeping his income and outlay closer on his official records. But he's not as smart as he thinks he is."

"But you're smarter than even he thinks he is." She paused, thought that through. "If you get me."

"Aren't we full of compliments tonight? I'll have to bang you against the wall more often."

She laughed, then picked up her coffee. She drank it even though it had gone cold. "I'll have the DNA match in the morning, maybe get lucky and get a blip of him on Kent's building's security. I'm going to corner the bartender and break down her corroboration of his bullshit alibi. I'll have him in a cage by noon. Then we can take his finances and his records apart, piece by piece. You can add weight to my hammer."

Roarke angled his head. "Except? I can hear an 'except' in your voice."

"Except it's too easy, Roarke. It's all too goddamn easy on his end. He gave up his blood without a blink, and with a smile."

"I particularly dislike his smile," Roarke commented.

"Yeah? With you on that. He has to know he left DNA at Kent's that can hang him, but he didn't demand I get a warrant. And the fact is, it might have taken me some fast talking to get one for it. He may not be as smart as he thinks, but he's not stupid either. He's not worried, and that worries me."

"So, he has an ace in the hole somewhere. You'll just have to trump it. Now, tell me, what else is it that worries you?"

"I don't know what you mean."

"You went somewhere else in your head once or twice when we were in the club. And you've been there again a time or two since. Where did you go that worries you?"

"I've got a lot to push through, think through," she began.

"Eve." It was all he said. All he needed to say.

"I saw my father. I stood there in that ugly place, and he

came toward me. Toward me," she repeated. "Not us, not the group of us, but me."

"Yes. Yes, he did."

"Like a dream, in a way. The fog, the lights, the noise. I knew it was for effect, for show, but . . . I got a hook in me, I guess, and then I looked in his eyes. You said sociopath. You said killer. And yeah, I saw that. But I saw more than that. When I looked into him I saw whatever monster it was that lived in my father. I saw it staring out at me. And it . . . it sickens me. It scares me."

Roarke reached down, took her hand. "Knowing monsters exist, as you and I do, Eve, may not always make for easy sleep, or even an easy heart. But it arms us against them."

"It was like he knew." She tightened her grip on his hand. There was no one else she could have told such things to. There had been a time when there'd been no one at all she could have told such things to. "I know it was my imagination, my own . . . demons, I guess you could say, but when he stared back into me, it was like he knew. Like he could see what was small and scared inside of me."

"You're wrong on that. What he saw was a woman who won't stand down."

"I hope so, because for a couple seconds I wanted to run. Just rabbit the hell out of there." She let out a shaky breath. "There are all kinds of vampires, you said that, too. Isn't that what my father was? Trying to suck the life out of me, trying to make me into something less than human? I put a knife into him instead of a stake. Maybe that's why he keeps coming back in my head."

"It's you who made you." He leaned down now, framed her face with his hands. "And what you are your father would never have understood. Neither would Vadim. No matter how he looks, he'll never really see you."

"He thinks he does."

"His mistake. Eve, do you want to talk to Mira about this?"

"No." She considered it another moment, then shook her head and repeated, "No, not now anyway. Dumping on you levels it out a little. Taking him down, all the way down—that'll take care of the rest."

For a moment she studied their joined hands, then shifted her gaze up to his. "I didn't want to tell you I'd been scared, much less why. I guess that was stupid."

"It was."

She scowled. "Aren't you supposed to say something like 'No, it wasn't'. Blah, blah, support, stroke, let me get you some chocolate'?"

"You haven't read the marriage handbook's footnotes. It's another *woman* who does that sort of thing. I believe I'm allowed to be more blunt, then ask if you'd like a quick shag."

"Shag yourself," she said and made him laugh. "But thanks anyway."

"Offer's always on the table."

"Yeah, yeah, and the floor, in the closet, or on the front stairs. Time to work, ace, not to play."

She pushed up to study and circle her murder board, and he knew she was soothed and settled.

"Prior bad acts, and plenty of them. Mysterious income. Contact with the vic, and the profile fits him like a tailor-made suit. Bullshit alibi. He's running a game in that club, skinning rich idiots with his vampire fantasy, maybe blackmailing them, selling illegals. But that's only part of the picture. He's got something," she said in a mutter now. "He's got something, and he's feeling fucking smug about it."

"Heads up, Lieutenant," Roarke warned.

She glanced his way, caught the candy bar he tossed across the room. She grinned, tore the wrapper, and biting in, continued to study her board.

When Allesseria finished her shift, she was careful not to rush, careful to do everything just as she did every night.

She closed down her tabs, keyed in her codes, passed her station off to her replacement.

She stretched her back as she walked, casually, to the employee-only area where she stowed her bag and her jacket every shift. Even there, behind closed doors, she kept her expression neutral and her movements routine. Everyone knew there were cameras in every section of the club, the boss had made that clear.

You never knew who was watching.

Her yawn wasn't entirely feigned. It had been a long shift, and a busy one as the crowds that patronized Bloodbath liked to stay thoroughly lubed. As she always did, she transferred her tips to her bag, zipped them into its inside pocket. After fitting the bag's strap across her body, she put her jacket over it.

She hung the illuminated cards, given to all employees, around her neck so that one glowed between her breasts, the other between her shoulder blades.

With the gleaming gold pentagram with its boldly red double B's in the center like a shield front and back, nobody would bother her on the way out of the club, on the nasty route through the tunnels. It was something else Dorian had made clear from the get-go, and he'd made an example of a souped-up chemi-head who'd tried a move on one of the waitresses the first week the club opened.

Rumor was the guy had ended up in pieces, and there hadn't been enough blood left to so much as stain the ground.

It was probably bullshit. Probably. But it was enough to keep the path clear for anyone coming or going from Bloodbath who wore the sign.

Still, she checked her pocket, as she always did, for her ministunner and panic button.

An ounce of prevention was worth a lot of peace of mind.

She headed out, and as was usual at shift changes, she left the club with a group of other employees. Safety in numbers. There wasn't much chatter, there rarely was, so she could huddle inside her own thoughts as they wound through the stink and the shadows, through the pounding music and wailing screams.

She'd thought she could handle it, the money was too good to pass up. With salary and tips, if she was frugal, she could move out of the city, plunk down a down payment on a nice little house.

A yard for her kid, a day job.

It seemed like the perfect plan, and she knew how to take care of herself. But it was too much, she had to face that now. The club, the tunnels, the boss himself. It was all too much, and she was going to have to go back to working street level, pulling doubles just to put a few extra aside every week. The house in Queens, the yard, the dog, would all just have to wait a few more years.

She'd walked out of Bloodbath for the last time.

She'd send in written notice, that's what she'd do, Allesseria decided as she finally came out to the sidewalk. She'd use her son as an excuse. Dorian knew she had joint custody, but she could use the night work as too strenuous, too difficult.

Nothing he could do about it, she assured herself as she pulled off the glowing cards and stuffed them in her pocket. Nothing, that she could think of, that he'd want to do. At the salary he offered, he'd replace her in one crook of the finger.

Let somebody else mix pig's blood—God, she *hoped* it was just pig's blood—in gin to make Bloody Martinis, or handle dry ice to make a Graveyard. She was done.

The cops had been the last straw. She couldn't take any more.

He'd made her lie for him, so there was a reason he needed the lie.

As Allesseria went underground again, this time to catch the subway home, she admitted she'd lied before he'd asked. Something had warned her she'd be better off playing dumb.

Never seen that face before.

Tiara Kent, who'd knocked back a half dozen Bloodies on her first visit to the club—and had spent a hell of a lot of time up in Dorian's private office.

Okay, she hadn't seen them leave together, but in fact, she hadn't seen either of them leave when Tiara had come to the club. Which meant they might have slipped out through Dorian's office.

And Allesseria hadn't seen Dorian from sometime before midnight last shift. He hadn't come down to work the floor as she'd told the cop he had. He hadn't worked the floor, not once that she'd noticed, after Tiara Kent had gone up those stairs with him.

And she always noticed him because of the way her skin started to crawl.

He could've killed Tiara Kent. He could've done it.

With her arms protectively crossed over her torso, Allesseria sat on the train, struggling with what she should do, could do. A dozen times she told herself just walking away was enough. It wasn't her responsibility, and she'd be smarter to just mind her own business. Quitting was enough. More than enough.

But when she got off at her stop, she thought of her son, how she tried to teach him to do the right thing, to stand up for what he knew was right. To be a good man one day.

So she pulled out the card the cop had left on the bar and her pocket 'link as she walked the dark street home.

Nerves prickled at the base of her spine, crawled up to the back of her throat. Even though she told herself it was foolish, she shot anxious glances over her shoulder. Nothing to worry about now, *nothing*. She was blocks from the club, and back on street level. As far as Dorian knew she'd backed him up, 100 percent.

She was nearly home. She was safe.

Still, she stayed in the streetlights where she could as she recited Eve's office code. When she reached voice mail, she took a long breath.

"Lieutenant Dallas, this is Allesseria Carter, the bartender at Bloodbath."

She paused, looking over her shoulder again as those nerves dug in like claws. Had she heard something? Footsteps, a rustle in the breeze?

But she saw nothing but light and shadow, the black, blank windows in the buildings.

Still, she increased her pace, felt her knees tremble as she hurried. "I need to talk to you, um, talk to you about Tiara Kent. If you could contact me as soon—"

He came out of nowhere, charging in like some dark and brutal wind. Shock had her sucking in air as she whirled around, as she stumbled back. She managed one choked-off scream as his hand closed over her throat, squeezing out even that single panicked gulp. The black eyes stared into hers when her 'link went flying. As if she weighed nothing at all, he lifted her off the ground.

"You," he said in a quiet, almost pleasant tone, "made a very tragic mistake."

She kicked, her legs dancing and dangling like a hanging man's when he dragged her out of the circle of light from the street lamp. Red dots exploded in front of her eyes while her lungs screamed for air and her hand fumbled wildly for her panic button.

Her feet thudded on broken steps, and tears spurted out of her eyes. They bulged in horror when he smiled and she saw, impossibly, the flash of fangs.

In the dark, those gleaming points sank into her neck.

The minute she was dressed in the morning, Eve snagged a second cup of coffee. "I'm going to check my home office machine, see if I got anything from the lab overnight."

"Being a bit obsessive, aren't you?" Roarke asked from

where he sat, scanning the morning financials on the bed-room screen. "It's barely seven."

"You have your obsessions." She nodded toward the maze of numbers. "I have mine."

"Check it from your pocket 'link, then. Have something to eat while you're about it."

"How am I supposed to check my office messages with my pocket 'link?"

Roarke only sighed, rose. He walked to her and held out a hand. "They're all connected, my technology-challenged darling, hence the term *'link.*"

"Yeah, yeah, but then you have to remember all these codes and sequences, and it's just easier to . . ."

He punched a command while she frowned at him. "Relay any new incomings on home unit Dallas," he ordered.

Acknowledged . . . There are no incomings since last operator use on home unit Dallas . . .

"Huh. Okay, not as complicated as I thought. Can I check my unit at Central?"

He only smiled. "Relay any new incomings on office unit Dallas, Cop Central."

Acknowledged . . . There is one new incoming trans-mission on voice mail . . .

"Damn it." She grabbed the 'link out of Roarke's hand. "I told them to contact me here as soon as they had—"

Lieutenant Dallas, this is Allesseria Carter, the bar-tender at Bloodbath.

"Conscience got to her," Eve decided, watching the face on-screen. "Walking home, it looks like. Looks spooked."

I need to talk to you, um, talk to you about Tiara Kent. If you could contact me as soon—

There was a sound—a rush of wind? Eve saw a

black-gloved hand, the blur of it whip in and close over Allesseria's throat.

"Fuck! Goddamn it." Eve's own hand clamped on Roarke's arm as the screen image blurred, the 'link struck the sidewalk, and the display went black.

"Play it back again," she ordered Roarke as she yanked out her communicator. "Dispatch, Dallas, Lieutenant Eve. I need a unit, closest possible unit at . . ." She flipped quickly through her memory to the address she'd pulled out of Allesseria's data, then snapped it out. Repeated it. "Possible victim of assault is Carter, Allesseria. Female, Caucasian, thirty-four, black hair, medium build. I'm on my way."

"I'll go with you," Roarke told her. "I'm closer than Peabody. You can contact her on the way. You know you won't find her in her apartment," he added as they rushed downstairs.

"Maybe she got away. Maybe he just wanted to scare her. Goddamn it, I picked her out for him. I set her up."

"You did nothing of the kind." He snatched up her jacket from the newel, tossed it to her as he snagged his own. "He chose her, the minute he asked her to lie for him, he chose her. I'll drive."

He'd get there faster, Eve knew, and it freed her to contact Peabody, then take the report from Dispatch. There was no response at Allesseria's apartment.

"Get inside," Eve snapped. "The victim's life is in immediate jeopardy. I have probable cause. Get the fuck inside."

She thumped her fist against her leg as she waited, waited, as Roarke maneuvered her police-issue through streams and clogs of morning traffic.

Dispatch, Dallas, Lieutenant Eve. Officers report the apartment is currently unoccupied. There is no sign of break-in or foul play.

No, Eve thought, there wouldn't be. He didn't take her there. "Start an immediate search in a five-block radius.

Repeating description. Subject is female, Caucasian, age thirty-four, black and brown, last seen wearing black pants, black shirt, red jacket."

Eve ended the transmission, stared out the windshield. "I know it," she said, though Roarke had said nothing. "I know it. He didn't leave her alive."

CHAPTER
SEVEN

Eve scanned sidewalks, the buildings as they approached Allesseria's apartment. It was a tough, low end of the lower-middle-class neighborhood. Most self-respecting muggers would hunt for scores a few blocks away in any direction.

Pickings would be slim here, and the population willing to fight for what they carried in their pockets. Street level LCs would troll for johns elsewhere, too. All in all, the handful of blocks were safe simply because they were poor enough not to warrant much trouble.

But Allesseria Carter hadn't been safe.

Eve's gaze zeroed in on a subway exit. "Pull over, park wherever you can. She'd take the subway, wouldn't she? Cheap and quick. If she did, this would've been her route home."

She slammed out of the car the minute Roarke stopped, then pulled out her 'link to replay the message. Looked for landmarks. "It's dark, and it's mostly her face, but . . ." She held up her own 'link as if relaying a message, then looked over her left shoulder. "See here, could be that building in the background."

She kept walking, studying the screen, the street. "Here, he took her right about here. Somebody would've picked up her 'link by now, or he did, but it was right about here he attacked."

She scanned again, focused on a narrow building sagging between a Thai market and a boarded-up storefront. It was plastered with graffiti, and what looked like an old, torn Condemned sign.

Eve took out her communicator, requested backup at the location. Then drawing her weapon, she started toward the door. "You carrying anything besides half the wealth of the world in your pocket?"

"Burglary tools, though this won't require them."

She nodded, reached down, and took her clutch piece out of its ankle holster. "You're deputized, ace." She sucked in a breath, kicked in the door.

She went in low and to the right while he took high and left in a routine they'd danced before. Sunlight dribbled through the broken windows, striking off shards of glass, filth, vermin droppings.

And blood.

Eve could smell it—not just the blood, but the death. That heavy human stench.

Roarke took out a penlight, shone it on the trail of smeared red.

He'd left her splayed on the floor, arms and legs spread out so her body formed a gruesome human X. Most of her clothes had been torn off, leaving only ragged remnants of black clinging to skin mottled with bruises.

Her blood spread out in a pool from the puncture wounds in her throat. Her eyes hadn't lost their horror with death, but stared at the ceiling in a fixed expression of abject terror.

"Didn't take her blood with him this time," Eve said

quietly. "Didn't come prepared for that. But he made sure to hurt her plenty before he bled her out. Got off on her pain, got off on the power. See how he spread her out? Mother-fucker."

Roarke touched a hand to Eve's shoulder. "I'll get your field kit."

She worked the scene; it's what she did. What she had to do. She could follow the trail of blood, of smeared foot-prints, and see Allesseria being dragged inside.

Kicking, Eve thought, her work shoes thudding hard against the broken concrete steps. Hard enough to cut through the cheap canvas before he'd hauled her inside.

He'd punctured her throat immediately, only steps inside the door. There was spatter against the dirty wall where she'd gushed. Where she'd collapsed. Dragged her uncon-scious from there, she noted. Gave himself a little more room to work. To beat her with his fists, to rape her. All while the blood ran out of her.

But he'd taken some, too. Ingested it, bottled it. She'd find out.

"Time of death oh-three-thirty," she said for the record. "Took her about an hour to die." She sat back on her haunches. "A block and a half from home."

She looked over at Roarke. He stood, his hands in the pockets of his jacket. The morning air fluttered in the broken windows, stirred his dark hair. And lifted the smell of ugly death all around them.

"He could've taken her in the club, anywhere in the underground. She might never have been found, and we'd never prove a thing if she'd been murdered down there."

"He wanted you to find her," Roarke agreed. "He's mak-ing a statement."

"Yeah, oh, yeah, because he didn't have to do this. Even if she recants, he'd find ten others to back his alibi. Ten others he'd bribe or intimidate. He didn't have to kill her, and certainly not like this."

"He enjoyed it." Roarke shifted his gaze, met Eve's eyes. "Just as you said. Payback was secondary to the killing."

"And he wanted it to be me who found her," Eve added. "Because of that click last night, that mutual recognition. But he's too cocky for his own good. There'll be DNA again, and he'll have picked up some of this dirt. Shoes, clothes. He'll have transferred some of this dirt, this blood, and the sweepers will find it."

"He attacked her while she was on the 'link—to you, Eve." Reaching out, Roarke took her hand, lifted her to her feet. "That's another statement."

"Yeah, and I'm hearing him. Just like he's going to hear me, really soon." She looked over as Peabody came in.

"Nothing on the canvass so far," Peabody reported. "I got in touch with the ex-husband. He lives a few blocks from here. He's on his way."

"We'll take him outside. He doesn't need to see this." Nobody needed to see what cops had to see. "Body can be bagged and tagged. There's nothing else she can tell us here. Let's see what she says to Morris."

She went out, grateful for the sunlight, and for the smell that was New York rather than death. She started to reach for her 'link to nag the lab yet again, when she spotted a six-and-a-half-foot black man with a body like a linebacker sprinting across the street against the light.

He wore short dreads, sweatpants, and a T-shirt, and an expression of fear in his topaz eyes. When he tried—and was well on his way to succeeding—shoving past the uniforms at the crime-scene barricade, she called out, went over.

"Rick Sabo?"

"Yes. Yes. My wife—my ex-wife. A detective called and said . . ."

"Let him through. I'm Lieutenant Dallas, Mr. Sabo. I'm sorry about your ex-wife."

"But are you absolutely sure it's her? She had a panic

button, a ministunner. She knew how to handle herself. Maybe—"

"She's been identified, I'm sorry. When did you—"

She broke off when he just crouched down, dropped his head in his hands as a man would if pierced by a sudden and unspeakable pain. "Oh, God, oh, God. *Aless*. I can't . . . I told her to quit that goddamn job. I told her."

"Why did you tell her to quit her job?"

He looked up, but since he didn't straighten, Eve hunkered down with him. "She worked in this cult club— vampire shit—which is bad enough. But it was underground, off Times Square. It wasn't safe, it's not safe down there, and she *knew* it."

"Then why'd she work there?"

"Made three times what she made on street level. Sometimes four with tips. No doubles. She wanted to buy a house, a little house, maybe in Queens. We've got a boy." His eyes watered up. "We got Sam, and she wanted a place out of the city. We share custody of Sam. But, Jesus, I told her it wasn't worth it. I went down to check it out right after she took the job. Goddamn pit in a goddamn sewer. Aless."

There was love here, Eve thought. Maybe not enough to make a marriage work, but there was love. "Did she talk about her work, the people she worked with? For?"

"No, not to me. Not after we went a round about it. Haven't fought like that since we split. Don't know that we fought like that before we split. I was scared, if you want to know the truth. Scared for her, and I handled it wrong."

His hands dangled between his knees now, and he stared at them as if they were foreign objects. "Flat out told her she was *going* to quit, and I know that's just the way to make her dig into something. If I'd handled it better, she might've . . ."

He looked up, looked past Eve. There were people gathered on the other side of the barricades, as people always did.

What happened? they'd ask, and as word trickled down,

they'd think how awful, how terrible, even as they continued to gawk, to linger, to hope to catch a glimpse of the dead body before they had to head off to work.

Because it wasn't them, it wasn't theirs the city had swallowed up. So they could gawk and linger and congratulate themselves that it wasn't them or theirs—and the next time it might be.

Sabo didn't see them, Eve knew that, too. Because for him, it was the next time.

"Mr. Sabo, did you meet any of her coworkers or her employer while you were in the club, or after?"

"What? No. No." He scrubbed his hands hard over his face. "Didn't want to. I only stayed about twenty minutes. Illegals passing around like party favors. People coming out of the private rooms licking blood off their lips, or it looked like it. She wanted a damn house in Queens."

"Mr. Sabo, I have to ask. It's routine. Can you verify your whereabouts between two and four a.m. this morning?"

"In bed, at home. I got Sam. I can't leave Sam alone at night." He rubbed at his eyes now before his hands dangled uselessly again. "I have building security. In and out. You can check. Whatever you have to do so you don't waste time, so you find who hurt Alless. Was she raped?"

Before Eve could respond, he shook his head. "No. No. Don't tell me. I don't think I want to know either way. Walk from the subway, after two in the morning, alone. Because of that damn job. Now what am I going to tell our boy? How am I going to tell our Sam his mama's gone?"

"I can have a grief counselor contact you, one who works with children."

"Yes. Please. Yes." His throat worked on a swallow. "I'll need help. Alless and I, well, we couldn't stay married, but we were a team when it came to Sam. I'll need help. I have to get back to my kid. I left him with the neighbor. I have to get back to Sam. Can you let me know when . . . when I need to do whatever I need to do?"

"We'll contact you, Mr. Sabo." Eve watched him walk away. "Peabody?"

"I'll take care of the grief counselor. Poor guy."

"Murder kills more than the victim," Eve said quietly. "We need to wrap up here, get into Central. Feeney may be able to clean up some of her last transmission from my unit. We get even a glimmer of this bastard . . ."

"I could help with that." Roarke stepped up beside her.

"You've got your own work."

"I do, but I'd be interested in, let's say, hammering one of those nails."

"If Feeney—" She broke off as her 'link signaled. "Hold on a minute." She moved aside, answered.

Roarke noted the instant change in her body language— the stiffening, the aggressive stance. When she turned back, he saw it mirrored in the temper that heated her eyes.

"DNA doesn't match Vadim's."

"But—"

"No but about it," Eve cut Peabody off. "There's a fuck-ing screwup somewhere. You want in," she said to Roarke, "you're in. You can round up Feeney at Central, do whatever the two of you can do with the transmission. Peabody, with me. We're going to the lab. Contact Morris." She moved quickly as she snapped out the order. "I want him to person-ally take the DNA samples from this vic, have them hand-delivered to the lab. That's red-flagged."

"Got it."

Eve glanced back at the building one last time. "No way, no goddamn way he slithers out of this."

Peabody had to all but leap into the car to keep up. "Maybe he didn't kill her."

"Screw that."

"What I mean is, maybe he had her killed. Set it up." Peabody jerked her safety harness tight as it looked like they were in for a hell of a ride.

"No. He wouldn't deny himself the pleasure of the kill."

Monsters didn't want to watch, to be *told*. They wanted to do. They wanted the smell of the blood. "He did them both. Kent because it's what he set out to do, Carter because he was smart enough to know she wasn't going to hold up his alibi, and it slaps at me. He picked her, put her on the spot, then he took her out. The lab screwed up, or I did. I did if he switched the vials."

"We were right there. He drew his own blood right in front of us."

"Hand's quicker than the eye," Eve muttered. "He worked as a magician, he's worked the grift all of his life. He offered the blood sample without a blink because he knew he could swing it so it wouldn't match."

And she'd been distracted, she couldn't deny it. Tight chest, dry throat, pumping heart. Her own fears had dulled her senses.

"Either way," Peabody commented, "without the match, with Allesseria vouching for him and being unable to recant, we've got nothing on him."

"That's what he's counting on. I played into it, and that pisses me off. Dark club, all that movement and noise. Guy draws his own blood at a bar. Not something you see every day." Looking into his eyes, she remembered. Caught in them for a few seconds too long, shuddering inside at what she'd seen there, and she's conned. "Son of a bitch."

She strode into the lab, only to be cut off by the chief, Dick Berenski.

His egg-shaped head was cocked aggressively as he jabbed one of his long, thin fingers at her. "Don't think about coming into my shop and saying we fucked up. I ran those samples twice myself. Personal. You want to argue with science, you go somewhere else. I can't make a match when there's no match."

He was called Dickhead for a reason, and it had every-thing to do with his personality. Eve throttled back. "I think he switched them on me. It's his DNA on the vic, but it's not his in the vial you have. I've got an idea how he pulled it off, but the question right now is: If it's not his blood in the vial, whose is it?"

It was obvious Berenski had been expecting a battle. Now, caught off guard, he was more accommodating than he normally would be without a substantial bribe. "Well, if we got the DNA in the system, I can find it for you."

"I did a standard search, crapped out."

"Global?"

"Yeah, do I look like this is my first day on the job? But I didn't run deceased."

"Blood from a corpse? How's that going to end up in some mope's veins?"

"Not in his veins, in a damn vial he palmed off on me. Can you do a global search, deceased donor?"

"Sure."

"How fast?"

He wiggled his spidery fingers. "Watch and learn."

He went back to his station, the long white counter with comps and screens and command centers. Sliding back and forth on his stool, he began to work—verbal orders, manual keys.

While he ran the searches, Eve drew out her 'link and tried Feeney.

Her old partner and the captain of EDD popped on her screen. He had a Danish in one hand, and a mouth full of the hefty bite missing from it. "Yo."

"Roarke's on his way in. Put him to work. I've got a 'link trans, voice mail, from a vic while she was being attacked. Lost the trans almost as soon. It's dark, it's jumpy, but if you can clean it up, I might burn this bastard quick."

"Take a look." He swallowed. "This your vampire?"

"Come on."

"Hey, before your time I took down this asshole who was grave robbing, then sewing body parts together. Thought he could make himself a Frankenstein. Weird shit happens. He take another one?"

"Yeah, early this morning."

Contemplatively, Feeney took another bite of Danish. "McNab said he pulled out a syringe and gave you blood right on the spot."

"Yeah. There was a screwup there. Looks like mine. I'll fill you in later. Anything you can do on the trans, Feeney, I'd appreciate."

"Your man gets here, we'll do some magic. Meanwhile, you go up against this guy, wouldn't hurt to take a cross along." He lifted his eyebrows when she just stared at him. "Kid, weird shit happens because people are fucking crazy."

"I'll keep that in mind."

She clicked off just as Berenski made a sound of victory. "Got your blood. And I'm forced to say, 'Damn good call, Dallas.'"

"I'm forced to say, 'Damn fast work.'"

"I'm the best. Pensky, Gregor." He tapped the ID picture on his screen.

Square face, Eve noted. Small eyes, pinched mouth. The data put him at two-ten and six-one, with a long sheet of violent crimes.

It also listed him as dead for nearly a year.

"How'd he get to be a corpse?" Eve demanded.

"Son of a bitch." Berenski pursed his thin lips. "Been running DNA on a DB." He called for the data.

"Body found in the woods in freaking Bulgaria, where it was believed he headed after escaping from a work program on his latest visit to their version of the State Pen." Eve shook her head. "Work program for a guy with this kind of sheet. Bludgeoned, partially dismembered, and how about this, exsanguinated. Peabody, let's get the full ME's report on this. I'm betting among his other injuries, there were a couple of puncture wounds in his throat."

"This vampire shit's creepy."

Eve glanced at Berenski. "It would be, if vampires existed. What happened to science?"

He jutted out what he called a chin. "You got science, you got the para side of it. I'd be sharpening stakes if I were you, Dallas."

"Yeah, that's on my list."

"Really?" Peabody asked when they got back into the car.

"Really what?"

"The stake-sharpening detail."

"Peabody, you're making my eye twitch."

"I know it's out there, but you have to consider all the information. Blood from a corpse. Vampires are corpses, essentially. No trace of Vadim on the first vic, scientifically at this point in time."

"Because he switched the fucking vials."

"Okay, okay." Peabody held up both hands, palms out. "But if you bought into the vampire lore, he could've sired this Pensky guy, then—"

"Then his body wouldn't have been real available for the Bulgarian ME."

Peabody considered. "There's that. But do we know, for absolute *sure*, that it stayed available?"

Give up, Eve told herself. Logical debates can't be made out of illogical theorems. "You be sure to check on that. While you do, I'll just stick with the more pedestrian theory that Vadim hooked up with Pensky, killed the shit out of him, and stored the blood he drained out for later use. It's smart, but it would've been a hell of a lot smarter to get blood from some unknown. We're also going to see if we can pin Vadim's whereabouts for the time of this Gregor's murder. What do you bet he was in Bulgaria?"

"He'd've been in Bulgaria if he vamped him, too," Peabody said under her breath. "Guy's got devil eyes."

"On the last part we heartily agree." She pulled into the garage at Central. "And we're going to give him a shot right between them. All data on Gregor Pensky's autopsy, Vadim's whereabouts at the time in question—and last night. Another DNA sample from that slippery son of a bitch."

Mentally kicking herself one more time on that score, Eve slammed the door of her police-issue. "This one spit— and it's going to be taken by a certified criminalist. Going to wrap him up before the day ends. He's not going to bite anyone else."

"Dallas?" Peabody scrambled inside the elevator. "Do you figure he's fatally bitten someone before? Bulgaria's a long way from Times Square. And there are places farther away. Places where bodies might never be found." Even if, Peabody thought, they stayed buried.

"I don't think he took a year off between Pensky and Kent." Eve scowled at the elevator doors. "So yeah, I think there'll be others."

"So do I. And listen, whether or not you—I mean we— believe in vampires, who's to say he doesn't? I know how he played it at Bloodbath. Like it was a show, a con—but a legal one this time. Maybe it isn't."

"Mira's initial profile allowed for him deluding himself into believing himself immortal, but his sheet screams con. We get him in the box," Eve decided, "we'll see how he plays it."

"I'm thinking if he does believe it, he's feeling pretty full of himself right now. Sucking out two vics in two nights."

"As of now, he's going on a no-hemoglobin diet."

Inside Central, Eve turned toward the Homicide bullpen. Stopped. Swags of garlic hung from the door frame like some odd holiday decoration. She caught the snickers from up and down the corridor, decided to ignore them, just as she ignored the surreptitious glances shot her way when she walked inside.

She arrowed in on Baxter, strolled to his desk. "How much did it run you?"

"It's fake." He grinned at her. "I'd have sprung for real,

even though it's steep, but it's hard to come by enough to make a real impact so we got the fake stuff, too. You gotta admit, it's funny."

"Yeah, inside I'm cracking up. I'm going back down to reinterview Count Dracula. Get your boy, you're backup."

"Underground." His grin vanished into a look of pure disgust. "I just bought these shoes."

"Now I'm crying on the inside." She pushed him aside with a satisfied grin, and commandeered Baxter's computer.

Moments later, her suspicions were confirmed. Two puncture wounds had pierced Gregor Pensky's carotid artery and had been attributed to an animal bite. She had news for Bulgaria, and the standing medical examiner. But for now, she contacted her own.

"What've you got?" she demanded of Morris.

"Saliva and semen, and I had my top man walk them to the lab. Exsanguination was COD. She was beaten pre- and postmortem, he used his fists on her, and wore gloves. Her larynx was partially crushed by manual strangulation. Tox just came back. Traces of the same cocktail inside Kent, administered through the neck wounds."

"He transferred the drug through the bite?"

"Yes. She didn't consume any blood, or alcohol."

"This one wasn't a party. Thanks, Morris." She sat back for a moment, organizing thoughts and strategy.

"Peabody," she said as she got to her feet. "Baxter, Trueheart. Let's move." She strode to the doorway, flicked a bulb of garlic with her finger. "You can take some of this along if that does it for you. Me?" She tapped her sidearm. "I'll stick with this."

CHAPTER

EIGHT

Baxter might like to joke and bitch about damage to his slick wardrobe, but he was a solid cop. His uniformed aide, Trueheart, hadn't shaken off all the green, but he was dependable as sunrise.

There wasn't a cop on the job—or not a sane one—who would be thrilled to traverse underground, day or night. But there weren't any who would back her up more reliably.

She took point, left Baxter to take the rear. Below the streets, time vanished. In the world, the day was sunny and heading toward warm. Here, it was as dark and dank as midnight in a winter graveyard. Still, at this hour most of those who inhabited the tunnels were huddled away in their holes and burrows.

Some of the clubs and arcades ran 24/7, and the harsh music still pumped, the ugly lights still glared. Those who came or stayed to do business were more interested in the pain or gain than confronting four armed cops.

A few threats and insults were hurled. One brave soul

invited *the girls* to have a taste of the appendage he was proud enough of to whip out and dangle in their direction.

Eve paused long enough to glance down. "Only thing down here interested in a taste of that is the rats, but they generally like bigger meals."

This comment caused hilarity among the flasher's companions.

"Sir," Peabody said, with feeling, "I really don't think you should tease the animals."

"The rats can handle it."

Eve turned down the next tunnel as the insulted flasher shouted inventive suggestions about what Eve might do with his pride and joy.

"Gotta give him points for originality," Baxter commented.

"And optimism," Trueheart added, and made his partner hoot with laughter.

Despite herself, Eve tossed a grin over her shoulder. His young, handsome face might have been pale and just a little clammy, but Trueheart was game.

The shouts echoed away as they reached Bloodbath. It was locked down tight.

She used the number Dorian had given her. With the video blocked, he answered in a slurred and sleepy voice.

"Dallas, official police business. Open up."

"Of course. One moment."

It took a bit longer than one, but the locks clicked, the security lights blinked to green. And the barred doors slid slowly open.

Eve saw the extra minutes had given Dorian time to set the stage.

Inside the lights were a dim and smoky blue with pulsing red undertones. The screen behind the stage flickered on, filled with images in black and white of women being attacked or willingly baring their necks for fangs. The blood that ran down flesh was black as pitch.

Dressed in black, his shirt open to the waist, Dorian stood above the screen on one of the open balconies. He seemed to float there on a thin river of fog, as if he could, at any moment, simply lift his arms and rise into the air. His face was ghost pale, his eyes and hair black as ink.

"I see you brought company." His voice flowed, echoed. "Please . . ." He gestured toward the steps. "Come up."

"That's a spider to the fly invite," Baxter murmured, glanced at Eve. "You go first."

She hated that her heart stuttered, that her blood ran cold under her skin. Though her stomach clenched in protest, she crossed the club floor where more fog was beginning to curl and snake, and her bootsteps echoed on the iron steps as she climbed.

Smiling, slowly smiling, Dorian stepped back. And vanished in the mist.

She drew her weapon. An instant later she had to fight not to jolt as he seemed to materialize directly in front of her. His eyes were so dark she couldn't tell pupil from iris. In them, if she let herself look, were all the horrors of her childhood.

"Nice trick," she said casually. "And a good way to get stunned."

"I trust your reflexes. My home." He gestured again, then led the way through an open door.

Black and red and silver. He'd played up the gothic touches, Eve noted, but didn't lack for plush. Iron chandeliers held white candles, wall niches showcased statuary of demons or nudes in pornographic poses.

There were curved black divans and black high-backed chairs studded with metal, and a single life-sized painting of a woman in a diaphanous white gown, bent limply over the arm of a black-caped man. Her eyes were wide with terror, her mouth open in a scream, as he bent toward her neck with fangs exposed.

"My humble home," Dorian said. "I hope you approve."

"A little too theatrical for my taste." She turned and looked him directly in the eyes. Eyes that triggered memories and fears she couldn't completely bury. "I'm going to need another sample, Dorian. I'll need you to come in for this one."

"Really? I'd think I gave you more than enough blood . . . for police purposes. A drink for you or your companions?"

"No."

"Excuse me while I get one. I'm not used to being up so early in the day." He moved to a bar, opened the mini fridge behind it. He took out a squat black bottle, poured red and thick liquid into a silver cup.

"We'll arrange your transport, have you back for your morning nap."

"I'd like to oblige you, but it's just not possible." He gestured an apology with one hand. "I'm under no legal obligation, after all."

"We'll discuss that at Central."

"I don't think so." Carrying his cup, he walked to a desk. "I have here a document that lists me—quite legally—as unable to tolerate sunlight. Religious reasons." He passed the document to her. "As to the sample, I'm afraid you'll need a warrant this time. I did cooperate."

He sat on the sofa, arranged himself in a lazy sprawl. "If this is about Tiara Kent, I have witnesses putting me here in the club at the time she was killed. You spoke with one yourself just last night."

Studying the paper, Eve answered without looking up. "Your alibi was killed early this morning."

"Really?" He sipped negligently. "That's a great pity. She was an excellent bartender."

"Where were you between two and four a.m. this morning?"

"Here, of course. I have a business to run and patrons to entertain."

Now her eyes flashed to his. Let him see, she told herself.

Let him see that I *know*. That I won't back down. "And witnesses to intimidate?"

"As you like." He shrugged a shoulder, and there was a laugh on his face now, a gleeful amusement smeared with viciousness. "I find religious prejudice tedious, but understandably . . . human. Those outside the cult often fear it, or smirk at it. For myself, I enjoy it and find it profitable. And there are other, more intimate benefits."

He rose again, moved across the room, opened a door. "Kendra, would you come out for a moment?"

She was covered in a robe so thin it might've been air, and it showed a generously curved body. Her hair was tumbled, her eyes blurry with sleep, and—Eve was certain—chemicals.

She recognized the blonde that had approached and pawed over Dorian the night before. She moved to him now, wrapped her arms around his neck, rubbed her body suggestively to his. "Come back to bed."

"Soon. This is Lieutenant Dallas, and her associates. Kendra Lake, a friend of mine. Kendra, the lieutenant would like to know where I was this morning, between two and four."

She turned her head, aimed eyes with pupils big enough to swim in toward Eve. "Dorian was with me, in bed, having sex. Lots of sex. We'd be having sex now if you'd go away. Unless you want to stay and watch."

"What are you on, Kendra?" Eve asked.

"I don't need to be on anything but Dorian." She rose on her toes, whispered something in Dorian's ear. He laughed, a low rumble, then shook his head.

"That's rude. Why don't you go back in, wait for me. I won't be long."

"Kendra," Eve said as the blonde started back toward the bedroom. "Did he promise you'd live forever?"

Kendra looked over her shoulder, smiled. Then shut the bedroom door behind her.

"Was there something else, Lieutenant?" Dorian asked. "I hate to keep a beautiful woman waiting."

"This might hold up." She set the document down. "Or it may not. Either way, we're not done. You shouldn't have used Gregor Pensky's DNA, because I'm going to link you to him." She stepped closer, ignoring the tickle at the back of her throat as those dark eyes pierced hers. "We'll talk again real soon, Dorian."

He grabbed her hand, brought it to his lips. She told herself she hadn't yanked it away to prove a point. But she wasn't entirely sure.

"I'll look forward to it."

Watching him, she dipped a finger in his cup, sucked the liquid off her finger. "Tasty," she said as his eyes blurred with what she recognized as excitement.

She walked out, down the stairs. With an effort she kept her expression cool as he once again materialized in front of her, in the mists that now clouded the club.

"I always escort my guests to the door. Safe travels, Lieutenant. Until we meet again."

"How'd he do that?" Even as her eyes tracked the tunnels, Peabody stuttered out the question. "How'd he do that?"

"Elevator, false doors. Smoke and fucking mirrors." It irritated Eve that he'd nearly made her jump, disturbed her so that her skin crawled as if he'd run his fingers over it.

She had to remind herself she'd bearded him in his own den, and she hadn't cracked. Her pulse wasn't steady, but she hadn't cracked.

"Damn good trick though," Baxter commented from the rear. "Did you get a load of the blonde? I might try a little blood sucking if you score that kind of action."

"She's an idiot, and a lucky one," Eve tossed back. "He needs to keep her alive, unless he's bone stupid."

"She was using. You were right on that one, Lieutenant." Trueheart's voice was just a little breathy. "I saw plenty of zoners and chemi-heads when I did sidewalk sleeper detail. She was zoned to the eyeballs."

"Okay, so he likes his women toked, and plays magic tricks. Not so scary," Peabody decided. "And the stuff he was drinking? Syrup, right? Just red syrup."

"No." Eve avoided a smear of some unidentifiable substance on the tunnel floor and aimed for the dim light ahead. "That was blood."

"Oh." Peabody gripped the cross at her neck. "Well."

On the street, Eve snapped out orders as she moved to her vehicle. "Baxter, I want you and Trueheart to find me a connection, any connection between Vadim and Pensky. Use EDD, if necessary, and see if you can pin Vadim in the area Pensky was killed. I'll get you the data I have. Peabody, push harder on the jewelry from the first vic. Turning the glitters liquid may be too hard to resist. We need to run this Kendra moron. My money says she's got a deep well. His pattern is to bilk rich women. However he's escalated, whatever the game, that's his base."

She shoved her way into traffic. "I'm going to the PA. I need a damn warrant, and I want to shatter his religious shield into a lot of tiny pieces."

But an hour later, Eve stood, stunned and furious, in APA Cher Reo's office.

"You've got to be kidding me."

"I'm giving it to you straight." Reo was smart, savvy, and ambitious, a small blond dynamo. And she tossed up her hands. "I'm not saying we couldn't have the order overturned, I'm saying it's a tricky business, and one that would take time and a lot of taxpayer dollars. The boss won't move on it, not with what you have. Bring us evidence, even a real glimmer of probable cause on the homicides, and we'll start the war. And war is the word. The courts don't like to mess with religious objections and predilections, even when they're obvious bullshit."

"This guy bled two women to death."

"Maybe he did. You say he did, I'm going to agree with you. But I can't give you a warrant for his residence, his place of business, on what you've got. I can't break down his objection to daylight hours with what you've got. Worse, the DNA you took—the vial with your initials on it, doesn't match."

"He switched them."

"How?"

"I don't know how." She kicked Reo's desk.

"Hey!"

"Reo, this guy's just getting started. He's pumped. He's using God knows what to keep pumped, and the killing's got him flying on his own importance. He's got a club full of opportunities every damn night. Like a damn all-you-can-eat buffet."

"Bring me something. I'll go to the wall for you, you know that. Bring me something I can use. Until you do, I'll do some research on precedents for breaking through a religious objection. If you can wiggle something that rings on the use or possession of illegals, I'll get you a warrant to search and seize on those grounds. It's the best I can do, Dallas."

"Okay. Okay." Eve raked her hands through her hair. "I'll get something." She thought of Allesseria's ex. Illegals passed around like party favors, he'd said. Add three cops and another civilian who had been in the club and they'd all swear they'd witnessed illegals bought, sold, and consumed. "Yeah, I can get something for an illegals raid."

"Make it work. And you know," Reo cast a glance at her office window, "I think I'm going to be damn sure I'm home and behind a locked door before sunset."

CHAPTER
NINE

Eve hunted up Feeney and Roarke in a lab in EDD. She could see them both standing, hands in pockets, as they studied a screen—in the same way she'd noted men often studied motors or other gadgets.

Physically, they couldn't have been less alike with Feeney nearly a head shorter even with the explosion of the mixed ginger and silver bush of his hair. Feeney habitually slouched, just as he was habitually rumpled and wrinkled. Roarke may have ditched his suit jacket and rolled up the sleeves of his crisp white shirt, but the contrast remained very broad.

Inside, she knew they often ran on the same path, particularly when it came to e-work. Geeks born of the same motherboard, she thought.

It was a relief to see them, and not so hard to admit. A relief to see these two men—so essential to the life she'd made—after coming from her confrontation with Dorian, and the demons he woke in her.

She stepped in. "Did you clean up the transmission?"

Feeney turned to her, droopy eyes, mournful expression. Roarke shifted, eyes of an almost savage blue. There was a click here, too, but a good solid one, one that made her smile.

Roarke angled his head. "Lieutenant?"

"Nothing." But she thought: *Who needs crosses and holy water to fight demons when you have two men like this?* Dorian would never have understood that bright and brilliant human link. Her father had never understood it.

"So." She crossed to them, and because it amused her, slid her hands into her pockets to mirror their stances. "What's the word?"

"Good news," Feeney began. "We got her clean. Bad news, there's not much of him."

"I don't need much."

"Going to need more than what we've got. Computer, run enhanced transmission."

Acknowledged . . .

Eve watched Allesseria's face. It was crystal clear now, as was the night around her, as was her voice. A streetlight beamed over her. The movement—rather than the jerky bounce of her quick walk—had been smoothed out, slowed down.

There was a sound, a *whoosh* of air, a ripple of fabric on the breeze. Eve watched the gloved hand snake in, between the 'link and the victim's face. There was an upward jerk, an instant of pain and terror in Allesseria's eyes. Then the image flipped as the phone tumbled: sky, street, sidewalk. Black.

"Crap" was Eve's comment, and her hands fisted in her pockets now. "Anything when you magnify and slow it down?"

"We can enhance so you can count the stitches in the seams of the glove," Feeney told her. "Can use the scale program to get you the size of it. We can give you the attacker's probable height calculated from the size, the angles. But we can't put on-screen what's not there. Got some snatches of audio though, for what it's worth."

He set the comp again, made the adjustments, then played it back.

What she heard first was silence.

"We backed out her voice, her footsteps," Roarke explained, "the ambient city noises. Now . . ."

She caught it. Feet on pavement, the faintest rustle, then the rush she identified as a run followed by a jump or leap. There was a breath, expelled in a kind of laugh as the hand shot out and clamped Allesseria's throat. And as the images rolled and tumbled on-screen, a single low word. *You.*

"Not enough for a voiceprint," Feeney pointed out. "Never hold up in court even if we could match it on one syllable."

"He doesn't have to know that." Eve narrowed her eyes at the screen. "Maybe what we've got is just enough to shake him, to make him think we have more."

Feeney grinned at Roarke, tapped a finger to his temple. "She's got something cooking up there."

"Yeah, I do. This time, we con the con."

Roarke stepped into Eve's office, closed the door. "I don't like it."

She continued across the cramped little room to her AutoChef, programmed coffee. "It's a good plan. It'll work." She took the two mugs of hot black out, passed him one. "And I didn't figure you'd like it. That's one of the drawbacks of having you inside an investigation."

"There are other ways to run him to ground, Eve."

"This is the quickest. There's no putting standard surveillance on him," she began. "There are dozens of ways in and out of those tunnels. I can't know what kind of escape hatch he might have in that club, up in his apartment. He decides he's bored here, or there's too much heat, he'd be in the wind before we got close."

"Find a way to shut down the club. Illegals raid will put him out of business."

"Sure, we could do that, we *will* do that. And if that's all we do, he'll be smoke. There are fronts to the business," she pointed out. "You said so yourself. And it'd take time we don't have to cut through them and dig down to him. By then he's gone."

He set the coffee down on her desk. "All right, even agreeing that all that's true, or very likely, it doesn't justify you going in alone. You're setting it up this way because the DNA crashed on you, and you're blaming yourself."

"That's not true." Or not entirely, she amended silently. "Sure, it pisses me off he pulled that over on me, but I'm not doing this to even the score." Or not entirely.

Logic, she decided, was the best way to lay it out. Not as satisfying as a fight, she thought, but quicker. "Okay, look. I go in there with troops or other badges, he's not going to talk, even if he sticks around long enough for me to corner him. He doesn't have to stick around at this point. I can't even pry him aboveground and get him in the box for interview. It has to be on his turf, and it has to be between him and me."

"Why—on the last point?"

"Why didn't you like him, from the get?"

She could see irritation cross Roarke's face before he picked up the coffee again. "Because he scoped my wife."

"Yeah. He'd like to take a bite, not only because I'm the cop looking at him, but because I'm married to you. Be a big ego kick for him to score off you. And if he thinks he has a shot at that, he'll take it, and I'll be ready."

"Eve—"

"Roarke. He'll kill again and soon. Maybe tonight. He has a taste for it now. You saw that, and so did I, the first time we met him. I'm telling you I saw more of it today. I see what he is."

This was the core, he knew, whatever she said. Whatever the other truths, this was the heart of it for her. "He's not your father."

"No, but there's a breed, and they're both of it. The smoke, the blood, the insinuation: Is he or isn't he an undead, blood-sucking fiend? That may tingle the spine, rouse superstitions, even tease the logical to entertain the illogical. But it's what's under it, Roarke. It's, well, shit, it's the beast that lives there that has to be stopped."

"The one you have to face," he corrected. "How many times?"

"As many as it takes. I want to walk away from it. Hell, I get within five feet of him, I want to run from it. And because I do, I can't."

"No." He traced his thumb down the shallow dent in her chin. "You can't." That, he knew, was what he had to face— again and again. Loving her left him no choice. "But this rush—"

"He's flying on the moment. Whatever drugs he's on, they're not as potent as the kill. As the blood. If I don't try this, and he gets another, how do I live with that?"

He searched her face, then lifted a hand to her cheek. "Being you, you don't. You can't. But I still don't have to like it."

"Understood. And . . ." She took his hand, squeezed it briefly. "Appreciated. Let's just count on me doing my job, and the rest of you doing yours. We'll shut him down, nail down that lid, before he knows what the hell's going on."

"He best not get so much as a nibble of you. That's my job." He leaned down, caught her bottom lip between his teeth. After one quick nip, he sank in, drawing her close, taking them both deep.

Her initial amusement slid away into the dreamy until

she could float away on the taste of him, glide off on the promise. When she sighed, eased back, her lips curved up.

"Good job," she told him.

"I do my best."

"Maybe later you can put in some overtime."

"Being dedicated to my work, I'll be available."

"But for right now, let's go get the team together for a full briefing. I don't want any screwups."

"Lieutenant." He caught her hand before she reached the door, and tugged her back around. Out of his pocket he drew a silver cross on a silver chain, and dangled it in front of her.

"Knew I forgot something." But when he draped it over her head, she goggled. "What? You're serious?"

"Indulge me." He planted another kiss on her lips, this one brief and firm. "I'm a superstitious man with a logical mind that can entertain the illogical."

Staring at him, she shook her head. "You're full of surprises, pal. Just full of them."

She used a conference room for the briefing. On-screen was a diagram of Bloodbath, and a second of the apartment—or the area of the apartment Eve had seen. Both were sketched from memory, with input from the others on the team who'd been inside the club.

As was often the case with underground establishments, no recorded blueprints or work orders could be located.

"There will be alternate exits," Eve continued. "It's likely at least some of the staff are aware of them, and will use them. Detaining and arresting waitresses and naked dancers aren't priorities."

"Speak for yourself," Baxter shot out, "on the naked dancers angle."

"Moving civilians out," Eve said, ignoring him, "without inciting a riot is a primary goal. Anyone wants to make collars for illegals, that's a personal decision and can be determined at the time. A couple dozen busts will add weight to the op, and hang on Vadim as manager. Anything and everything we get on him is a plus, but not at the expense of the primary target."

She scanned faces. "Nobody moves in, nobody tips the scales until I give the go. My communicator will be open for said go. Nothing, I repeat, nothing, is to be recorded from that source. I'm not having this slime skate on a technicality."

She paused, ordered the computer to show the diagram of the club only. "Our warrant covers only this area. No personnel are to move outside the club area in search or pursuit without probable cause. All weapons low stun."

Once more, she switched the screen image. Now Dorian Vadim's face filled it. "This is primary target. Unless specifically ordered or cleared, he is not to be detained or apprehended. If I can't pull this off, we have no cause for arrest. Suit up," she ordered. "Vests all around. Report to squad leaders for transportation to target."

She laid a hand on her sidearm. "Let's go kick ass."

As she bent to check her clutch piece, Baxter tapped her shoulder.

"What?"

"Got something for you." He held it out as she straightened.

"You're a laugh a minute, Baxter."

"Yeah, you gotta admit." He gave the wooden stake an agile toss.

Because she was amused despite herself, she caught the stake in one hand, then stuck it in her belt. "Thanks."

He blinked, then roared with laughter. "Eve Dallas, Vampire Slayer. One for the books."

CHAPTER

TEN

She went in alone, the way it had to be, as a cop, as a woman fighting her own demons.

She walked the now-familiar path down from the world to the underground, through the fetid tunnels with misery skulking in dirty shadows.

She'd come out of the shadows, Eve thought. So she knew what hid there, what bred there. What thrived there.

Light killed shadows, and it created them. But what loved the dark would always scuttle back from the light. Her badge had given her the light, Eve knew. Then Roarke had simply, irreversibly, blasted that light straight through her.

Nothing could pull her back again, unless she allowed it. Not the nightmares, not the memories, not whatever smear the man who'd made her had left in her blood.

What she did now, for the job, for two women, for herself, was only another way to cast the light.

She moved toward the ugly pulse of red and blue, the bone-rattling thrum of violent music.

The same bouncers flanked the arched door, and this time they sneered.

"Alone this time?"

Still moving, she kicked the one on the left solidly in the groin, smashed her elbow up and out into the bridge of the second's nose.

"Yeah," she said as she strode through the path they made as they stumbled back. "Just little old me."

She walked through the jostling crowd, through the sting of smoke, the crawl of fog. Someone made the mistake of making a playful grab for her and got a boot down hard on his instep for his trouble. And she never broke stride.

She reached the steps, started up their tight curve.

She felt him first, like the dance of sharpened nails along the skin. Then he was there, standing at the top of the stairs, mists swirling dramatically around him.

"Lieutenant Dallas, you're becoming a regular. No escort tonight?"

"I don't need an escort." She stopped on the step below him, knowing it gave him the superior ground. "But I'd like some privacy."

"Of course. Come with me." He held out a hand.

She placed hers in it, fought off a jitter of revulsion as his fingers twined with hers. He led her back, away from the crowd, then keyed in a code on his private door. "Enter Dorian," he said for the voice command, and the locks gave.

Inside candles were lit, dozens of them. Light and shadow, Eve thought again. On the wall screen various sections of the club were displayed, the sound muted, so people danced, groped, screamed, stalked, in absolute silence.

"Some view." Casually, she stepped away from him and stepped over as if to study the action on-screen.

"My way of being surrounded and alone at the same time." His hand brushed lightly over her shoulder as he walked behind her and over to his bar. "You'd understand that."

"You talk as if you know me. You look at me as though you do. But you don't."

"Oh, I think I do. I saw the understanding of violence, of power, and the taste for it in you. We have that in common. Wine?"

"No. Are you alone here, Dorian?"

"I am." Despite her answer, he poured two glasses. "Though I planned to entertain a woman later." This time his gaze traveled over her, boldly intimate. "How interesting it should be you. Tell me, Eve, is this a professional or a personal call?"

She let herself stare at him, into those eyes. "I don't know. I guess we'll find out. I know you killed those women."

He smiled slowly. "Do you? How?"

"I feel it. I see it when I look at you. Tell me how you did it."

"Why should I? Why would I? Lieutenant."

As if impatient, she shook her head. "I don't have a warrant. You know that. I haven't given you your rights. I can't use anything you tell me. You know that, too. I just need to know what you are. Why I feel the way I do around you. I don't believe in . . ."

There was no mistaking the *hunger* on his face as he walked toward her. "In what?"

She could hear her father's voice whispering in her mind. *There are things in the dark, little girl. Terrible things in the dark.*

"In the sort of thing you're selling out there." She gestured toward the screen. "Turn that off, will you? It feels crowded in here."

"You don't like to watch?" he said, silkily. "Or be watched?"

"Depends," she answered with what she hoped sounded like false bravado.

"Screen off," he ordered, and smiled again. "Better?"

"Yeah. It's better with it off."

"That's the signal." Feeney nodded to Roarke. **"All units,** move in. Move in. She's playing him," he said to Roarke. "She'll walk him right into it."

"Or he's playing her." With Eve's voice in his ear, Roarke rushed into the dark.

Into the terrible things.

"Hold it." There was the slightest hesitation in her order as she slapped a hand against Dorian's chest and shoved. "I have obligations. I have loyalties."

"None of which fill your needs."

"You don't know my needs."

"Give me five minutes to do as I like with you, and you'll know differently. You came to me." He trailed his fingers over her cheek. "You came to me alone. You want to know what I can give you."

She shook her head, stepped away. "I came because I need to understand. I can't settle, I can't focus. I feel like something's trying to crawl out of my skin."

"I can help you with that."

She glanced over her shoulder at him. "Yeah, I bet you could. But I'm not like Tiara Kent. I'm not looking for cheap thrills. And I'm not like Allesseria Carter. I don't need your goodwill. I'm not afraid of you."

"Aren't you? Aren't you afraid of what I could make you?"

She looked at the portrait. "Like that?" Her voice was just a little breathless. "I'm not that gullible."

He lifted one of the wineglasses, drank deeply. "There's more in the world that slips in and out of what's deemed reality."

"Such as?"

He drank again, and his eyes went even darker. "Such as powers, and hungers beyond the human. I'll take you there. I can show you a glimpse without causing you harm. You should drink. Relax. Nothing will happen to you here. It's not my way."

"No, you go to them. Kent practically spread rose petals on a path to her bed for you."

"Hypothetically, invitations are required."

"In an occupied building," Eve agreed. "Not in an abandoned one. Like the one where you dragged Allesseria, where you killed her."

"Does it excite you to think so, to look at me and see her death?"

"Maybe it does."

"You seek death." He laid his fingertips under hers, lifted her hand. "Surround yourself with it. Isn't that what I sensed, what I saw, in you that first moment our eyes met? It connects us, this . . . fondness for death in a way the man you give yourself to can never understand. He can't reach that dark bloom inside you. I can."

She let her fingers curl to his for an instant, then eased back again. "I don't know what connects us, but I felt something when I heard your voice come in on Allesseria's 'link message to me. It was a mistake to say anything, Dorian, a mistake not to make certain the 'link was down and the transmission broken before you spoke to her. We'll have your voiceprint match by morning."

He lowered the glass he'd lifted to his lips. "That's not possible."

"Would I be here now otherwise? Risking all this so I could see you tonight? This goes down tomorrow, and my part in it's over. I need answers for me. Why would I tell you we have evidence building that could take you down, give you time to poof? I have to know. For me."

"I have an alibi," he insisted.

"Kendra Lake? Another spoiled rich girl running on hormones, vanity, and chemicals. She won't help you. She'll crack, we both know it. She's on the juice, she's your lover. It won't hold."

"You're lying." He gulped down the rest of the liquid in the glass, heaved the glass aside. "You're lying. You bitch."

Okay, Eve thought, time to change directions.

Outside the apartment it was hell. Screams and shouts echoed through the mist some clever soul had boosted up when the small army of cops had burst in, announcing a raid.

Roarke flung one attacker aside, dodged the swipe of a knife from another. Preferring fists to stunner, he used them viciously. Despite the cacophony, he heard Eve's voice clearly in his head.

"She's losing him," he yelled to Feeney. Whirling, Roarke sprinted for the stairs through streams of stunner fire.

"Caught me," Eve said. "I'm lying about any pretense I find you attractive or compelling on a personal level. About the rest, that's a wrap. You not only ran your mouth where it could be heard on Allesseria's 'link, EDD's working on cleaning and enhancing a few seconds on-screen during the trans. You moved partially into view.

"Added to that," she continued, "we're about to link you to one Pensky, Gregor. Shouldn't have used a former known associate as a fall guy. Even a dead fall guy, Dorian. Little slips, they'll kill you every time."

She glanced idly around the room. "I bet you saved some of Tiara Kent's blood for a souvenir. I get that warrant in the morning, I'm going to find it, and the jewelry you took off her dead or dying body. You scum. That'll put you down for three counts of murder. Anything else you want to add to the menu?"

"Do you think you can threaten me?" His eyes were black pools. "Play with me?"

"If you're trying for thrall, you're missing. I'll have you locked on Allesseria in a matter of hours. The rest will tumble right into the pile. You're done. I just wanted the satisfaction of telling you personally before—Don't," she warned. She laid her hand on her stunner when she saw the move in his eyes. "Unless you want to add assaulting an officer to the mix. In which case, I can haul you out of here. Sun's down, Dorian."

"Yes, it is." He smiled, and to Eve's absolute shock, showed fangs.

He leaped, almost seemed to fly at her. She drew her weapon, pivoted, but she wasn't quick enough. Nothing could have been. She got off two shots as he hurled her across the room. He took both hits, and just kept coming. She felt it in every bone as she hit the stone wall, and though the stunner spurted out of her hand on impact, she managed to roll, then kick up hard with both feet. The force knocked him back far enough to give her room to flip up.

She braced for the next attack, but instead he hissed like a snake, cringed back. She flicked her gaze down, saw he was staring at the cross that had come out from under her shirt.

"You've got to be kidding me." He snarled as he circled her. "You actually believe your own hype."

Whatever he'd drunk had juiced him up good, she determined. So good, she'd never be able to take him in hand-to-hand. She held up the cross as she tried to gauge the distance to her stunner, and her chances of reaching it.

"I'll drink you dry." His tongue ran over his long incisors. "Almost dry. And make you drink me. I'll change you into what I am."

"What? A babbling lunatic? Why didn't Tiara change?"

"She wasn't strong enough. I drank too much of her. But she died in bliss under me. As you will. But you're strong,

strong enough to be reborn. I knew it when I saw you. Knew you'd be the first who'd walk as I walk."

"Uh-huh. You have the right to remain silent."

He sprang, leaping like a great cat. She blocked the first blow, though she felt the force of it sing down her arm, explode into her shoulder. But the second sent her sprawling. She thudded hard against one of his metal tables, and tasted her own blood in her mouth as she rolled painfully onto her back.

He was standing over her now, fangs gleaming, eyes mad. "I give you the gift, the ultimate kiss."

Eve swiped the blood off her mouth. "Bite me."

Grinning, he fell on her.

Outside the door, Feeney pulled out his master and a bag of electronic tricks to bypass the locks.

"I've got it." Blood seeped through the ragged tear in Roarke's jacket where a knife point had slipped through. He flipped out a recorder, closed his eyes to focus first on the tones of the beeps.

Quickly, he played his fingers over the keypad in the same order, then held the recorder to the voice command.

"Enter Dorian," the recorder replayed.

"Hey, Dallas said nothing was to be recorded."

Roarke spared one glance over at Feeney's wide grin. "I'm a poor team player."

They pushed in the door, Roarke going low as he knew Feeney preferred high.

She was flat on her back, blood soaking her shirt. Even as Roarke rushed toward her, she pushed herself up on her elbows. "I'm okay. I'm okay. Call the MTs before that ass-hole bleeds to death."

Roarke barely spared a glance at the man lying on the floor with a wooden stake in his belly. His own stomach muscles were knotted in slippery fists. "How much of this is yours?"

She looked down at her shirt in some disgust. "Hardly any. Missed the heart. Bastard was on top of me. Gut wounds are messy. Feeney?"

"Contacting the MTs," he told her. "Situation below is nearly contained. Hell of a show. But looks like you're the headliner here. Jesus, what a freaking mess."

"I can't believe I'm going to have to thank Baxter for being a smart-ass. Lost my weapon. He'd've done some damage before you got through if I hadn't had the pointy stick."

She started to stand, and with Roarke's help made it to her feet. Once there, she swayed and she staggered. "Just a little shaken up. Hit my head on various hard objects. No, no, don't carry me."

He simply scooped her into his arms. "You're doomed to have me disobey." Then he pressed his lips to the side of her throat where he saw the faint wounds. "Got a taste of you, did he?"

She heard the rage, and tried to tamp it down. "Told him to bite me. It's the first time anyone's ever taken that suggestion literally. Except you." She turned Roarke's face with her hand so that he looked at her rather than Dorian. "Put me down, will you, pal? This seriously undermines my authority."

"Hey, hey!" Crouched over Dorian, Feeney stopped even his half-hearted attempt to stanch the blood flow. "Is this guy sporting fangs?"

"He must've had them filed down that way," Eve said. "Then had them capped. Easy on, easy off. We'll sort it out."

Peabody ran in. There was a darkening bruise on her cheekbone and a nasty scrape along her jaw. "Unit's heading out to escort the MTs in. Holy crap!" she added when she saw Dorian. "You staked him. You actually staked him."

"It was handy. Let's get those medics in here. I don't want this guy skipping out on multiple murder charges by dying on me. I want to know the minute he's able to talk. I think we're going to get an interesting confession."

"It's supposed to be the heart," she heard Peabody mutter. "It's really supposed to be the heart."

Eve blew out a long breath. "Keep it up, Peabody, and I may have Mira shrink your head after she's done with this second-rate Dracula. I want some damn air. I'm going up to the real world."

Once she had, she took the bottle of water Roarke passed her and drank like a camel. She lifted her chin at the blood on his sleeve. "Is that bad?"

"It damn well is. I liked this jacket. Here, take a blocker. If you don't have the mother of all headaches yet, it's only due to adrenaline. Take the blocker, and I won't haul your stubborn ass into a health center for an exam."

She popped the blocker without a quibble. Then since it was there, she sat on the edge of the floor through the open door of the police van.

"He believed it," she said after a moment. "He actually believed he was a vampire. Drugs probably pushed the act into his reality. Mira nailed the profile from the get. It was the pretending to be the Prince of Darkness that was the pretense, for him."

"More likely he was just pushing the con as far as it would take him—and gambling to use it to plead insanity."

"No. You didn't see his face when he looked at this." She held up the cross. "And thanks, by the way. It bought me a few minutes when it counted."

Roarke sat beside her, rubbed a hand over her thigh. "Illogical superstition. Sometimes it works."

"Apparently. He's got himself some kind of super-Zeus recipe, is my guess. Not just the whacked brain it causes, or the temporary strength. Speed, too. The bastard was fast. Magician training, grift experience, drugs. I wonder when it turned on him, stopped being a way to case marks."

Gently, Roarke traced a fingertip over her neck wounds. "There are all kinds of vampires, aren't there? Darling Eve."

"Yeah." Very briefly, since all of the cops running around were too busy to notice, she leaned her head against Roarke's shoulder. "Under it, he wasn't really like my father. Not the way I thought. My father wasn't crazy. Dorian, he's bug-shit."

"Evil doesn't have to be sane."

"No, you're right about that." And she'd faced it—and she'd beaten it. One more time. "Well, the bad news is he's going to end up in a facility for violent mental defectives, not a concrete cage. But you take what you can get."

Roarke's hand rested on her knee. She laid hers over it, squeezed. "And right now, I'll take a hot shower and a fresh shirt. I've got to go in and clean myself up, and clean this up, too."

"I'll drive."

"You should go home," she told him, but her hand stayed over his. "Get some sleep. It's going to take hours to close this up."

"I have this image I can't shake." He got up, drew her to her feet. "Of the sun rising, all red and gold smears over the sky. And you and I walking toward home in that lovely soft light. So taking what I can get, I'll take sunrise with you."

"Sunrise it is."

She kept her hand in his as she pulled out her communicator to contact Feeney, Peabody, the team leaders to check on the status below.

With her hand linked with Roarke's, the demons that plagued her were silent. And would stay silent, she thought, through the night. And well past sunrise.

RITUAL IN DEATH

One owes respect to the living;
to the dead one owes only the truth.

—VOLTAIRE

The belief in a supernatural source of evil
is not necessary; men alone are quite capable
of every wickedness.

—JOSEPH CONRAD

ONE

Her feet were killing her. And made her imagine traveling back in time, hunting down whoever had invented stiletto heels, and beating the crap out of him.

What was the point of them other than throwing a woman off balance, making it next to impossible to run, and inducing foot cramps?

The question occupied Eve's mind as she tuned out the bulk of the party conversation buzzing around her like a hive of drunk hornets. What if one of the guests at this shindig went off and . . . stabbed somebody in the eye with a shrimp fork, for instance? How was she supposed to take him down dressed like this? And a foot pursuit in these stilts? Forget about it.

It was a hell of a getup for a cop, to her way of thinking. The flimsy excuse for a dress left most of her exposed. And she glittered. You couldn't have diamonds hanging all over you and blend.

Of course, you couldn't go to any sort of snazzy function with Roarke and blend.

The only advantage to the ridiculous damn shoes that she could see was the fact that they boosted her up so that she and Roarke were eye-to-eye.

They were stupendous eyes, bold and brilliantly blue. A look from them could give her a tingle in the belly—even after nearly two years of marriage. The rest of him didn't suck either, she reflected. The black silk fall of hair framed a billion-dollar jackpot of a face. Even now, as he glanced at her that sculpted, delicious mouth curved up in a slow, secret smile.

All she had to do, Eve reminded herself, was tolerate the goddamn shoes a couple more hours, then she'd have that mouth—and the rest of the package—to herself. Screaming arches were probably a small price to pay.

"Darling." Roarke took a glass of champagne from the waiter passing them, and handed it to her. Since the glass he'd traded it for had still been half full, she interpreted it as a signal to tune back in.

Okay, okay, she thought. She was here as Roarke's spouse. It wasn't as if he demanded she gear up like this and attend excruciatingly boring parties every day of the week. He was smooth about it—and as the man had more money than God and nearly as much power and position—the least she could do was play the part when they were doing the public couple thing.

Their hostess, one Maxia Carlyle, glided over in some kind of floaty number. The wealthy socialite was—by her own words—kicking into New York for a few days to catch up with friends. All of whom, Eve supposed, were wandering around Maxia's expansive tri-level hotel suite gorging on canapés and sloshing down champagne.

"I haven't had a minute to talk to you." Maxia put her hand on Roarke's arm, tipped her face to his.

They looked, Eve decided, like an ad for the rich and the gorgeous.

"And how've you been, Maxi?"

"Oh, you know how it goes." She laughed, shrugging one perfect bare shoulder. "It's been about four years, hasn't it, since we've seen each other. Never seem to land in the same place at the same time, so I'm especially glad you could make it tonight. And you," she added with a sparkling smile for Eve. "I was hoping I'd get the chance to meet you. Roarke's cop."

"Mostly the NYPSD considers me theirs."

"I can't even imagine it. What it must be like. Your work must be so fascinating and exciting. Investigating murders and murderers."

"It has its moments."

"More than moments, I'm sure. I've seen you on-screen from time to time. The Icove case in particular."

And wasn't that one going to dog her forever? Eve mused.

"I have to say you don't look anything like a police-woman." Maxia's perfect eyebrows arched as she gave Eve's dress a quick scan. "Leonardo dresses you, doesn't he?"

"No, I usually do it myself."

Roarke gave her a little elbow poke. "Eve's oldest friend is married to Leonardo. Eve often wears him."

"Mavis Freestone is your oldest friend?" Now, in addition to interest and curiosity, considerable warmth infused Maxia's face. "I love her music, but my niece is a slathering fan. I took her to one of Mavis's concerts, in London, and arranged for a backstage pass. She was so sweet with my niece, and I've been the undisputed champion of aunts ever since."

She laughed, touched Eve's arm. "You *do* have a fascinating life. Married to Roarke, friends with Mavis and Leonardo, and chasing killers. I suppose it's mostly head work, isn't it? Studying evidence, looking for clues. People like me glamorize it, think about policework the way it is on-screen and at the vids. All danger and action, chasing mad-men down dark alleys and firing off your weapon, when in reality it's brain and paperwork."

"Yeah." Eve controlled the urge to smirk. "That's about it."

"Being married to Roarke's action enough. Are you still dangerous?" Maxia asked him.

"Domesticated." He lifted Eve's hand, kissed it. "Entirely."

"I don't believe that for a minute. Oh, there's Anton. I need to snatch him away and bring him over to meet you."

Eve took a long, long drink of champagne.

"We'll meet this Anton, mingle another twenty," Roarke said, the faint hint of Ireland in his voice, "and slip out and away."

Eve felt a tingle of joy, right down to her numbed toes. "Seriously?"

"I never intended to stay above an hour or so. And certainly owe you for the points I'm making by bringing a Homicide cop to the party."

"It's all paperwork," Eve said dryly.

He skimmed a finger down her arm, where a knife had slashed only days before. "Yes, your work is nothing but tedium. But I have to agree with Maxi. You don't look very coplike tonight."

"Good thing I don't have to chase down any psycho killers. I'd fall off these stupid shoes and embarrass myself." She curled her toes in them—or attempted to while she flicked a hand at the short, choppy crop of brown hair she'd recently taken the scissors to herself. Old priceless diamonds dripped from her ears. "I don't get parties like this. People standing around. Talk, talk, talk. Why do they have to get all dressed up to do that?"

"To show off."

She thought about that over another sip of wine. "I guess that's it. At least I don't have to gear up like this for the shower deal for Louise. Still, another party. More talk, talk, talk."

"It's a ritual, after all. When a friend's about to marry, her friends gather together, with gifts, and . . . well, I have no idea what happens then."

"If it's anything like mine, some of them drink till they puke, and others strip it off and dance."

"Sorry I'll miss it."

"Liar." But she grinned at him.

"Here we are!" Maxia came back, towing a portly, mustachioed man somewhere on the shady side of sixty. On his arm like a whippy vine twined a woman well shy of thirty with full, pouty lips, a bored expression, and a short red dress that covered very little of her expansive breasts.

"You simply must meet Anton and his lovely companion. It's Satin, isn't it?"

"Silk," the bored blonde corrected.

"Of course it is."

Eve caught the quick glint in Maxia's eyes and understood she'd *mistaken* the name deliberately. And liked her better for it.

"Actually we met a few years ago." Anton stuck out a wide, pudgy hand. "At Wimbledon."

"It's nice to see you again. My wife, Eve."

"Yes, the American cop. A pleasure, Detective."

"Lieutenant." Eve glanced down at Silk's sky-high heels. Just heels, she noted, with the feet arched into them bare on top. "I heard about those." She pointed. "People are actually wearing invisible shoes."

"They're not available to the public for another three weeks." Silk tossed her long mane of hair. "Sookie pulled some strings." She plastered herself against Anton/Sookie.

"Anton's produced several films about crime and police and so on," Maxia commented. "So I thought he'd enjoy meeting one of New York's Finest."

"British-style procedurals." Anton patted Silk's hand as she tugged at him like a petulant child. "What we like to think of as crackling whodunits—with plenty of sex and violence," he added with a laugh. "And a slight connection with reality, as you'd know. I have been thinking about using an American setting, so I—"

"I don't see why a girl would want to be a cop." Silk frowned at Eve. "It's not very feminine."

"Really? It's funny because I don't see why a *girl* would want to be a bimb—"

"What is it you do?" Roarke cut Eve off, smoothly— giving her only the slightest pinch on the ass.

"I'm an actress. I just finished shooting a major role in Sookie's next vid."

"Victim, right?" Eve asked.

"I get to die dramatically. It's going to make me a star, isn't it, Sookie?"

"Absolutely, sweetheart."

"I want to go. There's nothing happening here. I want to go dancing, go some place with some *action*." She tugged hard enough to pull Anton back a few steps.

"He used to be such a sensible man," Maxia murmured.

"Guys of a certain age are especially vulnerable to bimboitis."

Maxia laughed. "I'm so glad I like you. I wish I wasn't due in Prague in a couple of days so I could get to know you better. I should mingle, make sure everyone isn't as bored as Linen over there."

"I think that's Polyester. Definitely man-made fibers."

Laughing again, Maxia shook her head. "Yes, I really like you. And you." She rose to her toes to kiss Roarke's cheek. "You look awfully happy."

"I am. And awfully glad to see you again, Maxi."

As Maxia started to turn, Silk's strident voice whined out. "But I want to go *now*. I want to have *fun*. This party is *dead*."

Someone screamed. Something crashed. As people stumbled back, as some turned, shoving through small packs of others, Eve pushed forward.

The man staggered like a drunk, and wore nothing but spatters and smears of blood. The knife clutched in his hand gleamed with it.

A woman in his path fainted, and managed to take out a waiter holding a full tray of canapés with her. As shrimp balls and quail eggs rained, Silk shrieked, turned, and in a sprint for the terrace bowled over guests like pins in an alley.

Eve flipped open the next-to-useless bag she carried, tossed it to Roarke as she pulled out her weapon.

"Drop it. Drop it now." She sized him up quickly. About five feet, ten inches, roughly one-sixty-five. Caucasian, brown and brown. And the eyes were glazed and glassy. Shock or drugs—maybe both.

"Drop it," she repeated when he took another staggering step forward. "Or I drop you."

"What?" His gaze skidded around the room. "What? What is it?"

She considered and rejected just stunning him in a matter of seconds. Instead she moved to him, gripped the wrist of his knife hand, twisted. "Drop the goddamn knife."

His eyes stared into hers as his fingers went limp. She heard the knife hit the floor. "Nobody touch it. Stay back. I'm the police, do you get that? I'm a cop. What are you on?"

"I don't know. I don't know. The police? Can you help me? I think I killed someone. Can you help me?"

"Yeah. You bet. Roarke, I need a field kit ASAP, and for you to call this in. I need everyone else upstairs for now. I need you people to clear this room until the situation is contained. Move it!" she snapped when people stood, gaping. "And somebody check on that woman lying in the shrimp balls over there."

Roarke stepped up beside her. "I've sent one of the hotel staff down to the garage to get the field kit out of the boot of the car," he told her. "I've notified your Dispatch."

"Thanks." She stood where she was as the naked party crasher sat on the floor and began to shudder. "Just remember, you're the one who wanted to come tonight."

With a nod, Roarke planted a foot on the hilt of the knife to secure it. "No one to blame but myself."

"Can you get my recorder out of that stupid purse?"

"You brought a recorder?"

"If you need the weapon, you're going to need the recorder."

When he handed it to her, Eve pinned it to the frothy material over her breasts, engaged it. After reciting the basics, she crouched down. "Who do you think you killed?"

"I don't know."

"What's your name?"

"It's . . ." He lifted a blood-smeared hand, rubbed it over his face. "I can't think. I can't remember. I can't think."

"Tell me what you took."

"Took?"

"Drugs. Illegals."

"I . . . I don't do illegals. Do I? There's so much blood." He lifted his hands, stared at them. "Do you see all this blood?"

"Yeah." She looked up at Roarke. "It's fresh. I'm going to need to do a room-to-room, starting with this floor. He couldn't have walked around for long like this. We start with this floor."

"I can arrange that. Do you want security to start on that, or sit on him while you do the room-to-room?"

"Sit on him. I don't want them to talk to him, touch him. What's that room over there?"

"It would be a maid's room."

"That'll do."

"Eve," Roarke said as she straightened. "I don't see any wounds on him. If that blood's someone else's—that much blood—they can't possibly still be alive."

"No, but we push the room-to-room first."

CHAPTER

TWO

She needed to move fast. The amount of blood on her naked guy made it doubtful she'd find anyone alive—if she found anyone at all—so she couldn't putz around. While she didn't much like leaving her suspect with hotel security, even once she'd clapped on the restraints from her field kit, she couldn't afford to wait for her uniformed backup, or her partner.

For lack of better, she set her suspect on the floor of the maid's room, ran his prints.

"Jackson Pike." She crouched down on his level, looked into the glazed brown eyes. "Jack?"

"What?"

"What happened, Jack?"

"I don't . . ." He looked around the room, dazed and stoned. "I don't . . ." Then he moaned in pain and clutched his head.

"Uniformed officers are on their way," she said to the pair from security as she straightened. "I want him exactly where I've left him, and those people upstairs contained until I get back. Nobody comes in except NYPSD officials. Nobody goes out. Let's move," she said to Roarke.

"Guy's a doctor," she continued as they started out the door. "Thirty-three years old. Single."

"He didn't walk in off the street like that."

"No. Your hotel. Find out if a Jackson Pike, or anyone with a variation of that name's registered. How's this floor set up?"

Roarke pulled out his 'link as he gestured. "Four triplexes, one on each corner. One minute."

While he spoke to the hotel manager, Eve turned left. "Well, he left a trail. That's handy." Moving quickly, she followed bloody footprints over the lush carpet.

"No Jackson Pike, or any Pikes for that matter," Roarke told her. "There's a Jackson, Carl, on thirty-two. They're checking. On this floor Maxia has 600. Six-oh-two is occupied by Domingo Fellini—actor—I saw him at the party."

"Pike didn't come from there, trail's down this way." She picked up the pace as they started down the long corridor. "It's the sixtieth floor. Why isn't it 6002?"

"The sixth floor is the health club, the pool, and so on. No guest rooms. The triplexes cater to those who can afford the freight, and we bill them as penthouses, or apartments. So it's Suite 600. Perception."

"Yeah, your perception's pretty screwed with all this blood on your carpet. Anyone in 604?"

"Not tonight."

"Empty suite's a nice spot for bloody murder, but the trail heads off." She kept moving, her weapon in her hand, her eyes scanning. "Does every suite have the private elevator like Suite 600?"

"They do, yes. Those elevators in the center of the floor are also private, in that you need a key card or clearance for the trip up."

Emergency exits, all four corners, she noted, via stairs.

But Jackson Pike hadn't used them. His trail led straight to the carved double doors of Suite 606.

Eve saw the faint smear of blood over the ornate zero.

Suite 666, she thought. Wasn't that just perfect?

She signaled for Roarke to stay back, then tried the knob. "Locked. I don't have my master."

"Lucky for you, you have me." He drew a slim tool out of his pocket.

"Handy, but have you ever considered how a cop's supposed to explain—should it come up—why her husband's got burglary tools in his pockets?"

"For bloody emergencies?" He straightened. "Lock's off."

"I don't suppose you're carrying."

He flicked her a look, his eyes very cool. "While I didn't think it necessary to bring a weapon to a cocktail party, I got this from security." He drew out a stunner. "Civilian issue. Perfectly legal."

"Hmm. On three."

It wasn't their first time through a door. She went low, he went high into a large living area lit by hundreds of candles. In the flickering light blood gleamed as it pooled over the black pentagram drawn on the polished marble floor.

A body floated on that pool, the arms and legs spread to form an X at the center of the sign.

Gone, Eve thought, bled out. Throat slashed, multiple body wounds. She shook her head at Roarke, gestured to the left.

She moved right, in a suite the mirror image of Maxia's. Sweeping her weapon, she cleared a dining room, a short hallway, a kitchen, a powder room, making the circle that brought her back to Roarke.

"Bed and bath clear, this level," he told her. "Both were used. There's considerable blood—smears not spatters. Hers, I expect."

He wasn't a cop, she mused, but he could think like one.

"We're going up." She did a chin point toward the elevator and tried to ignore the stench—not just death, but a kind of burning on the air. "Can you block that? Shut it down?"

Saying nothing, he walked to it, took out his tool again. While he worked, Eve circled the pentagram to clear the terrace.

"Done."

"What's the layout on the second floor?"

"Bed and bath, small sitting room to the left. Master suite—living area, powder room, dressing area, bed and bath to the right."

"I'll take the right."

The place felt empty, she thought. It felt dead. The metallic reek of the blood, the sickly sweet overlay of death mixed with candle wax smeared the air. And something more, that burning and a kind of . . . pulsing, she thought. Spent energy, the shadows of it still beating.

Together they cleared the second level, then the third.

She found evidence of sexual frenzy, of food, of drink, of murder. "The sweepers are going to be hours in here, if not days."

Roarke studied the glasses, plates, half-eaten food. "What kind of people do murder, and leave so much of themselves behind?"

"The kind who think they're beyond or above the law. The worst kind. I need to seal this place off, all three levels, until Crime Scene gets here. Who was registered in this suite?"

"The Asant Group." On the steps, he stared down at the body posed on the pentagram. "Jumble the letters, and you've got—"

"Satan. God, I hate this kind of shit. People want to worship the devil, be my guest. Hell, they can have horns surgically implanted on their forehead. But then they've just got to slice somebody up for their human sacrifice and drag me into it."

"Damned cheeky of them."

"I'll say."

"Naked Jack didn't do this on his own."

"Nope. Let's go see if his memory's a little clearer."

The uniforms had taken over. Eve directed them to take names and contact info from the guests, then clear them out.

She sat on the floor with Jackson. "I need a sample of the blood you're wearing, Jack."

"There's so much of it." His body jerked every few seconds, as if in surprise. "It's not mine."

"No." She took several samples—face, arms, chest, back, feet. "What were you doing in 606?"

"What?"

"Suite 606. You were in there."

"I don't know. Was I?"

"Who's the woman?"

"There were a lot of women, weren't there?" Again he shuddered in pain. "Were you there? Do you know what happened?"

"Look at me, goddamn it." Her voice was like a slap, shocked him back to her. "There's a woman in 606. Her throat's slashed."

"Did I do it? Did I hurt somebody?" He pressed his forehead to his knees. "My head. My head. Somebody's screaming in my head."

"Do you belong to the Asant Group?"

"I don't know. What is it? I don't know. Who are you? What's happening?"

With a shake of her head, Eve rose as the med-techs she'd ordered stepped in. "I want him examined. I want a blood sample. I need to know what he's on. When you're done, he'll be transported to Cop Central."

"Whose blood is it?"

"You're too late for her." She walked back into the living area to leave them to it just as her partner came in the main door.

Peabody's hair was pulled back in a stubby little tail that left her square face unframed and seemed to enlarge her brown eyes. She wore baggy dark pants and a white tee with a red jacket tossed over it. She carried a field kit.

"Who died?"

"An as yet unidentified female. Prime suspect is in there." Eve jerked her head. "Naked and covered with what is most likely her blood."

"Wow. Must've been a hell of a party."

"It happened on the other side. Let's go work the scene."

Outside the doors of 606 they coated hands and feet with Seal-It while Eve gave Peabody the rundown.

"He just walked into the cocktail party? And doesn't remember anything?"

"Yes, and so it seems. He doesn't come off as faking it. Both pupils are big as the moon. He's disoriented, motor skills are off, and he appears to have one major headache."

"Stoned?"

"Be my first guess, but we'll see what the MTs have to say about it." Eve unsealed the door, and now used the key Roarke had acquired for her.

When she stepped in, the sturdy Peabody blanched. "Man. Oh crap." She bent over at the waist, pressed her hands to her thighs and took long, slow breaths.

"Don't you boot on my crime scene."

"Just need a minute. Okay." She kept breathing. "Okay. Black magic. Bad juju."

"Don't start that shit. We've got a bunch of assholes who had an orgy, topped it off with ritual murder using Satan as an excuse. Used the private elevator," Eve added, gesturing toward it, "most likely, coming and going. We'll want the security discs for that. Cleaned up after they did her. Evidence of that in the bathrooms, of which there are six in this place. Beds show signs of being used, and food and drink were consumed. Since I doubt the pentagram is part of the room's original decor, somebody drew it on the floor. A question might be 'Why?' Why use a fancy, high-dollar hotel suite for your annual satanic meeting?

"Let's get her prints, get an ID and a time of death." Since Peabody still looked pale, Eve opted to take the body herself. "Do a run on Pike, Jackson. His prints came up with age thirty-three, and an addy on West Eighty-eighth. He's a doctor. See if he's got a sheet."

Eve stepped over to the body, doing what she could to avoid the blood. Not to preserve her shoes, but the scene. The air chilled, teased gooseflesh on her arms, and once more she felt, sensed, a pulsing.

She lifted the victim's hand to the Identi-pad, scanned the prints.

"Marsterson, Ava, age twenty-six, single. Mixed-race female with an address on Amsterdam. Employed as office manager at the West Side Health Clinic."

Eve tipped her head at the tattoo—a red and gold serpent swallowing its own tail—that circled the left hip. "She's got a tat on her hip, and it's not listed on her ID. Maybe a temp, or maybe fresh."

She took out her gauge. "TOD, twenty-two-ten. That's nearly an hour before Pike crashed the party down the hall." She replaced the gauge and studied the body. "The victim's throat is deeply slashed, in what appears to be a single blow with a sharp blade, right to left, slightly downward angle. A right-handed attacker, facing. He wanted to see your face when he sliced you open. Multiple wounds, slices, stab wounds, over shoulders, torso, abdomen, legs. Varying sizes and depths. Various blades held in various hands? Victim is posed, arms and legs spread, in the center of a black pentagram drawn directly onto the floor. Bruising on the thighs. Possible rape or consensual sex, ME to determine. No defensive wounds. None. Didn't put up a fight, Ava? Did they just take you down by slashing your throat, then have a party on you? Tox screen to determine presence of alcohol and/or drugs."

At the knock on the door, Eve called out for Peabody.

"I got it." Peabody hustled over, used the security peep. "It's Crime Scene."

In minutes the room filled with noise, movement, equipment, and the somehow cleaner smell of chemicals. When the crew from the morgue rolled in, Eve stepped away from the body.

"Marsterson, Ava. Bag and tag. Peabody, with me. Run this Asant Group," she ordered. "We're going in to shake what we can out of Pike."

"There had to be at least a dozen people in there, Dallas. Twelve, fifteen people by the number of trays and the glasses. Why come here to do this? You can't cover it up this way, and hey, party down the hall going on at the same time with a cop right there. By the way, you look totally mag. The shoes are up to wicked."

Eve frowned down at the shoes she'd forgotten she was wearing. "Shit, shit. I've got to go into Central in this getup." She'd also, she realized, forgotten Roarke.

He leaned against the wall outside Maxia's suite doing something that entertained or interested him on his PPC. And looked up as she approached.

"Sorry. I should've told you to go home."

"I assumed you'd want the code for the car since it's not one of yours. I had the garage bring it out front. Hello, Peabody."

"Hey. You guys look superior. It's really too bad the evening got screwed for you."

"It got screwed bigger for Ava Marsterson," Eve commented. "Maxia?"

"Took a soother and went to bed. I'll get myself home." He caught Eve's chin in his hand, skimmed his thumb down the dent, then kissed her. He handed her a mini memo cube. "Code's on it. Take care, Lieutenant. Good night, Peabody."

Peabody watched him walk away. "Boy, sometimes you just want to slurp him up without a straw." She wheeled her eyes to Eve. "Did I say that out loud?"

THREE

Grateful she kept some workout gear in her locker, Eve stripped off the party dress, pried her aching feet out of the hated shoes, then pulled on loose cotton pants and a faded gray tee. Since she couldn't walk around Central or successfully intimidate a suspect dripping in diamonds, she had no choice but to secure them in her locker.

Safe enough, she thought. If they'd been a candy bar, odds were lower that her property would be there when she opened the locker. But a small—probably not so small— fortune in diamonds, no problem.

After stepping into an ancient pair of skids, she met Peabody in the corridor.

"No criminal. Nothing, Dallas. He had a detained and released for disturbing the peace when he was twenty. Some college fraternity party. It wouldn't be on his record except the campus cops slapped the whole fraternity over it. He's from Pennsylvania, just moved here a couple of weeks ago. He's a doctor, pretty much brand-spanking-new, and just took a position on staff at—"

"The West Side Health Clinic."

"It's annoying to do the run if I don't get the payoff. Interview A. They got him cleaned up."

"The victim?" Eve asked as they walked.

"Clean to the squeaky level. Moved to New York about two years ago from Indiana. Both parents and younger brother still back there. We'll have to notify them."

"We'll take Pike first. They can wait a few hours to have their lives shattered." She pushed open the door to the interview room, nodded to the uniform.

The uniform stepped out, and Eve walked to the table where Jack sat in the orange pants and shirt of a con. "Record on. Dallas, Lieutenant Eve, and Peabody, Detective Delia, in interview with Pike, Jackson, regarding the investigation into the death of Marsterson, Ava."

"Ava?" Jack looked up, his face squeezed tight as if he struggled on the name. "Ava?"

"That's right, Ava. You've been read your rights, Mr. Pike, is that correct?"

"Ah, I don't know."

"Then we'll refresh you." Eve recited the Revised Miranda. "Do you understand your rights and obligations?"

"I think. Yes. Why? Why am I here?"

"You don't remember?"

"My head." He pressed both hands to his temples. "Was I in an accident? My head hurts."

"What do you remember about today?"

"I . . . I went to work. Didn't I? What day is it? Is it Tuesday?"

"It's Wednesday."

"But . . ." Jack stared up at her. "What happened to Tuesday?"

"What drugs did you take, Jack?"

"I don't, I don't take drugs. I don't do illegals. I'm a doctor. I'm on staff at . . ." He held his head again, and rocked. "Where? Where?"

"The West Side Health Clinic."

He looked at Eve, his eyes, his face slack with relief. "Yes. Yes. That's it. I just started. I went to work. I went to work, and then . . ." He moaned, shuddered. "Please, can I have a blocker? My head's pounding."

"You've got something in you, Jack. I can't give you a blocker until I know what it is. Did you go to the Palace Hotel with Ava? To Suite 606?"

"Ava . . . I can't . . . Ava works at the clinic." Sweat shone on his face from the effort. "Ava, manages . . . Ava. We . . ." Then horror covered it. "No. No. No."

"What happened to Ava, Jack?"

"No. No."

"What happened in 606?"

"I don't know. I don't—"

"Stop!" She reached over, grabbed a fistful of his shirt. "You tell me what happened."

"It's not real. It didn't happen."

"What isn't real?"

"The people, the people." He surged to his feet, and Eve signaled Peabody to stay back. "The lights. The voices. Smoke and fire. And hell came." He lurched around the interview room, holding his head. Tears leaked out of his eyes. "Laughing. Screaming. I couldn't stop. Did I want to stop? We had sex. No. Yes. I don't know. Bodies and hands and mouths. They hurt her. Did I hurt her? But she was smiling, smiling at me. Then her blood."

His hands ran over his face as if wiping at it. "Her blood. All over me."

His eyes rolled up in his head. Peabody managed to break the worst of his fall by going down with him. "Jesus, Dallas, no way this guy's faking it."

"No. Let's get him into a cage. I want him on suicide watch. I want eyes on him." She stepped to the door at the knock.

"Screening on your suspect, Lieutenant. They said you wanted it ASAP."

"Thanks." She took the report from a tech, scanned it. "Jesus, what doesn't this guy have in him? Erotica, Rabbit, Zoner, Jive, Lucy."

"Sleepy, Dopey, and Doc," Peabody finished. Then shrugged at Eve's frown. "Bad joke. No wonder his head's screaming. Coming down off a cocktail like that's gotta rip it up."

"Get him into a cage, have a medic treat him. He's had enough for one night."

"He doesn't come across like somebody who could do what was done to that woman tonight."

"That much junk inside him, you don't know what he could do. But he's not a regular user. No way he could be a regular with that kind of habit and not have a single pop."

Eve started back to her office. A couple of uniforms led a weeping woman away in the opposite direction. Outside the bullpen a guy wearing a torn and bloody shirt sat laughing quietly to himself while he rattled the restraints that chained him to the seat.

She swung into the bullpen while he went back to giggling. In her office she hit the AutoChef for coffee first, then sat at her desk. She gulped caffeine while she booted up the security discs from the hotel.

She ran the VIP check-in first, the elaborate parlor reserved for guests in the tonier suites and the triplexes. She ordered the computer to coordinate with the time stamped on the Asant Group's check-in. And watched the parlor fuzz into white static. She ran it back, noted the glitch began thirty minutes before the log-in, and continued to twenty-three hundred.

The pattern repeated when she ran the security discs for the private elevator, and again when she ran the main lobby discs.

"Son of a bitch." She turned to her interoffice 'link. "Peabody, wake up your cohab. I need McNab in here to dig into the security discs. They're wiped."

If the boy genius from the Electronic Detectives Division couldn't dig out data, she had someone who could. She contacted Roarke.

"Why are you awake?" she demanded when her 'link screen showed him at his desk.

"Why are you?"

"Oh, just a little something about a ritual murder. I thought you'd want to know that all the security discs from your hotel are compromised. Nothing but static on all starting thirty minutes before the log-in for the Asant Group."

"Are you bringing them to me or am I coming to you?"

"I've got McNab coming in, but—"

"I'm on my way."

"Wait. Listen, grab me some work clothes, will you? And my weapon harness, and—"

"I know what you need."

Her screen went black. Pissed off, she thought, and couldn't blame him. She imagined a few heads would roll at Roarke's Palace, and in short order. But meanwhile, she had useless discs on her hands, a suspect with drug-induced memory blanks, and a mutilated body at the morgue.

And it was still shy of dawn.

She opened her murder book, set up her board. According to the hotel records, the Asant Group had booked the triplex two months prior, and secured it with a credit card under the name of Josef Bellor, who carried an address in Budapest.

She fed the data into her computer, ordered a standard run. Only to learn Josef Bellor of Budapest had died there five years before at the ripe age of one hundred and twenty-one.

"Gonna be hard-pressed to get him to pay the bill," she muttered.

One night's booking, she thought, going over the notes. All room service delivered through the suite's AutoChefs or pre-ordered and delivered prior to check-in. Five cases of wine, several pounds of various European cheeses, fancy breads, caviar, pâtés, cream cakes.

No point in ritual murder on an empty stomach.

So they ate, drank, orgied, she thought, pushing up to pace the small space of her office. Popped whatever illegals suited their fancy. Three floors of revelry, soundproofed high-collar digs with the privacy shades activated.

Would've saved the best for last, she decided. The sacrifice would've been the evening's crescendo.

Just how did a nice girl from Indiana end up the star of the show? How did a transplanted young doctor from Pennsylvania get invited and left behind?

"Lieutenant."

She turned to the sleepy-eyed McNab in her doorway. He wore pants of screaming yellow that matched the fist-sized dots shrieking over a shirt of eye-tearing green. His long blond hair was pulled back from his thin, pretty face into a tail. She wondered if the hank of it somehow balanced the weight of the tangle of silver loops in his ear.

"Doesn't it ever give you a headache?" she wondered. "Just looking in the mirror."

"Huh?"

"Never mind. Discs." She gathered them from her desk, pushed them at him. "Find something on them. Roarke's on his way."

"Okay. Why?"

"They're his discs. Palace Hotel security. I've already shot a report to your unit in EDD. Read it, work it. Get me something."

He stifled a yawn, then focused on her board. "Is that the vic?"

Eve only nodded, said nothing when he came in to study the board. He'd work better and harder, she knew, if he was invested. "That's fucked up," he said. "That's seriously fucked up. And that's gotta be more than one killer." He slipped the discs into one of the pockets of his pants. "If there's an image on these, we'll get it."

If there were no images, she thought when McNab left, it meant the security had been compromised on site. Knowing how tightly any ship in Roarke's expansive fleet ran, that would've taken some serious magic.

She turned toward her 'link with the idea of tagging Roarke on his way in. And he walked into her office.

"That was quick."

"I'm in a hurry." He set a bag on her visitor's chair. "Where are the discs?"

"I just passed them off to McNab. Wait." She shot out a hand as he turned. "If the security was breached on site, how could it be done?"

"I don't know until I see the discs, do I?"

"Be pissed off later. How could it be done?"

He made an obvious effort to settle himself, then walked to her AutoChef to program coffee for himself. "It would have to be through security or electronics, and one of the top levels. Most likely both, working in tandem. No one at that level would consider a bribe of any kind worth their position."

"Threat, blackmail?"

"Anything's possible, of course, but doubtful. It would be more to their advantage to come to me with the problem than to circumvent security."

"I'll need names anyway."

He set the coffee aside, took out his PPC. After a moment's work, he nodded toward her machine. "Now you have them. And if any of my people had a part in what happened to that girl, I want to know when you know."

He walked out, his barely restrained fury leaving a bolt of energy behind. Eve blew out a breath, and since he'd forgotten his coffee, picked it up and drank it herself.

FOUR

Though she had no doubt Roarke's screening process was more stringent than the Pentagon's, she ran the names he'd given her. She got clean and clear on all. If, she decided, the word from EDD was an on-site screwup, she'd run their spouses, when applicable, and family members.

But for now she couldn't put off informing next of kin.

It took, Eve thought when she'd finished, under thirty seconds to shatter the world of two ordinary people, with ordinary lives. More time, she reflected as she turned back to her board, than it had taken to slash Ava Marsterson's throat, for her brain to process the insult. But not much. Not much more.

She rubbed the heels of her hands over eyes gritty with fatigue, then checked the time. A couple of hours until she could bitch at the lab for any results, or go to the morgue for the same on the victim's autopsy.

Enough time for a shower to clear her head before nagging EDD. She picked up the bag Roarke had left her.

"Take two hours in the crib," she ordered Peabody when

she stepped back into the bullpen. "I'm going to grab a shower."

"Okay. I ran the Asant Group from every possible angle. It doesn't exist."

"It's just a cover."

"Then I tried a search for any occult holidays, or dates of import that coordinate with today—or yesterday now. Nothing."

"Well, that was good thinking. Worth a shot. It was a damn party, that's for sure. Maybe they don't need an occasion. No, no," Eve corrected herself. "It was too elaborate, planned too far in advance to just be for the hell of it."

"For the hell of it. Ha-ha. God." Peabody rubbed her eyes. "I need those two hours down."

"Take them now. It's the last you'll be seeing of the back of your eyelids for a while."

She headed to the showers. In the locker room she checked the contents of the bag, noted that Roarke hadn't missed a trick. Underwear, boots, pants, shirt, jacket, weapon harness, her clutch piece, communicator, restraints, spare recorder, PPC, and cash. More than she normally carried on the job. She stuffed it all in her locker, grabbed a towel, then wrapped herself in it once she'd stripped off.

In the miserly shower cube she ordered the water on full at 101 degrees. It came out in a stingy lukewarm trickle, so she closed her eyes and pretended she was home, where the shower sported multiple and generous jets that pummeled the body with glorious heat. Then spun around, soaking wet, when her instincts tingled to see Roarke standing in the narrow opening, hands in pockets.

"If this is the best the NYPSD offers it's no wonder you're prone to hour-long showers at home."

"What's wrong with you? Close the door. Anybody could walk in here."

"I locked the door, which you neglected to do."

"Because cops aren't prone to sneaking peeks while another cop is in the damn shower. What are you doing?"

"Taking my clothes off so they don't get wet. That's the usual procedure."

"You can't come in here." She jabbed a finger at him when he draped his shirt over a bench. "Cut it out. There's barely room for me. Besides—"

"The security was breached on site. It's going to be a very long day. I want a shower, and since she's naked, wet, and here, I want my wife."

He stepped in, slid his arms around her. "Not only is this excuse for a shower stall the approximate size of a coffin, but it's bloody noisy for the amount of water dripping out."

"Who's the most likely to have compromised—"

"Later," he said, and drew her in. "Later," and covered her mouth with his.

She'd seen his eyes before their lips met; seen the worry and the fatigue in them. It was so rare for him to show either, even to her, that she instinctively wrapped around him. Need. She understood the need, not just for the physical, but for the unity.

Touch, taste, movement. Knowing who you were, each to the other, and what you became when that need brought you together.

"Anybody finds out about this," she murmured in his ear, "I'll get razzed for years." She bit lightly at his lobe. "So make it good."

Her heart slammed against her ribs when he drove into her. "Okay. That's a start."

He laughed, an unexpected and welcome zing of humor along with the pleasure. The old pipes clanged and rattled as he slowed his thrusts, smoothed the pace down from urgent to easy. He turned his head, found her mouth again, and drew them both down, deep, deep. Filled them both from the shimmering well of sensation and emotion.

He felt her rise up, the cry of her release tangled in the kiss. And let himself follow.

On a long, long breath, she dropped her head on his shoulder. "This is not authorized use of departmental facilities."

"We expert civilian consultants need our perks, too." He tipped her head up. "I adore you, Lieutenant."

"Yeah? Then shove it over some, pal. You're hogging what there is of the water."

When they stepped out and she began toweling off, he lifted a brow. "Towel over drying tube? Not your usual."

"I don't trust them in here." She gave the tube a suspicious glare. "You could get fried, or maybe worse, trapped. Anyway, I gave Peabody some crib time, but I'm going to cut it short, see if they've gotten to the vic at the morgue."

"I'll be going with you."

She didn't argue; it was a waste of time. "You're not responsible for what happened to Ava Marsterson."

He watched her as he buttoned his shirt. "If you put one of your men in charge of an op, and there was a screwup, if a civilian lost her life, who does it fall on?"

She sat to pull on her boots, tried another way. "No security, not even yours, is completely infallible."

He sat beside her on the bench. "A group of people came into my place, breached the security from the inside, and ripped a woman to pieces. I need to know how, and I need to know why. If one of my people was part of it, I'm going to know who."

"Then I'd better roust Peabody. I hope you came down in my ride," she added. "That toy we drove last night won't hold the three of us."

"I drove something that will."

"This is so mag!" Peabody bounced on the backseat of the muscular and roomy all-terrain. "First we get to zip in that way-uptown Stinger, and now we're pumping the road in this."

"Glad you're enjoying yourself," Eve commented. "We wouldn't want murder to dampen your day."

"You've got to take your ups where you get them. I've never even seen one of these before." Peabody petted the seat as she might a purring cat.

"It's a prototype," Roarke told her. "It won't go on line for a couple of months yet."

"Sweetness."

"Peabody, as soon as you finish enjoying yourself, run the heads of security and electronics in the file. Run their spouses, parents, siblings, cohabs, offspring, spouses and cohabs of offspring. I want to know if anyone has a sheet. I want to know if anyone's family pet has a sheet."

"They've been screened," Roarke told her. "Caro can forward you all the data."

Eve had no doubt his efficient admin could gather and transmit data in record time. "We need to confirm, and confirm through official channels."

When he said nothing, she took out her own PPC, copied all data to Dr. Mira's office unit. She wanted the department's top profiler and psychiatrist to review and analyze. Added to it, Eve thought, one of Mira's daughters was Wiccan. Maybe, just maybe, they'd tap that source.

The cold white tiles of the morgue echoed with their footsteps. Eve scented coffee—or what passed for it here—as they strode past Vending. She scented death long before they pushed through the double doors of the autopsy room.

Ava lay naked on a slab with Chief Medical Examiner Morris working on her. His delicate and precise Y-cut opened her, exposed her. Eve heard Peabody swallow hard behind her.

Morris straightened as they came in. The protective gown covered his silver-edged blue suit. He wore his dark hair pulled back in a long, sleek tail. "Company," he said, and the faintest of smiles moved across his exotically sexy face. "And so early in the morning. Roarke, this is unexpected." But his eyes tracked over to Peabody. "There's water in the friggie, Detective."

"Thanks." Her face glowed with sweat as she hurried over for a bottle.

"What can you tell me?" Eve asked him.

"We haven't gotten very far. You flagged her for me specifically, and I've only been in about an hour. And that's because the ME on duty was pissy that he couldn't get his hands in."

"I didn't want anyone but you on her. I'd rather wait. I have a pretty good idea how it went anyway. Can you tell me if she was raped?"

"I can tell you she had rough sex—very rough—multiple times. As to whether it was consensual or not? She can't tell us. But from the tearing, I'd say rape. Gang rape."

"Sperm?"

"They doused her—vaginally, anally, orally to remove. I've already sent samples to the lab, but I wouldn't hold my breath for DNA. I'd say multiple partners. She was brutally used, pre- and postmortem." He looked down at the body. "There are so many levels of cruelty, aren't there? And they all walk in our doors."

"What about the tat? It looked fresh and real."

"It's both. Inked within the last twelve to fifteen hours."

"They wanted her marked," Eve mused. "The throat wound came first. Death blow. Right-handed assailant, facing."

"If I were a teacher, you'd be my pet. There are sixty-eight other wounds, several of which would have been mortal on their own, some of which are relatively superficial. I want to run a closer analysis, but on a first pass, at least a dozen different blades were used on her. The bruising, from finger grips, hands, fists, feet. Some premortem. And yet—"

"Not one defensive wound," Eve finished. "No sign she was restrained. She took it. I need to know what she took or what they gave her."

"I've flagged the tox screen priority. I can tell you she wasn't a user, unless it was very rare, very casual. This was a very healthy woman, one who tended to her body, inside and out. There'll be a rape drug in her, something potent enough to cause her to tolerate this kind of abuse without a struggle."

"I've got somebody in the tank. He was loaded. I sent a sample to the lab. Her parents and her brother are coming in from Indiana."

"God pity them." Morris touched one sealed and bloodied hand to Ava's arm. "I'll see she's cleaned up before they view her." Morris glanced over at Roarke, with understanding in his dark eyes. "We'll take care of her," he said. "And them. You can be sure of it."

As they walked down the white-tiled tunnel, Roarke spoke for the first time. "It's a hard life you've chosen, Lieutenant. A brutal road that brings you to that so often."

"It chose me," she said, but was grateful to step outside, and into the cool air of the new spring morning.

CHAPTER
FIVE

Eve gave Roarke an Upper West Side address when they got back into the AT.

"Mika Nakamura's worked for me for nine years." He pulled out of the parking slot. "Four of those as head of security at the hotel."

"Then she must be good," Eve commented. "And should be able to explain what the hell went wrong last night. She was on the log from noon until just after twenty-three hundred. Do you usually work your people for an eleven-hour stretch?"

"No. She should have logged out at eight." His eyes stayed on the road, his voice remained cool and flat. "Paul Chambers came on at seven. I spoke with him last night, and again this morning. He took the main hotel as Mika told him she'd handle the VIP and Towers, as she had other work to catch up on. She also told him she'd be running some maintenance on the cams."

"Is that usual?"

"As head of security, Mika would have some autonomy. She's earned it."

Touchy, Eve thought. *Very touchy.* "Have you spoken with her?"

"I haven't been able to reach her. And, yes, I fully intended to see her in person before you contacted me about the discs." The tone, very cool, very level, spoke of ruthlessly restrained fury. "She wouldn't hold the position she does if she hadn't passed the initial screening, and the twice yearly screening thereafter."

In the backseat, Peabody cleared her throat. "She comes up clean. So does her husband of five years. One child, female, age three. Um, born in Tokyo, and relocated to New York at age ten when her parents—who also come clean—moved here for career purposes. Attended both Harvard and Columbia. Speaks three languages and holds degrees in Communications, Hotel Management, and Psychology."

"How did she end up yours?" Eve asked Roarke.

"I recruited her right out of college. I have scouts, you could call them, and they brought her to my attention. It's not in the realm of any reality that she had any part in what was done to that girl."

"She logged out about ten minutes before Pike walked into Maxia's party. And minutes before the security for the elevators and lobby cleared. We have to look at that. She could've been forced, threatened."

"There are fail-safes." He shook his head. "She's smart. She's too damn smart to get herself trapped that way."

Better to let it lie, Eve decided, until they spoke to the woman in question.

Security paid well enough, in Roarke's domain, to warrant a tidy duplex in a tony neighborhood. People clipped along the sidewalk wearing suits and style while they sipped what she assumed was fancy fake coffee out of go-cups. Pretty women with bouncy hair herded pretty children toward what, she assumed again, would be private schools. A couple of teenagers whizzed by on airboards while a third chased after them on street blades.

Eve climbed the short steps to the door. "You can take the lead with her," she told Roarke, "but when I step in, you have to step back."

Rather than respond, he rang the bell.

Privacy screens shielded the front windows, and the security lock held a steady red. As the seconds ticked away, Eve wondered how a woman might go into the wind with a husband and a kid. They had a weekend home in Connecticut, she mused, and relatives in Japan. If . . .

The security light blinked green.

Mika Nakamura was a stunner. Eve had seen that from the ID shot. But at the moment, she looked hard used. Sallow skin, dull, bloodshot eyes, the tangled mess of ebony hair all spoke of a hard night, or an illness.

"Sir?" the voice rasped. Mika cleared her throat, opened the door a bit wider. She wore a long scarlet robe messily tied at the waist.

"I need to speak with you, Mika."

"Of course. Yes. Is something wrong?"

She stepped back. Eve noted the house was dim, that the privacy screens had been boosted up to block the light. Even so, the interior was splashed with vibrant colors from rugs and art.

"Please come in. Won't you sit down? Can I get you some coffee? Tea?"

"Aren't you well, Mika?"

"I'm just a little off. I had my husband take Aiko out for breakfast because I can't seem to pull it together."

"Long night?" Eve asked, and Mika gave her a puzzled look.

"I . . . sorry?"

"My wife, Lieutenant Dallas, and her partner, Detective Peabody. I've been trying to reach you, Mika."

"You have?" She pushed her hands at her hair in an absent attempt to straighten it. "Nothing's come through. Did I . . ." She pressed her fingers to her temple. "Did I turn the 'links off? Why would I do that?"

"Sit down." Roarke took her arm, led her to a chair in as bold a red as her robe. He sat on the glossy black coffee table to face her. "There was an incident at the hotel last night."

"An incident." She repeated the words slowly, as if learning the language.

"You were on the com, Mika. You ordered Paul to cover the main hotel, though it was already covered. And you dismissed the tech from the screen room, telling them you'd be running some maintenance on the cameras."

"That doesn't sound right." She rubbed at her temple again. "It doesn't sound right."

Eve touched Roarke's shoulder, and though impatience flashed into his eyes, he rose. Eve took his place. "Just before sixteen hundred, you shut down the cameras in the VIP lobby and the private elevator for Suite 606. They remained off until approximately twenty-three hundred."

"Why would I do that?"

Not a denial, Eve noted. A sincere question. "A group checked into that suite. The Asant Group. Do you know them?"

"No."

"During the time the cameras were shut down, from your com, a woman was murdered in that suite."

Even the sickly color faded from Mika's cheeks. "Murdered? Oh, God. Sir—"

"Look at me, Mika," Eve demanded. "Who told you to turn off the cameras, to send your relief away, to dismiss the tech?"

"Nobody." Her breath went short as her pale face bunched with pain. "I didn't. I wouldn't. Murdered? Who? How?"

Eve narrowed her eyes. "Got a headache, Mika?"

"Yes. It's splitting. I took a blocker, but it hasn't touched it. I can't think. I don't understand any of this."

"Do you remember going to work yesterday?"

"Of course. Of course I do. I . . ." Her lips trembled; her eyes filled. "No. No. I don't remember. I don't remember anything, it's all blurred and blank. My head. God." She dropped it into her hands, rocked herself, much as Jackson Pike had. "When I try to remember, it's worse. I can't stand the pain. Sir, something's wrong with me. Something's wrong."

"All right now, Mika." Roarke simply nudged Eve aside, crouched, and put his arms around the weeping woman. "We'll take care of it. We'll get you to a doctor."

"Peabody, help Ms. Nakamura get dressed. We'll have her taken down to Central."

"Damn it, Eve." Roarke shoved to his feet.

"Dr. Mira can examine her," Eve said evenly, "and determine if the cause is physical or psychological. Or both."

Roarke eased back, turned to help Mika to her feet. "Go with Detective Peabody. It's going to be all right."

"Someone's dead. Did I do something? If I did—"

"Look at me. It's going to be all right."

It seemed to calm her. But as she continued to tremble, Peabody put an arm around her to lead her from the room.

"Same symptoms as Jackson Pike," Eve commented. "Down the line."

"Eve—"

"I'm cutting you a break by not getting pissed off. Don't push it."

He merely nodded. "I'll stay until she's ready to go. Then I've other things to see to."

"Good." She took out her communicator to arrange for Mika's transportation, then contacted Mira's office. She plowed through Mira's admin. "I'm pulling rank, are you hearing me? If necessary I'll go to the commander on this, and nobody'll be happy about that. I'm ordering a priority. Dr. Mira will clear her schedule as of now. Jackson Pike, currently in custody, will be brought down to her for examination. She has the file. If she has any questions, she can reach me. In an hour, she will examine Mika Nakamura, who will be brought to Central shortly. If you have a problem, you can take it up with me later, but you'll do exactly what I've told you, and you'll do it now."

Eve clicked off. "Ought to hook her up with Summerset," she muttered. "Couple of tight-asses." While Roarke watched thoughtfully, she contacted her own division and arranged for two uniforms to deliver Pike to Mira's office, ASAP. Satisfied, she shoved the communicator back in her pocket.

"Someone used her," Roarke began.

"Maybe."

"Used her," he repeated. "And a woman's dead because of it. Mika won't ever forget that."

"You can worry about that now. I can't."

"Understood. We're not on different sides, Eve. Just slightly different angles. She's in pain, and afraid, and confused. And she's mine. You understand that."

"Yeah." She understood that right down to the bone. "And Ava Marsterson's mine. Do I think your head of security suddenly thought it would be fun to help a bunch of lunatics carve someone up in the name of Satan? No. But there's a reason they used her, a reason they used your place, that room, that victim. There's a reason for Jackson Pike."

Eve stepped over as Peabody led Mika back into the room.

"Ms. Nakamura, do you use the West Side Health Clinic?"

"What? Yes. Aiko's pediatrician is there, and my doctor."

"Do you know Ava Marsterson?"

"I—" Mika staggered back, one hand pressed to her head. "Who? I can't think through the pain."

Eve glanced at Roarke. "I take that as a yes."

"She's straight, Dallas." Peabody brooded out the window of the AT. "She could barely stand for the pain, but she fought to push through it. Worried about her husband and kid, sick—seriously sick—at the idea someone died while she had the com." She glanced at Eve. "Just like Pike. So you have to think, given the circumstances . . . Ritual magic, on the black side, the gathering of, well, power. By all appearances and all evidence, the ability to cause two straight arrows to behave in a way opposed to their character. We could be dealing with a spell."

Eve's brown eyes narrowed. "I knew you were going to get around to that."

"It's not unprecedented," Peabody insisted. "There are sensitives, unscrupulous sensitives who've used their gifts for their own gain, their own purpose. Black magic's taking those gifts, that power, and distorting it."

"Jackson Pike was loaded with drugs."

"Add drugs to the mix, it's easier to bend the will. There was something in that suite, something left over." Peabody rubbed her arms as if suddenly chilled. "You felt it, too."

She didn't argue, because that much was true. "I'm not buying that some witch can . . ." Eve waved a hand in the air. "And get some normal guy to start hacking someone with a knife."

"I don't think he did. I think he was supposed to be another sacrifice—or maybe just the patsy." When Eve didn't respond, Peabody scowled. "You don't want to buy into the power deal, but going straight logic, why does this group plan all this and include some young doctor who's only been in New York a couple of weeks, and has no ties, *none* to anything off prior to that? You don't bring some newbie in on the big deal. You don't—"

"You're right."

"Listen, I'm just saying . . . I'm right?"

"About Pike, yeah, you're right. Maybe they were going to off him, too. Or maybe they pulled him in to take the rap. Drugged the shit out of him, left him behind. He's got no defense. Naked, full of illegals, covered with the vic's blood, and carrying around one of the knives used on her. Still, they'd have to figure we'd know he didn't do it alone, and once the drugs wear off, we examine him, work with him, he could start to remember some details."

Peabody pondered on it a moment. "Okay, look, you don't buy the magic, but you'll agree that people who get together to light candles, have orgies that end in human sacrifice probably do."

"I'll give you that."

"And can be persuasive—especially if they have a gift, are a sensitive, especially if the person they're persuading is doped up."

"Okay." Eve nodded.

"So, to *dissuade* we need someone with a gift, someone who believes, to break the spell."

"You want to bring in a witch? Christ."

"It's an option," Peabody pushed.

"Mira's going to examine them, and determine the root of the physical and/or psychological blocks. Let's stick with reality, for just a little while."

She shot up to a slot on a second-level street parking. "Trosky, Brian, on the desk at the time of the group check-in. Let's see what he remembers, or if he's got himself a really bad headache this morning."

Eve strode across the sidewalk and into the apartment building. As it didn't boast a doorman or clerk, she went straight to the intercoms, pressed the one labeled Trosky.

When no response came, Eve bypassed the elevator lock. "Third floor," she ordered.

The music blasted out the moment the doors opened on three. A woman stood beating on the door of 305, Trosky's apartment. "Brian, for Christ's sake, turn it *down*."

"Problem?" Eve asked at close to a shout.

"Yeah, unless you're frigging deaf. He's had that music blaring like that for over an hour. I work nights. I gotta get some sleep."

"He doesn't answer the door? Did you try his 'link?"

"Yeah. It's not like him, I gotta say. He's a nice guy. Good neighbor." She beat on the door again. "Brian, for Christ's sake!"

"Okay, move aside."

When Eve pulled out her master, the woman goggled. "Hold on, hold on a minute. You can't just go breaking into somebody's place. I'm calling the cops."

"We are the cops." Eve nodded at Peabody as she used the master, and Peabody pulled out her badge.

"Oh, wow, oh, shit. Is he in trouble? I don't wanna get him in trouble."

Eve pushed open the door, felt her eardrums vibrate at the force of the music. "Mr. Trosky, this is the police!" she shouted. "We're coming in. Music, off," she ordered, but the roar of it continued. "Peabody, find the source of that noise and kill it. Trosky! This is the NYPSD!"

She drew her weapon, but kept it down at her side as she scanned the living area—trashed—then the bump-out of the kitchen. She moved to the open bedroom door.

He lay across the bed, tangled in the bloody sheets. She swept the room and the adjoining bath, though instinct told her Brian Trosky hadn't been attacked, that the hammer that had caved his skull—to stop the pain?—had been wielded by his own hand.

CHAPTER
SIX

Same side, Roarke thought as he walked into Spirit Quest, different angles. Eve would always search for the logical, the rational. He was a bit more flexible. And so he'd come to talk to the witch.

The shop was pretty, even festive in its way with its crystals and stones, its bells and candles, its colorful bowls and thriving herbs. Its scent was spring meadow, he thought, with a hint of moonlight.

In the small space with the murmur of harps and flutes as background, people browsed. He watched a woman in a flowing white dress carry a ball of smoky crystal to the counter where the young, fresh-faced clerk instructed her solemnly on how to charge the ball by moonlight, how to cleanse it.

When the purchase had been made, wrapped and bagged, Roarke took a step toward the counter. He needn't have bothered, as she stepped out of the back room with an awareness in her dark eyes that told him she'd sensed him—or in the more pedestrian method, had seen him on a security screen.

"Welcome back."

"Isis." He took the hand she offered, held it—and yes, felt that frisson of something. Some connection.

"You're not here to shop," she said in her warm, throaty voice, "which is too bad considering the depths of your pockets. Come upstairs, we'll be comfortable and you can tell me what you need to know."

She led the way, through the back, up the stairs. She moved gracefully, athletically, an Amazon goddess of considerable height and generous curves. Her flaming hair fell in mad curls nearly to the waist of the snug white top she wore, just teasing the back of the first of the many layers of her skirt, a rainbow of hues. She turned at the door, smiled at him out of those onyx eyes. Her face was bold, broad featured with skin of a dull, dreamy gold.

"Once, in another life, we sought comfort together for more than talk." Her smile faded. "But now it's death, again it's death that brings you here. And weighs on you. I'm sorry."

She stepped into the living area of an apartment as exotic and appealing as her shop. "Your Eve is well?"

"Yes. Chas?"

She let out a laugh. "Snuck down to the deli for coffee," she said, referring to her lover. "We pretend he's having a walk. But you can't live with and love another and not know at least some of their secrets."

He stared into her dark eyes, so compelling—so eerily familiar. "Did I know yours, once upon a time?"

She gestured to a chair, took her own. "We knew each other, and loved very well. But I was not your love, your only. You found her then, as you've found her again. And always will. You knew when you first saw her. At the first scent, the first touch."

"I did. It was . . ." He smiled a little, remembering his first contact with Eve. "Annoying."

"Does she know you've come?"

"No. We don't always follow the same lines, even though

we usually end in the same place. I don't know if you can help, or if I have a right to bring death to your door."

"Not ordinary death." Isis took a long, slow breath. "Has someone used the arts to cause harm?"

"I don't know. They have, at least, used the illusion of them to kill an innocent woman. You haven't heard of this?"

"We've only just opened this morning, and I don't listen to the media reports." Rings glittered and gleamed on her fingers as she laid her hands on the arms of her chair, settled back. "What would I have heard?"

He told her then, watched her lovely skin pale, her eyes go darker yet. "Do you know of them? The Asant Group?"

"No, and I would have." Her fingers stroked the smooth blue stone of the pendant she wore, as if for comfort. "I hear both the dark and the light. Suite 606. Or 666 with such little change. You didn't know this girl?"

"No."

"You brought nothing of hers, nothing she owned, wore, touched?"

"I'm sorry, no."

Still pale, Isis nodded. "Then to help you, you need to take me there. To where they sacrificed her."

Eve shot over to the West Side Health Clinic. "They had to troll for the victim here. Scoop up the new doctor, connect with Mika. Somebody on staff, a patient, one of the god-damn cleaning crew."

"Do you really think Pike or Mika might try to kill them-selves like Trosky?"

"Mira's notified. It won't happen. It's not even noon," Eve replied.

"Sure could use lunch though."

"Maybe he did slip out on them, or came to sooner than they figured. Walked into the party. Impromptu party, Maxia just planned it the day before. Couldn't know he'd walk right in to another penthouse. Couldn't know a cop and the owner of the hotel would be right there, that we'd find the body minutes later."

"Without the party he might've wandered around the floor for hours, or . . . gotten down to a lower floor, even the lobby," Peabody agreed. "Nobody would've zeroed right in on 606."

"What you'd get is a lot of civilian screaming, running, security taking him down. Cops get called in. At some point, they're going to check the discs, but they don't know the exact time frame, so it'd take a while, and a while longer to pinpoint 606 and find her. If three of the key players kill themselves before we interview them thoroughly, before they're examined by a professional, what've we got?"

"What looks like the new guy in town luring a pretty girl to her death, and being in league with the other two, being part of a cult."

"Yeah, you could waste some time on that. They may not be ready for us." Eve swung toward the curb, coldly double-parking. "Not quite ready." She flipped on her On Duty sign, stepped out, and walked to the clinic.

Babies cried. Why, she wondered, did they always sound like invading aliens? People sat with the dead-eyed stare of the ill or the terminally bored. Eve crossed over to the check-in desk where a brunette looked at her with tear-ravaged eyes.

"I'm sorry, we're not taking walk-ins today. I can refer you to—" She broke off when Eve laid her badge on the counter. "Oh. Oh. Ava." Tears popped out, fat and fast. "It's about Ava."

"Who's in charge here?"

"I—I—Ava really managed the clinic. She really handled everything. I don't understand how—"

"Sarah." Another woman in a smart suit stepped up, touched the receptionist's shoulder. "Go on into the break room for a little while. It's all right."

"I'm sorry, Leah. I just can't *stand* it." She rose, fled.

"I'm Leah Burke." The older brunette held out a hand, gave Eve's a firm shake. "One of the nurse practitioners. We only heard about Ava a couple of hours ago. We're all just . . . Well, we're reeling. Please, come back. I need to find someone to cover the desk. We can use Dr. Slone's office, he's with a patient. Left, then right, then the third door on the right. I'll be right with you."

Eve tried to ignore the images of what might be going on behind the closed doors of examination rooms. She hated clinics, hospitals, doctors, MTs. If they were medicals, she wanted them to keep their damn distance.

Slone's office was polished and prim. Diplomas in black frames made the walls important, while a photo of a hot blonde on the desk added that personal touch. Sturdy, straight-back chairs ranged in back and in front of the wide desk.

"Run her," Eve told Peabody.

"Already am. Forty-eight years old, divorced. One child, female, deceased. Aw, jeez, hit while crossing the street. Drunk driver. Graduated Columbia Medical School. Put in ten years at the free clinic in Alphabet City, took five years as professional mother, did another two in Alphabet City, unemployed for a year after her kid died, then came here. Six years in. No criminal. She—"

At Eve's signal, Peabody lowered her PPC. A moment later Leah hurried in. "I'm very sorry. We're all turned around and upset today. We're scrambling to reschedule appointments, and deal with patients when we can't. Do you want Ava's medical and employment records? Dr. Collins authorized us to turn them over to the police if you came for them."

"Yeah, we'll take them. And Dr. Pike's."

"Jack?" She seemed to sink. "We were afraid . . . We haven't been able to reach him, and he didn't come in for his shift. They were together last night. Their first date."

"Is that so?"

"Ava was so nervous, and Jack was so sweet. I can't believe they're dead."

"She is; he isn't. Where were they going?"

"What? He's all right?" Her eyes widened, went shiny with tears. "Jack's all right?"

"He'll do. Do you know where they were going?"

"Ah, just something casual. Dinner and vid, maybe a club. What happened? Can you tell us what happened? The reports don't make any sense, and when we call for information, we can't get any. We're all—"

She stepped aside as the door opened. He was an imposing man, maybe six-two, lean as a whip with a sharply chiseled face. His eyes were green with a touch of gold, his hair a deep bronze.

"Dr. Slone, this is . . . I'm sorry, I'm so turned around. I didn't get the names. The police."

"Lieutenant Dallas, Detective Peabody."

"Yes, of course. Leah, see to Sarah, will you? She should go home." He went to his desk, sat behind it. "What happened to Ava?"

"She was murdered."

"Mutilated, the reports say. The word was 'mutilated.'"

"That would be accurate."

He breathed slowly in, slowly out. "In a hotel room. I find it hard to believe Ava would go to a hotel room with Jack on a first date. With anyone for that matter."

"She was a young healthy woman. Young healthy women often go to hotel rooms on a date."

"She was shy, and what I'm sure you'd think of as old fashioned." The flare of anger brought out the gold in his eyes. "She must have been forced to go there, and Jack would never force her, or anyone. Where is Dr. Pike?"

"He's in custody."

Now Slone rose from his seat. "You've arrested him? For this?"

"I said he was in custody, not that he was under arrest."

Disdain tightened his face as he stared holes through Eve. "Does he have a lawyer?"

"He hasn't requested one."

"I won't have that boy accused of this. I brought him here. Do you understand? I brought him here."

"You recruited him," Eve said, thinking of Roarke's earlier statement.

"He's a fine doctor, a fine young man. A healer, not a killer. I'll personally arrange for his counsel."

"That's your choice. Where were you last night, Dr. Slone?"

"I beg your pardon?"

Eve often wondered why people used that phrase when they really meant "fuck you."

"It's routine. What time did you leave the clinic?"

"I left about four, and walked home. I believe I arrived close to five."

"Can anyone verify that? Your wife, your staff?"

"It was our housekeeper's day off," he said stiffly. "My wife was out. She got home shortly after seven. I resent the implications of this."

"I'm going to implicate the same to the rest of the staff and employees of the clinic. I can use your office, or conduct the implications downtown."

"We'll see what my lawyer has to say about that."

Before he could reach for his 'link, Eve snatched Peabody's bag, and pulled out the still of Ava at the crime scene.

"Take a look, take a good one." Eve slapped the photo on his desk. "Then curl your lip at my *implications* and call your damn lawyer."

He didn't pale; he didn't tremble. But he looked for a very long time. And when he raised his head his eyes were hard, and they were cold. "She was hardly more than a child. Use the office. I'll notify the others. They'll have to speak with you between patients."

He strode out, shut the door behind him.

"He's got a mean bedside manner," Eve commented.

"So do you, sir."

With a shrug, Eve dipped her hands into her pockets. "Run him. Run them all."

CHAPTER

SEVEN

While Isis gathered what she needed, Roarke took out his 'link to contact Eve. He struggled against the resentment that burned through him at the idea that he felt obligated to get clearance from his wife to enter his own property. And, he realized, resented the struggle *against* the resentment.

Bloody cops, he thought, and their bloody procedure. And then, bloody hell when he was dumped straight to her voice mail.

"Well then, if you can't be bothered to answer your 'link, I'll tell you that I've my own expert. I want her to have a pass at the crime scene, so I'll be taking her there shortly. Any problem with that, well, you'll have to get back to me, won't you? And we'll see if I can be bothered answering my 'link."

When he clicked off he saw Isis watching him with amusement dancing in her eyes. "Two strong-headed, strong-willed people, both not only used to giving orders but to having them obeyed. It must be an interesting and stimulating life you have together."

"There are times I wonder how we ever managed to get through two hours together much less two years. And other times I wonder how either of us survived before we found each other."

"She'll be angry with you for taking me to this place."

"No, what she'll be is right pissed. But they used my place, you see, and at least one of my people. So pissed she'll have to be. I'm grateful to you for doing this."

"Gifts aren't free. What I have, what I am makes its own demands. Will you take this?" She held out a small white silk bag tied with a silver cord.

"What is it?"

"A protection charm. I'd like you to carry it when we go in that room together."

"All right." He slipped it in his pocket, felt it bump lightly against the gray button he habitually carried there. Eve's button, he mused, and wasn't that a kind of charm? "I've been in before."

"Yes. And what did you feel?"

"Beyond the anger, the pity? I suppose if I were a fanciful man I'd say I caught the scent of hell. It's not sulphur and brimstone. It's the stench of cruelty."

Isis took a long breath. "Then we'll go. And we'll look."

In Slone's office, Eve glanced at the readout on her 'link, and let the transmission go to voice mail. Roarke would have to wait, she decided, and turned back to Sarah Meeks. The receptionist had a soother in her now, but tears still trembled.

"Where were Ava and Jack going?"

"They weren't sure. They both wanted to keep it light, you know? First date, and you work in the same place, so if it doesn't work out . . ."

"Did they leave together, from here?"

"No—I mean, I don't think so. She was—they were—

still here when I left. But I know she planned to go home first. Even though it was casual, Ava wanted to fuss a little, so she was going home to change."

"What time did you leave?"

"About three. I came on at seven yesterday, and left around three."

"Who else was here when you left?"

"Oh, let's see. Dr. Slone, and Dr. Collins, and Dr. Pratt. Um, Leah, Kiki, Roger, one of our physician assistants, and . . ."

Eve took notes as Sarah listed names.

"Was Ava seeing anyone else?"

"No. I mean, she dated sometimes, but not a lot, and nothing serious. There was just this spark, you know, between her and Jack. We all thought they might . . ."

"Did she have any interest in the occult?"

"The what? You mean, like ghosts or something?"

"Or something."

"I don't think so. Ava was . . ." She trailed off again, as if trying to find the word. "Grounded. That's it. She was just really real. She loved her job here, and was so good at it. Good with the staff, the patients. She remembered people's names, and what they came in for, and what everybody liked in their coffee."

"Was there anyone who showed a particular interest in her—other than Jack?"

"Everyone did. She was like that. Everybody loved Ava."

Eve sent Sarah out, sniffling. "Anything pop on those runs?" she asked Peabody.

"Nothing that sings. You've got a lot of highly educated people on staff. Slone's married, two kids, no criminal. Wife's an interior designer. Homes in the city, in the Hamptons, and in Colorado. Collins, Dr. Lawrence, second marriage, two offspring from each, no criminal. Current wife is professional mother. Upper West Side digs here, and a home in Costa Rica. Pratt—"

"Copy the data to my pocket unit." Eve paced the office. "This is going to take a while. We need to split up. Go over and check Ava's apartment. Have EDD pick up her electronics. I'll meet you back at Central when we're done here."

"Okay. You know, Dallas, we're both going to need sleep at some point."

"We'll get to that. Tell them to get someone else in here."

At least one of the killers was here, Eve thought. She was sure of it. The vic hadn't been in the city two full years, and from what Eve had learned, most of her time and energy and interest funnelled into her work. These were her contacts, her people.

Pike, brand-spanking-new.

It was possible they'd run afoul of someone at Ava's apartment—and Peabody would ferret that out, if so. But logic said both Ava and Jack had known at least one of her killers well enough to trust.

And what easier place was there to drug someone than in a health center? The place was full of drugs—and people who, in Eve's opinion, just loved sticking them into other people. Subdue them here, she speculated, give them enough happy juice to make them compliant and transport them to the hotel, where one or more partners has already dealt with Mika and Trosky.

Get them upstairs, she imagined, and let the party begin. Had to be early. The whole thing had been done by twenty-three hundred, latest. It took time to eat, drink, orgy, and perform a human sacrifice.

She glanced up as the door opened. The man who hurried in was about five-ten and carrying a good five excess pounds in the belly. His round face held a pleasant if harried smile. Eyes of faded green radiated both fatigue and kindness. He scooped his hand through his short tangle of brown hair.

"I'm so sorry to keep you waiting. We're . . . well, we're short-staffed today, as you know. We didn't have enough time to notify all the staff, the patients, and close today."

He sat, wearily. "I think we're all running on sheer nerves. Sorry, I'm Dr. Collins, Larry Collins."

"Lieutenant Dallas. I'm sorry for your loss."

"It's incomprehensible. At least a half dozen times today I've started to ask Ava for something. In the six months or so since she's been here, she's become the hub of the practice."

"You're aware she was planning to see Dr. Pike last night, socially."

"Yes. We were all invested, a bunch of matchmakers." His lips compressed on the term. "And now . . . Jack couldn't have hurt her, Lieutenant. It's just not possible."

"What time did she leave yesterday?"

"Ah, let me think. I believe she was still here when I left, and that would have been close to five. Yes, yes, because I said good night to her and—" He broke off, looked away, struggled for composure. "—and good luck."

"Where did you go?"

"I went home, and had a drink." He smiled a little. "My last patient of the day was a very, let's say, active and opinionated five-year-old."

"You're a pediatrician?"

"That's right."

Eve nodded, watching him. "I have to ask, it's routine. Is there anyone who can verify your whereabouts from five p.m. to midnight?"

"My wife. She fixed me the drink, bless her. We had a quiet evening at home as the kids were spending the night with friends."

"All right. Who was here when you left, other than Ava?"

"I'm not entirely sure." He furrowed his brow in thought. "I think Rodney, one of our nurses, and Kiki, a lab tech. I know the waiting room was clear, because I commented on it to Ava. We try to close at five, but realistically it's nearer to six most days."

"Dr. Pike? Was he still here?"

"I didn't see him. Of course, he may have been with a patient."

"Thanks for your time. I may have some follow-ups later, but for now, that's it. Would you send either Kiki or Rodney in?"

"I think Rodney's on his lunch break, but I'll see that Kiki's told you're waiting." He rose, walked to the desk where she sat, offered a hand. "Thank you, Lieutenant, for all you're doing."

She got to her feet first so their eyes would be level. She thought of when she might grab a meal, and took his hand. "It's my job."

"All the same." He held her hand, her eyes a moment longer, then released it. "Thank you."

She waited until he'd left the room before she spoke for her recorder. "Note, Dr. Lawrence Collins is a sensitive. And one who doesn't mind poking into another's mind without permission."

Hope he enjoyed her thoughts of pepperoni pizza, Eve mused. Then checking the time, pulled out her 'link to check her messages.

She was snarling and steaming before Roarke's message played out. "Son of a bitch!" She tagged him back. "You'd better answer, goddamn it, you'd just better—Stay out of my crime scene," she snapped out when his face came on-screen.

"That crime scene is a suite in my hotel."

"Look, pal—"

"You look for a change. One of my people is in custody. Another, I've just been informed, is dead by his own hand. I won't sit and do nothing."

"I'm getting somewhere here, and I'll be in contact with Mira within the hour. She'll have finished the initial exams, and if she gets the results I think I may have enough for a search warrant."

"That's all very well and good for you. Meanwhile, I've

my own line to tug, and at the end of it, you may have enough for arrest warrants."

"You can't just walk into a crime scene and take someone with you. Who the hell is with you?"

"Isis."

There was a long, stunned silence. "You're taking a witch into my crime scene? What the hell's wrong with you? If the two of you compromise—"

"Your sweepers and techs have been through, the scene's been recorded and photographed, evidence removed and logged. You've been over that suite top to bottom yourself. Added to that, goddamn right back at you, I didn't come down in the last shower of rain. I know what's to be done to protect the bleeding scene."

"You both need a nap," Eve heard Isis say, very pleasantly.

"Listen. I'm on the Upper West Side, finishing up interviews with the staff at the health center. I'll be done in about thirty minutes, and can be at the hotel in forty. Wait. Just wait until I get there."

There was another silence, then she saw him nod. "Forty minutes," he said and clicked off.

Eve hissed out a breath, kicked Slone's desk. She might have kicked it a second time, but the door opened.

The woman who came in reeked of Neo-Goth. The black hair, red lips, and the silver hoop through her pierced left brow projected a kind of careless defiance that merged with the tattoo that peeked out from the slope of her breast.

Eve might have considered it all a matter of personal style, along with the snug black top and pants, the chunky black boots, but for the smug gleam in the black-lined eyes.

Weak link, Eve thought, and smiled. "Hello, Kiki."

"I'm swamped." She dumped herself in a chair. "So let's cut to it. I left about five—Ava, the pure and wholesome— was still here, all shiny-eyed about her date with Dr. Dull. I lit out, met up with some friends downtown. We hit some clubs, got trashed, hung out, and I got home about two. Is that it?"

"Not quite. I'll need the names and contact information for your friends."

Kiki shrugged, rattled off names and 'link numbers.

"You didn't like Ava?"

"Wasn't my type, that's all. Too bad she's dead and all that. Saint Jack probably freaked when she wouldn't put out, and did her." Now those eyes glittered. "But since I wasn't there, I don't know. Ava and I weren't buds, so I got no clue what she was into. You need more, you'll have to catch me later. I'm backed up."

"Thanks for your time."

"Whatev."

Eve waited a few seconds, then walked to the door, stepped out. She saw Kiki at the end of the corridor in an intense conversation with Leah Burke. The moment Leah spotted Eve coming toward them, she squeezed a hand on Kiki's arm to silence her, and started forward. "Lieutenant, can I help you?"

"I'd like to speak to Rodney."

"He's not back from his break." She checked her wrist unit. "He should be only a few more minutes. He's very prompt."

"Okay, I'll take Dr. Pratt."

"He's still with a patient. I can't—"

"I'll keep it short. I'm sure we'll all be happy when this is done. Before you interrupt him, what time did you leave last night?"

"Me? Ah, just after five."

"Was Ava still here?"

"No, she'd just left. I, ah, scooted her along, actually, so she could get ready for her date. I closed up last night."

"You were the last to leave?"

"That's right."

"And where did you go?"

"I went home. I, ah, walked home, changed, had some dinner."

"You didn't go out again?"

"No."

"Make or receive any calls, have any visitors?"

"No, it was a quiet night. Lieutenant, I have patients myself."

"Okay. I've only got a couple more staff members, and I'll be out of your hair."

Eve stepped back into Slone's office. Collins, Burke, and Kiki, she thought, were top of her suspect list. She scanned Silas Pratt's data, but he didn't keep her waiting long.

He strode in, a sharply handsome man with an air of confidence. His eyes were a laser blast of blue, and she could admit they gave her a jolt. When he offered his hand she allowed herself to think just that: *Here's a great-looking man with killer eyes.*

He smiled at her. "Lieutenant, I'm Silas Pratt."

Her heart pumped a little harder as he squeezed her hand. She felt the probe of his gaze, and yes, of his power, like heat along her brain. "Have a seat, Dr. Pratt," she said and removed her hand from his.

"Can you tell me if you have any leads? Other than Jack. No one who knows him will believe Jack did this to our Ava."

"You've only known him a couple of weeks."

"That's true. Peter recruited him, but I like to think I'm a good judge of character. What they're saying was done to Ava, well, it's monstrous, isn't it? And to someone so young, so vibrant."

Now he did sit, and passed a hand over those potent eyes. "I thought of her almost as a daughter."

"You don't have children. According to your official data."

"No. But it was easy to feel a paternal kind of affection for Ava."

"I don't want to intrude any longer than necessary." And she wanted out, Eve admitted. There was a heat in the room now, a kind of singeing of the air. "When did you leave yesterday?"

"About quarter to five. Ava was getting ready to leave, I remember. Leah was shooing her out. She and Jack—well, you know about all that."

"Yes. Did you approve of that? One of your doctors dating your office manager."

He looked surprised by the question, even bemused. "They were both adults—and frankly, they seemed besotted with each other from the first minute."

"Where did you go when you left?"

"Home to change. My wife and I had a small dinner party last evening. A few friends."

"I apologize, but it's routine. I'll need the names and contact numbers."

"Of course." He smiled at her. "No apology necessary." And he gave her six names. She thanked him, dismissed him. Then added those names to her list of suspects.

CHAPTER
EIGHT

Roarke arranged lunch for himself and Isis in the owner's suite of the hotel, and passed the forty minutes eating food that didn't interest him while making polite small talk with a witch.

"When's the last time you slept?" Isis asked him.

"I suppose it's been about thirty-two hours now. She'll push herself until she drops, you see. Eve."

"And you relax and recreate?"

"More often than she. But no, in this case, in this particular case, I suppose we'll both push. Her time's up, so if you've finished, I'll take you to 606."

"First." She rose, stepped to him, and placed her hand on his head. "No, relax, just for a moment. Clear your mind. You can trust me."

A warm flow, he thought. Not the quick burst of energy that came from popping a booster, but more of a slow, steady build of stamina.

"Better?"

"Thank you, yes."

"It won't last long, but between that and the little you ate, it should get you through. What you need is some rest." She picked up her bag. "I'm ready."

He led her to the elevator.

"You said there's a private elevator that opens into the suite, as well as the doors to the hallways."

"That's right."

"I want to see it from the outside first. I want to go through the door, not through a machine."

"All right. Sixtieth floor," he ordered. "Main bank."

"I'll ask you, whatever happens, not to leave me alone."

"I won't." When the elevator doors opened, Roarke took her hand.

The bloody footprints still walked the carpet. Blood smears marred the walls where Jack had laid his hand for balance. In Roarke's hand, Isis's fingers tensed.

"People think of it as a cliché." She stared at the door where the tail of blood made a six from the middle zero. "But it has power and meaning. It should be cleaned—all of this—with blessed water as soon as possible."

Roarke stepped forward, drew out his master. And Eve strode off the elevator like vengeance.

"Wait. Didn't I tell you to wait?"

"And so I did." Roarke turned to her, his gaze as icy as hers was hot. "You're late."

She put herself between him and the door. "I know who did this. At least I know some of them. I can close this without the mumbo."

"Nice to see you again, Eve."

Eve shifted her gaze to Isis. "No offense. I appreciate you being willing to help, and in fact, have some questions you may be able to answer. You don't have to see what's in there."

"I've already seen some of it, through him and now through you. Seen what's trapped in your minds. But I can't feel unless I go in. I can't feel or see what she saw and felt unless I go in. I might help, I might not, but he needs it."

Isis took Eve's arms so that for a moment, she stood as the link between Eve and Roarke. "You know that."

Eve yanked out her master and turned to the door. "When I say it's done, it's done," she stated.

Roarke slipped the protection charm into her pocket as she unsealed the door.

She stepped in first. "Lights on full." She turned quickly when she heard Isis let out a quick, shuddering breath. But Isis put out a hand, and took another step into the room.

"It reeks still, and will until it's cleansed. No one can stay here until a cleansing. You feel it, do you feel it? This is not the work of a dabbler, not the vile work of one who only seeks blood and death for their own sake. This is power and purpose, and it brought the dark."

"You're going to tell me they called up Satan?"

Isis turned her black eyes on Eve. "I imagine he has more important things to do than answer a summons. But evil can be called, and it can be fed. You can't do what you do and believe otherwise. Or see what you see."

She stared at the pentagram, and the pools and rivers of blood that washed over it. "She doesn't know me, neither in body nor spirit. I need some of her blood. Get that, while I prepare."

She knelt and began taking items from her bag.

Eve said, "Crap," but she stalked off to get swabs from the bathroom amenities.

"I'll need three. Head, heart, hand." Isis set out candles, crystals, herbs.

Though she rolled her eyes, Eve crossed to the pentagram. If she felt a pull when she stepped into it, she willfully pushed it away. She slapped a look toward Roarke as she coated the swabs. "If it ever gets out that I not only allowed but participated in some voodoo bullshit—"

He crouched beside her, took her free hand. "My lips are sealed as long as you want them to be. I owe you for this."

"Damn right you do."

"You're so tired, darling Eve." Before she could evade, he leaned to her, brushed her lips with his.

"There's power there, too," Isis murmured. "We'll need it. Light the candles, please, and stand with me. Together with me while I cast the circle. Hurry. I can't stay here long.

"The power of three in light," she said as Roarke lit the candles. "The power of three in flesh." She took a bag and walked a circle of salt around them. "Order the lights off," she commanded, and when only the candles lit the room, she began to chant in a language Eve didn't recognize.

With a curved knife she turned, like the hand of a compass. Her face glowed; her eyes burned. She placed crystals at the compass points of the circle, then sprinkled herbs into the water she'd poured into a small copper bowl.

Whether it was fatigue or the power of suggestion, Eve felt something cold, cold, brutally cold push against the air.

"It cannot enter what is light. It cannot enter what is bright. And we will not *open*!" Isis threw her hands high, and her biceps quivered with the strain. "I am daughter of the sun, sister of the moon. I am child and servant of the goddess. In this place, at this hour, I call upon her power. Into me, into mine, bring both light and sight divine. Set the murdered spirit free, send her essence into me.

"The power of three, by her blood."

Isis smeared Ava's blood on her forehead, on her breast, on her hand. And falling to her knees, she shook. Her eyes glazed like black glass while her face went white as wax. Horror etched into her features. Both Eve and Roarke dropped down beside her. Her hands grasped theirs, her fingers tightened like wires.

"She's in some sort of trance. We have to get her out."

"We gave our word," Roarke reminded her. "Christ, she's cold as ice."

Isis bowed back until her head nearly touched the floor. And screamed. For one mad moment, Eve imagined she saw a gash open and gush blood from her throat. And when the witch slumped, Eve wasn't certain if she was unconscious or dead.

"Fuck this, we're getting her out of here now."

"Don't leave the circle." Isis's voice was weak, but her eyes fluttered open. "Don't. The red bottle there. I need it, and a little help to sit up."

They eased her up, and taking the bottle, she sipped slowly from it. "It's not an illegal," she said, with both pain and humor in her eyes. "A potion. There's always a price for power."

"You're in pain," Eve said flatly. "We need to get you out of here."

"The circle needs to be closed as it was opened. Properly. Then, yes, we all need to get out of here."

When it was done, and her tools gathered again, Isis leaned on Roarke while Eve resealed the door.

"Can we go back to where we had lunch? I'll tell you what I can tell you, but I want to be away from here."

In the owner's suite, Roarke helped her to the couch, tucked pillows behind her head. "What do you need?" he asked her.

"A really big glass of wine."

"I can get that for you. Lieutenant?"

"Coffee. I understand you're a sensitive," Eve began, "and you believe, strongly believe in your . . . faith."

"You sometimes hear the cries of the dead. Feel their pain, and know their need for you. We're not so far apart." Isis closed her eyes a moment, opening them when Roarke brought her wine. She drank slowly, as she had her potion. "She was a lovely child. I saw some of what they did to her. Not all, I think, not all, but enough. She was inside herself, screaming to get out, but trapped there. There are ways to trap a spirit, with drugs, and other methods. She drank what they gave her, ate, let them touch her. She had no choice. They marked her with a serpent."

Eve thought of the tattoo, said nothing.

"Sex for power. Well, for some of them, it was only sex— the greed for it, the meanness of it. No love, not even lust. Just greed and violence and power. The one they brought her first, not one of them. Trapped as she was. Something there."

Isis touched a hand to her forehead, sipped more wine. "Something light between them," she continued. "Light and new, twisted now when they coupled on the sign. Snuffing out that fragile light with chants and drugs and power until it, too, turned mean. They raped her, took him away and raped her, again and again while she lay unable to fight, to resist. And her trapped spirit screaming, screaming."

"Easy now," Roarke murmured, and took Isis's hand. "Easy."

She nodded, gathered herself again. "They pulled her up, dragged her to the one who leads them. She looked at him. He said her name, and she looked in his eyes when he cut her throat.

"And they fell on her like beasts. I couldn't bear any more. I couldn't bear it."

Eve rose and walked away while Isis wept in absolute silence, while Roarke sat with her, held her hand. She walked to the wide glass doors, yanked them open, and stepped out into the spring air that buzzed like a mad hive from the city.

When Roarke came out, she continued to stare out at the snarls of traffic, the rush of people below. "What am I supposed to do with this?" she demanded. "Go to the PA and tell him I want to arrest these people because a witch communed with the tragic spirit of the victim?"

"Eve."

He laid a hand on her shoulder, but rather than turn to him, she curled her hands on the rail until they were fists. "I know she didn't bullshit that, okay? I may be cynical, but

I'm not stupid. And I'm *sick* at the thought that she saw what she saw. Nobody should. Nobody should have to see that, feel that."

"No one but you?" he asked, and turned her to face him.

She shook her head. "I looked right in the faces of some of the people who did this to that girl. And I looked right in the eyes of one of them, the one I think cut her throat. And for a second—hell, longer—I was scared right down to my guts." She let out a breath. "Now, I'm just pissed off."

He pressed his lips to her forehead. "Then take them down, Lieutenant."

"I damn well will." She put her arms around him first, squeezed. "You pissed me off."

"Same goes. Now, it seems, I'm not. And I just love you."

"I'm still a little pissed." But she tipped her head back, looked into his eyes. "But I love you, too."

Stepping away, she went back to Isis. "Are you steady enough to look at some pictures?"

"Yes."

"Let's hope I don't need your statement, your ID, or . . . the rest of it to take these bastards down. But just in case." Eve pulled a stack of ID photos from her bag, spread them on the coffee table.

"Yes." Shifting to sit up, Isis took another sip of wine. Then, without hesitation, pointed out Ava's murderers.

CHAPTER
NINE

Eve rushed through Central, dodging other cops on the glides on her way to Homicide. The time with Isis had put her behind. She needed to meet with Mira, go over her notes, organize them. Then talk the PA into issuing more than a dozen arrest warrants.

And God, she needed coffee.

She veered toward her bullpen just as Peabody came out.

"I was about to tag you. Grabbing an energy bar first. You want?"

Eve started to decline, the things were disgusting. But they worked. "Yeah. I need to put a couple of things together, then meet with Mira."

At Vending, Peabody plugged in some credits. "You want the Razzmatazz or the Berry Burst?"

"What difference does it make? They're both revolting."

"I kinda like the Berry Burst." As Peabody made the selections, the machine cheerfully congratulated her on her choices, then listed the ingredients and nutritional information. "I checked in with Mira since you were late getting back."

"Ran into stuff. Fill you in. Coffee."

Peabody hiked after Eve to Eve's office. "She said she needed another thirty minutes, that was about five minutes ago. Down-the-hall neighbor at the vic's apartment states the vic never came home after work yesterday. They were supposed to do the girl thing together for the date. Hair, outfit, like that. Ava never showed. Nothing in her apartment to indicate an interest or connection with the occult. EDD's got her electronics."

"She never went back to the apartment because they took her at the clinic." Eve took a bite of the energy bar, washed it down with coffee. She filled Peabody in, and as expected, her partner's eyes went big as planets.

"You—*you* did like a ritual?"

"You had to be there," Eve muttered.

"No, really happy to pass. Was it scary?"

"The point is, while I'm not sure how much weight the woo-woo might carry in court, Isis fingered every single one of the people on my list. Damn smug is what they are, alibied up. Alibiing each other. Break one, break all. If Mira's got anything solid, we top it off. We've got enough to push for a search warrant on the clinic—and if we push right, on the residences of the staff. Contact the PA. Get them."

"Me? Me?" If she'd just been ordered to run naked through the bullpen, Peabody would've been less stunned. "But you should do it. They listen to you over there. What am I supposed to do?"

"Jesus, Peabody. Sing, dance, shed a goddamn tear. Put the package together and get it done. I've got Mira in fifteen. Go."

She all but shoved Peabody out the door, then closed it. Locked it. She two-pointed the rest of the energy bar into the trash. It wasn't doing the job. She needed five minutes down, she admitted. Just five. She set her wrist unit to alarm, sat at her desk, laid her head down on it, and shut her eyes.

She went straight under.

A sound woke her, a kind of humming. Voices, tinny with distance, tapped on her subconscious. One—young, male—spiked with excitement.

"Look! Flying cars. Look out the window! That is so *cool*."

Eve allowed herself a groan, started to slap at her wrist unit. Opening bleary eyes, she stared groggily at the swirl of luminous blue light, and the man, woman, and child cloaked in its circle. Instinct had her reaching for her weapon even as she registered them—tall man, a lot of gold hair, slim brunette with startled green eyes, and a shaggy-haired boy.

She thought she heard the woman say, "Oops." Then they were gone, and her wrist unit was beeping.

"Okay, with a dream that weird, I need more than five minutes down." She turned off the alarm, scrubbed her hands over her face. After downing the rest of her now luke-warm coffee, she gathered what she needed for Mira.

As she left the office, she shot a frown over her shoulder. Weird, she thought again. The whole damn day was weird.

Mira's admin gave Eve a glare that turned the room into an arctic cave. Knowing the way to Mira lay at the dragon's feet, Eve cut through the bull. "I kicked you, and kicked you hard this morning." She pulled out one of the crime-scene photos. "She's why." And laid it on the desk.

The admin sucked in a breath, held it, let it out slowly. "I see. Yes. She's waiting for you, Lieutenant."

"Thanks." Eve picked up the photo and walked into Mira's office.

Mira wasn't at her desk but standing at the window, her

back to the room. She looked smaller somehow, Eve thought. Almost delicate in her quiet lavender suit.

"Dr. Mira."

"Yes. Such a lovely day. Sometimes you need to remember the world is full of lovely days. You've had a very long one, haven't you?"

"It's got a ways to go yet."

Mira turned. Her sable hair curled around her pretty face, but her eyes looked tired and troubled. "Where do you want me to begin?"

"I know what happened, and I know who's responsible. At least the main players. I need to know what was done to Jackson Pike and Mika Nakamura, how it was done, and who did it. What was done to them was also done to the desk clerk at the hotel, and he bashed his own brains out with a hammer. So I need to know if it was done to anyone else."

Rather than sit in one of her cozy scoop chairs as was her habit, Mira continued to stand. "First, the toxicology screening showed a combination of drugs in their systems. I have that list for you. Both had a hallucinogenic in their bloodstream and a drug we sometimes use to control patients with violent tendencies. As you know, both Pike and the victim were also given sexual drugs."

"Would that explain the headaches, the memory blanks?"

"The combination would likely result in a kind of chemical hangover, but no, not the violent pain. There may be blank spots as well, but again, no, that's not my conclusion."

She did sit now. "The drugs were used to begin a process, and to enhance it."

"They've been hypnotized."

"You're ahead of me."

"No, but I'm hoping we're on pace. At least two of the suspects are sensitives. They took a pass at me. Since I've dealt with a homicidal psychic before, I used the same method to block them, to steer them away. One of them, Silas Pratt, he's . . . Look, I know you've got a daughter who's Wiccan, and I get there are theories and faiths and even documentation, studies, blah, blah. I'm not big on that. But this guy?"

It went against the grain to admit it. "He's got a punch," Eve told her.

"You don't want to use the word 'power.'"

"It doesn't take power to load people up with drugs, or to hypnotize them. It's a technique. You use it." She stuffed her hands in her pockets and began to pace. "One of these bastards is Mika's kid's doctor. She took the kid in for a standard checkup three weeks ago. So, we theorize Pratt hypnotizes her. Maybe they slip her something first to make her more susceptible, but he takes her under, and gives her the assignment. Posthypnotic suggestion, right?"

"Yes."

"It needs a trigger—something she sees, hears. Easy enough to take care of that while she's on her way to work, maybe give her a booster shot. She goes in, shuts down the cameras. They had to get to the desk clerk. We'll find the intersect there, but they turned him on like a damn droid. They waltz Pike and the victim right in. They go along like puppies. They're loaded by then, and under . . ."

"A spell?"

"If that's the word. Pike's left as patsy, with that trigger still cocked in his head. The pain's impossible, and trying to remember takes it up to excruciating."

"I believe if you hadn't gotten them to me, into a controlled, medical environment when you did, they'd have ended it as the desk clerk did. I've had to use that pain to try to get to the trigger. It's . . . difficult."

Understanding, Eve moved to Mira's AutoChef. "What's that tea you're always drinking?"

Mira managed a smile. "It varies. I think jasmine would be nice. Thank you."

Eve programmed a cup, brought it to Mira, took a seat. "You're not hurting them. You know that. The one who cocked the trigger is."

"They, both of them, begged me to kill them." Mira sipped the tea, then eased wearily back in the chair. "It's taken hours for me to find the right method to dial the pain down. Not turn it off, not yet, but lower it from inhuman to hideous. Enough that Jack remembered a little. He remembered that Dr. Pratt called him into his office at the end of the day. He's not sure of the time, it's cloudy, but thinks it was after his last patient. Pratt gave him a cup of coffee, and after he drank it, it's more jumbled. He remembers being in a limo with Collins and Ava. He thinks there were more. I recorded everything, of course. He remembers having sex with Ava."

"Does he remember the murder?"

Her eyes troubled, Mira shook her head. "He's suppressing. Even without the trigger, his mind's not ready to go there. He next remembers waking in a bed, covered with blood, and a woman he called Leah sitting beside him, crying."

"Leah Burke. Good, that's good. I can break her, and she'll take them all down with her."

"It wasn't just a young woman killed in that suite, Eve. Parts of the two people I have sedated and restrained for their own safety were murdered in there. When I find the way to remove the trigger and they remember what was done, their part in it however unwilling, they'll never be the same."

"You'll help them deal with it, or find someone who'll help them deal with it. It's what you do."

"Take them down, Eve. Take them down hard. When I can tell Mika and Jack that's been done, we can start on the healing."

In all the time they'd worked together, Mira had never asked. Eve rose. "Like you said, it's a lovely day. Before it's over, they'll be down."

As she walked out, Eve whipped out her communicator to contact Peabody. "Search warrants?"

"It's looking good on the clinic. I just need to—"

"Put a hold on it. We've got a wit who puts Leah Burke in Suite 606. We're bringing her in. Book an interview room."

"You want me to have her picked up?"

"Here's how it goes. Two uniforms at her door. If she's not home yet, I need to know ASAP. She's not under arrest, and she's not to be read her rights. Got that?"

"Got it."

"She's needed down here for further questioning. That's all they know. She's not to be permitted to contact anyone. She's not under arrest. I'll finish up with the search warrants."

Eve was still listing the names for the APA when she approached Homicide. What sounded like a small riot had her quickening her steps.

Then she smelled the pizza. "Yeah, I mean even the house in the Caribbean. I've got goddamn probable cause right down the line. I've got witness statements, and within two hours I'm going to hand you a confession on a goddamn platter that will take down every son of a bitch on the list I just gave you. They're going to have hoodoo voodoo crap tucked away," Eve said meeting Roarke's eyes as she stepped into the bullpen. "Because they believe it. A dozen blades were used on the vic. We're going to find some, most, or all of them."

She clicked off. "Figured you'd be back around after you got your witch home."

"You haven't eaten." He picked up a box of pizza while her men swarmed like ants over the five others he'd brought in. "Eat now."

She grabbed a slice, chomped a huge bite. "Oh. God. Good." She swallowed, took another. "I got them."

"I can see that. Can I watch?"

She took the tube of Pepsi he offered, guzzled. "It's a good bribe. Take Observation."

Revived and revved, Eve stood with Roarke in Observation and watched Leah pace the interview room in her smart suit.

"She's already sweating. Ten minutes in, and she's already sweating. She's scared and guilty, and the doctors aren't here to tell her what to do, what to say."

"Why her? Out of all of them?"

"She cried." She glanced over as Mira came in.

"Word's out that you have one of them in," Mira said. "I wanted to see for myself."

"I haven't arrested her yet. Listen, I'm going to ask you not to turn on the audio until I give you the go. Actually, I'm not asking. I've got to get started."

"Will I be able to see Mika?" Roarke asked Mira after Eve stepped out.

"Not yet. She's comfortable for the moment. I've spoken with her husband."

"So have I. Is there anything I can do for her?"

"There will be." Mira laid a hand over Roarke's, and

watched Eve enter Interview. "What she's going to say needs to be off the record. At least for my ears."

"Do you object?"

"No." Mira stared at Leah Burke through the glass. "No, I don't."

Inside, Leah spun toward Eve. "I demand to know why I was brought here, why I'm being treated this way. I have rights. I have—"

"Shut the fuck up. You've got nothing here until I give it to you. Sit down."

The words, the tone, had Leah's whole body recoiling. "I will not—"

"I'll put you down, bitch. Believe it."

The threat, so hot and hard in Eve's eyes, had Leah sitting at the small table. "You'll lose your badge." But her voice trembled, just a little. "Worse. There are laws."

Eve slammed both fists on the table, hard enough to have Leah covering her face in defense. "Laws? I bet you were thinking about *laws* when Ava Marsterson was being hacked to death. Jack remembers, Leah." She leaned close, snapped her fingers in front of Leah's face. "Boom. Spell broken. You've got one shot. One, then I move on to the next. But I'll hurt you first."

"You can't touch me. You can't put your hands on me. I want—"

"I know how to hurt you so it won't show." Eve let the heat burn in her eyes as she circled the table. "Your word against mine. Decorated cop against murder suspect. Guess who they'll believe? I haven't put this on record. I haven't read you your rights. And we're all alone here, Leah. One shot once I turn on the record. You don't take it, I move to Kiki or Rodney, to Larry's wife, and down the line—and you go back to a cage blubbering with the pain.

"Everybody gets one shot. Take it, I deal down to Murder Two. You'll do life, but you'll do it on planet. Pass? And you'll find out what hell really is because you'll be in some concrete cage in an off-planet penal colony where I will personally see that word gets out you fucked with tiny little children. Do you know what cons like to do to people who fuck with tiny little children?"

"I've never touched a child—"

"I'll lie." Eve grinned. "And I'll love it. One shot, and if you so much as *think* lawyer, it's done. You only get the chance because Jack's soft-hearted enough to think you feel real bad about what happened. Me? I'm hoping you pass so I can look forward to getting the reports on how many inventive ways the other cons and the guards rape you over the next, oh, fifty years."

She came around the table, whispered in Leah's ear. "They find ways to get sharp, ugly tools into those cages, Leah. They'll slice and dice you, let them stitch you up again just so they can slice and dice some more. The more you beg, the more they'll enjoy it."

She watched tears plop on Leah's trembling hands, on the rough surface of the table. And thinking of Ava, felt no pity. "She trusted you, you bitch."

"Please. Oh, please."

"Screw you." Eve walked to the door, stepped out. She took a deep breath, signaled Peabody. "Let's do it." Walking back in, she nodded toward the observation glass. "Record on. Dallas, Lieutenant Eve—"

"Please, please. I'll tell you everything."

"Hey, great." Eve slid into her chair, composed and easy. "Let's just get everything on record first, and read you your rights."

When she'd finished, she nodded to Leah. "What do you want to tell us, Ms. Burke?"

"I didn't know it would be like that. I swear, I swear I didn't know."

"Like what?"

"So much blood. I never thought they would really kill her."

"Be more specific."

"I thought it would be a symbolic death."

"Bullshit." Eve leaned back in her chair with the warning in her eyes clear. *Lie, and your one shot dies.* "You knew exactly what was going to happen, and when it did, you couldn't handle it. If you want me to go to the PA and say you came in, you confessed, you gave the details and feel remorse, don't bullshit me. Did you participate in the ritual murder of Ava Marsterson?"

"Yes. I didn't understand. Believe me, I didn't under-stand. I thought I did, but . . . She didn't accept, and neither did Jack. Not like Silas said they would."

"Silas Pratt participated in the murder of Ava Marster-son?"

"He cut her throat. She just stood there, and he cut her throat, and the blood gushed out of her. She didn't accept. She didn't know what was happening, so how could she accept?"

"Accept what?"

"Her sacrifice. That she would be the gift."

"Whose gift?"

"The gift from us to the prince. To Lucifer."

"How long have you been a satanist?"

"I am *not* a satanist. I am a disciple of the One."

Eve gave it a moment, unsure if she was amused or irri-tated by the obvious insult in Leah's voice. "Okay. And does the One demand the murder of innocents?"

"Your God murdered my child." Leah's hands balled into fists, beat lightly on the table. "He took her, and what had she ever done? She was just a baby. I found my way back. I found my strength and my purpose."

"Silas Pratt showed you the way back."

"He's a great man. You'll never understand. A man of power. You'll never hold him with your pitiful laws and your bars."

"But he lied to you, this great man, this man of power," Peabody put in. "He lied to you about Ava and Jack."

"No, I think . . . No, he wouldn't lie. I think he miscalculated, that's all. She just wasn't ready. Wasn't as strong as Silas thought. Or maybe it's me. Maybe I'm weak. I couldn't stand what they did to her."

"Tell me who they are. Every name of everyone who was in Suite 606."

"Silas and his wife, Ola. Larry—Dr. Collins—and his wife, Bria." In a dull, empty voice, she gave Eve a dozen names in addition to her own. "And Ava and Jack."

"Dr. Slone?"

"No. Peter and the others from the clinic who weren't there aren't disciples or priests. It's important, Silas thinks, that there are those who aren't part of us—and to know who is open to our faith, and who would be closed. Everyone who is of our group attended. It was an important ritual, a celebration."

"A celebration?"

"Yes. It was Silas's birthday."

"I've seen his records. It wasn't his birthday."

"His date of rebirth in the One."

"Right." Eve sat back again. "Why Ava and Jack?"

"Ava was the gift. Silas recognized her as such the day she came in to interview for the position. And Jack . . . the sexual energy between them would be a vital element to the ritual."

"Why that room?"

"We'd considered other venues, but . . . A palace, it seemed right. And Larry's connection to the head of security gave us the way in. I'm only a disciple. I don't plan." She folded her hands now, bowed her head. "I follow."

"You followed them into that suite. But first you helped drug Ava and Jack at the clinic."

"We gave them what would open them to the coming ritual, what would help them accept, and embrace Silas's power."

"He used hypnosis, Leah, on top of hallucinogens."

Tears continued to gather and spill. "You don't understand. You're closed."

"Fine. You used chemicals to open Ava and Jack, without their knowledge or permission."

"Yes, but—"

"And once they were under that influence, you took them to the hotel. Correct?"

"Yes."

"There, Mika Nakamura and Brian Trosky had also been drugged, and *embraced* by Silas's power. That power caused them to shut down the security cameras to the lobby, and to the elevators for the sixtieth floor. It also, as had been done to Jack, caused them to forget what had been done, or suffer pain."

"The pain is only if they refuse to accept, only to help them—"

"Inside the room, you ate and you drank, you engaged in sexual activity."

Color flushed into her cheeks. It was amazing, Eve mused, what embarrassed murderers.

"Sex is an offering."

"Ava didn't offer, did she? After you'd feasted and stoked up, painted your pentagram, lit your candles, said whatever it is you people say, you stretched out a drugged, helpless, naked woman on the floor, and told a drugged, helpless man to have at her. He cared for her. They cared for each other, isn't that true?"

"Yes, yes, but—"

"And when he finished what he'd have never done of his own will, the rest of you raped her."

"Yes." Tears rolled down her cheeks. "Everyone was required to take from the gift, and to give of ourselves. But I felt . . ."

"What?"

"Cold. So cold. Not the heat, not the fire, but ice. I heard her screaming in my head. I swear I *heard* her." She covered her face with her hands. "But no one would listen. They pulled her to her feet. Kiki and Rodney. Silas stepped into the circle, and the cold, the cold was terrible. Her screaming was like spikes in my head. But no one heard her. He slashed her throat, and her blood sprayed all over him. Everyone rushed forward when she fell to take more blood, to make more blood. Jack passed out, so they coated him with her blood. They took him upstairs, left him in bed while they finished with her. Larry told me to go up, to take one of the knives and put it in Jack's hand, and to give him another round of drugs so he'd overdose."

"The plan was to kill Jack, leave him behind, so it looked as if he'd killed Ava."

"Yes. Yes. But I couldn't. I couldn't give him more. Her blood was on my hands, and I could hear her screaming." She laid down her head and wept.

"Give her five minutes to pull it together," Eve told Peabody. "The charge is Murder in the Second, two counts," she added, thinking of Trosky. "Additional charges are kidnapping, two counts, rape, inducing chemicals without consent or knowledge, including illegals. Have her booked and bolted. I'm going to go get us a shitload of warrants."

Lack of sleep didn't put a hitch in Eve's stride as she walked to Silas Pratt's front door. Big, fancy house, she noted. Well, he'd seen the last of that. The droid that answered looked down its nose. "Dr. and Mrs. Pratt are unavailable at this time. Please leave your name and state your business, and—"

He didn't get any further as Eve shoved him aside. "Shut that thing down," she ordered the uniforms that trailed after her and Peabody. She walked into the spacious living area where the doctor and his wife were sipping martinis.

"Exactly what is the meaning of this?" Silas demanded as he surged to his feet.

"Deal with the woman, Peabody. He's mine. Silas Pratt, you're under arrest. The charges are Murder in the First Degree in the death of Ava Marsterson, a human being. Murder in the First Degree in the death of—"

"This is absurd. You're absurd."

Eve felt that *punch* of his, accepted the ice that coated her belly. Even welcomed it. "Don't interrupt. Resist, by all means, because I'd love to spend the next several minutes kicking your ass. Jesus, Peabody, can't you shut her up?"

"She's a screamer," Peabody said cheerfully as she passed the hysterical Ola to waiting uniforms.

"Now where was I? Oh yeah, the death of Brian Trosky, another human being. We've got kidnapping charges, illegals, fraud, medical abuse, and just for fun, destruction of property. You guys seriously trashed that suite. You have the right to remain silent," she began.

"You can go to hell."

"Thanks, but New York's close enough for me." She grabbed one of his arms to pull it behind his back as she read him the rest of the Revised Miranda. When he tried to shake her off, she gave herself the pleasure of slamming the heel of her boot into his instep. He cursed at her, snarled at her as she clapped the restraints to his wrist. "What is that, Latin? Greek? Or is it just all made up?"

He struggled as she frog-marched him across the room, which, she thought, it could be argued was the reason his head smacked into the doorjamb. "Gee, I bet you're going to have a headache now. Cut it out, before you hurt yourself."

"I'll drink your blood from a silver cup."

"That's just disgusting." She moved her mouth close to his ear. "You don't have any power here, asshole. Getting arrested, dragged out of your fancy house in front of your fancy neighbors, and hey, look, it's Channel 75." She beamed, pleased her heads-up to her contact there had brought the media. "Nothing like humiliation to water down power. I bet even the devil himself's embarrassed."

She muscled him into the back of the police car. She fixed dark glasses over his head, over his eyes. "Remember he's a sensitive," she told the cops she'd put in charge. "He goes straight into isolation."

She slammed the door, put her hands on her hips. "Go home, Peabody," she said when her partner stepped beside her and yawned until her jaw cracked. "Get some sleep."

"I am so on that. Some day, huh?"

"Yeah, some day." Eve stood where she was, watched Roarke come to her. Gosh, she thought, pretty. And realized sleep deprivation had gooed up her brain.

"I imagine this arrest will be playing on-screen for some time."

"That's entertainment." Eve gave him a quick smile.

"Please tell me you're not going to make all the other arrests personally, then deal with the ensuing paperwork tonight."

"Nah, I just wanted this one, 'specially. I delegated, and the paperwork'll wait till morning. I'm pretty close to falling on my face."

He put his arms around her, amused that she was tired enough not to resist even though some of the media remained. "I want to go home, sleep with my wife. For days."

"Settle for eight straight hours?"

"Deal."

With their arms around each other's waist they walked to the car. Roarke got behind the wheel; Eve slid into the passenger's seat. And, he noted, got started on that eight hours immediately.

EPILOGUE

Jack sat up in bed when Eve entered his treatment room.
He was pale, and bruises of fatigue dogged his eyes. No
doubt she'd had a more restful night than he had. "Doctor?"
he began.

"Lieutenant. Lieutenant Dallas. Do you remember me?"

He stared through her for a moment. "Yes. I remember."
He held up a hand, a signal to wait. And shutting his eyes,
breathed. "I remember. You were at the hotel, but not, not
in that room. And you were talking to me in another room.
The police station. Am I under arrest?"

"No, Jack. I know you're working with Dr. Mira. She
says you're better than you were, and you'll be better yet."

"The drugs are out of my system. It helps. The headaches . . . it's not as bad. Ava's dead. I was there." The words
trembled out. Once more he closed his eyes, breathed. "I
was there. I raped her."

"No, you didn't. They used you both. You're a doctor,
Jack. I know Mira told you what they'd put in you, and you
know what those chemicals can do. You were drugged, put

under hypnosis. Kidnapped. Nothing that happened was your fault or responsibility. You were a victim."

"I'm alive. She's not."

"I know. That's hard. You're afraid to remember, afraid to ask if you used the knife you had in your hand."

His eyes welled, and tears leaked out. "How can I live with that? Whatever they put in me, whatever they did, how can I live with that?"

"You don't have to. You didn't use the knife. I have a number of statements from people who were there, who were involved. Every one of them says you passed out. They put the knife in your hand when you were upstairs, unconscious."

"The blood. Her blood."

"They put it on you. You were supposed to die, holding the knife, covered in her blood. There would have been questions, sure, a lot of questions. Who else was with you. They had two other people they believed would be dead who'd be tied in. One of them is dead, Jack—he didn't do anything, and he's dead. Another is across the hall in a room like this, struggling to deal with what happened. They drugged her, used her. Do you blame her for Ava?"

"No. God."

"Why blame yourself?"

"I couldn't get out. I couldn't get *out* of . . . myself, and help her. Even when I heard her screaming. In my head."

"Thirteen people killed Ava. You weren't one of them. Because you lived, we found them. Every one of them is locked up. Every one of them is going to pay. You lived, and you found me, Jack. I was in Suite 606. I saw what was done to her. I had her blood on my hands. She was in my head, too, Jack. I'm telling you, she doesn't blame you. She doesn't want you to carry this."

He put out a hand, took hers. "They're going to pay?"

"Every goddamn one."

"Thank you."

She stepped out, and watched through the observation window as Roarke leaned over and kissed Mika on the brow.

"How is she?" she asked when he came out.

"Better. Better than I'd hoped, really. Mira said she has a strong mind. How about your Jack?"

"He'll get there."

Roarke took her hand. "Another long day, Lieutenant, with all your interrogations and reports and media conferences."

"You had one, too, I imagine, making up for the time lost yesterday. Buying up wide chunks of the universe takes it out of a guy."

"Yet I feel surprisingly . . . fresh."

"Good, because I want to go home and sleep with my husband—in a much more active sense than last night." She let him keep her hand as they walked away from the treatment rooms. "You know, I found this little bag full of stones and flowery things in the pocket of the jacket I had on yesterday. How do you suppose that got there?"

"Hmm. Magic?"

She gave him a shoulder bump and let it go. As far as she was concerned, the only magic she'd ever need was the good strong grip of his hand in hers.

MISSING IN DEATH

CHAPTER
ONE

On a day kissed gently by summer, three thousand, seven hundred and sixty-one passengers cruised the New York Harbor on the Staten Island Ferry. Two of them had murder on their minds.

The other three thousand, seven hundred and fifty-nine aboard the bright orange ferry christened the *Hillary Rodham Clinton* were simply along for the ride. Most were tourists who happily took their vids and snaps of the retreating Manhattan skyline or that iconic symbol of freedom, the Statue of Liberty.

Even in 2060, nearly two centuries after she'd first greeted hopeful immigrants to a new world, nobody beat "The Lady."

Those who jockeyed for the best views munched on soy chips, sucked down tubes of soft drinks from the snack bars while the ferry chugged placidly along on calm waters under baby blue skies.

With the bold sun streaming, the scent of sunscreen mixed with the scent of water, many jammed the decks for the duration of the twenty-five-minute ride from Lower Manhattan to Staten Island. A turbo would have taken half the time, but the ferry wasn't about expediency. It was about tradition.

Most planned to get off at St. George, jam the terminal, then simply load back on again to complete the round trip. It was free, it was summer, it was a pretty way to spend an hour.

Some midday commuters, eschewing the bridges, the turbos, or the air trams, sat inside, out of the biggest crowds, and passed the time with their PPCs or 'links.

Summer meant more kids. Babies cried or slept, toddlers whined or giggled, and parents sought to distract the bored or fractious by pointing out the grand lady or a passing boat.

For Carolee Grogan of Springfield, Missouri, the ferry ride checked off another item on her Must Do list on the family vacation she'd lobbied for. Other Must Dos included the top of the Empire State Building, the Central Park Zoo, the Museum of Natural History, St. Pat's, the Metropolitan Museum of Art (though she wasn't sure she'd success-fully harangue her husband and ten- and seven-year-old sons into that one), Ellis Island, Memorial Park, a Broadway show—she didn't care which one—and shopping on Fifth Avenue.

In the spirit of fairness, she'd added on a ball game at Yankee Stadium, and fully accepted she would have to wan-der the cathedral of Tiffany's alone while her gang hit the video heaven of Times Square.

At forty-three, Carolee was living a long-cherished dream. She'd finally pushed, shoved and nagged her husband east of the Mississippi.

Could Europe be far behind?

When she started to take a snapshot of her "boys," as she called Steve and their sons, a man standing nearby offered to take one of the whole family. Carolee happily turned over her camera, posed with her boys with the dignified lady of liberty behind them.

"See." She gave her husband an elbow poke as they went back to looking out at the water. "He was nice. Not all New Yorkers are rude and nasty."

"Carolee, he was a tourist, just like us. He's probably from Toledo or somewhere." But he smiled when he said it. It was more fun to yank her chain than to admit he was having a pretty good time.

"I'm going to ask him."

Steve only shook his head as his wife walked over to chat up the picture taker. It was so Carolee. She could—and did—talk to anyone anywhere about anything.

When she came back she offered Steve a smug smile. "He's from Maryland, *but*," she added with a quick finger jab, "he's lived in New York for almost ten years. He's going over to Staten Island to visit his daughter. She just had a baby. A girl. His wife's been staying with them the past few days to help out, and she's meeting him at the terminal. It's their first grandchild."

"Did you find out how long he's been married, where and how he met his wife, who he voted for in the last election?"

She laughed and gave Steve another poke.

"I'm thirsty."

She glanced down at her youngest. "You know, me, too. Why don't you and I go get some drinks for everybody." She grabbed his hand and snaked her way through the people crowded on deck. "Are you having a good time, Pete?"

"It's pretty neat, but I really want to go see the penguins."

"Tomorrow, first thing."

"Can we get a soy dog?"

"Where are you putting them? You had one an hour ago."

"They smell good."

Vacation meant indulgence, she decided. "Soy dogs it is."

"But I have to pee."

"Okay." As a veteran mother, she'd scoped out the

restrooms when they'd boarded the ferry. Now she detoured to steer them toward the nearest facilities.

And, of course, since Pete mentioned it, now *she* had to pee. She pointed toward the men's room. "If you get out first, you stand right here. You remember what the ferry staff looks like, the uniforms? If you need help, go right to one of them."

"Mom, I'm just going to pee."

"Well, me, too. You wait for me *here* if you get out first."

She watched him go in, knowing full well he rolled his eyes the minute his back was to her. It amused her as she turned toward the women's room.

And saw the Out of Order sign.

"Shoot."

She weighed her options. Hold it until Pete came out, then hold it some more while they got the dogs and drinks— because he'd whine and sulk otherwise—then make her way to the other restroom.

Or . . . maybe she could just peek in. Surely not all the stalls were out of order. She only needed one.

She pushed open the door, hurried in. She didn't want to leave Pete alone for long.

She made the turn at the line of sinks, her mind on getting the provisions and squeezing back to the rail to watch Staten Island come into view.

She stopped dead, her limbs frozen in shock.

Blood, she thought, could only think, so much blood. The woman on the floor seemed bathed in it.

The man standing over the body held a still-dripping knife in one hand and a stunner in the other.

"I'm sorry," he said—and, to her shocked mind, sounded sincere.

Even as Carolee sucked in the air to scream, took the first stumbling step back, he triggered the stunner.

"Really very sorry," he said as Carolee fell to the floor.

*   *   *

Racing across New York Harbor in a turbo wasn't how Lieu-tenant Eve Dallas expected to spend her afternoon. She'd played second lead that morning to her partner's primary role in the unfortunate demise of Vickie Trendor, the third wife of the unrepentant Alan Trendor, who'd smashed her skull with an inferior bottle of California chardonnay.

According to the new widower, it wasn't accurate to say he'd bashed her brains out when she simply hadn't had any brains to begin with.

While the prosecutor and the counsel for the defense hammered out a plea arrangement, Eve had made a dent in her paperwork, discussed strategy with two of her detectives on an ongoing case and congratulated another on closing one.

A pretty good day, in her estimation.

Now, she and Peabody, her partner, were speeding across the water in a boat she judged to be about the size of a surfboard toward the orange hulk of a ferry stalled halfway between Manhattan and Staten Island.

"This is absolutely mag!" Peabody stood near the bow, her square-jawed face lifted to the wind, her short, flippy hair flying.

"Why?"

"Jeez, Dallas!" Peabody lowered her shades down her nose, exposing delighted brown eyes. "We're getting a boat ride. We're on the water. Half the time you can forget Manhattan's an island."

"That's what I like about it. Out here, it makes you wonder, how come it doesn't sink? All that weight—the buildings, the streets, the people. It should go down like a stone."

"Come on." With a laugh, Peabody pushed her shades back in place. "Statue of Liberty," she pointed out. "She's the best."

Eve wouldn't argue. She'd come close to dying inside the

landmark, fighting radical terrorists bent on blowing it up. Even now, she could look at its lines, its grandeur, and see her husband, bleeding, clinging to a ledge outside the proud face.

They'd survived that one, she mused, and Roarke had defused the bomb, saved the day. Symbols mattered, and because they'd fought and bled, people could chug by on the ferry every day and snap their pictures of freedom.

That was fine, that was the job. What she didn't get was why Homicide had to zip off the island because the Department of Transportation cops couldn't find a passenger.

Blood all over a bathroom and a missing woman. Interesting, sure, she decided, but not really her turf. In fact, it wasn't turf at all. It was water. It was a big orange boat on the water.

Why didn't boats sink? The errant thought reminded her that sometimes they did, and she decided not to dwell on it.

When the turbo approached that big orange boat, she noted people ranged along the rail on the tiers of decks. Some of them waved.

Beside her, Peabody waved back.

"Cut it out," Eve ordered.

"Sorry. It's knee-jerk. Looks like DOT sent out backup," she commented, nodding toward the turbos at the base of the ferry with the Department of Transportation logo emblazoned on the hull. "I hope she didn't fall over. Or jump. But somebody would notice that, right?"

"More likely she wandered off from the passenger areas, got lost and is currently trying to wander back."

"Blood," Peabody reminded her, and Eve shrugged.

"Let's just wait and see."

That, too, was part of the job—the waiting and seeing. She'd been a cop for a dozen years and knew the dangers of jumping to conclusions.

She shifted her weight as the turbo slowed, bracing on long legs while she scanned the rails, the faces, the open areas. Her short hair fluttered around her face while those eyes—golden brown, long and cop-flat—studied what might or might not be a crime scene.

When the turbo was secured, she stepped off.

She judged the man who stepped forward to offer his hand as late twenties. He wore the casual summer khakis and light blue shirt with its DOT emblem well. Sun-streaked hair waved around a face tanned by sun or design. Pale green eyes contrasted with the deeper tone, and added an intensity.

"Lieutenant, Detective, I'm Inspector Warren. I'm glad you're here."

"You haven't located your passenger, Inspector?"

"No. A search is still under way." He gestured for them to walk with him. "We've added a dozen officers to the DOT crew aboard to complete the search, and to secure the area where the missing woman was last seen."

They started up a set of stairs.

"How many passengers aboard?"

"The ticker counted three thousand, seven hundred and sixty-one boarding at Whitehall."

"Inspector, it wouldn't be procedure to call Homicide on a missing passenger."

"No, but none of this is hitting SOP. I have to tell you, Lieutenant, it doesn't make sense." He took the next set of stairs, glancing over at the people hugging the rail. "I don't mind admitting, this situation is above my pay grade. And right now, most of the passengers are being patient. It's mostly tourists, and this is kind of an adventure. But if we hold the ferry here much longer, it's not going to be pretty."

Eve stepped onto the next deck where DOT officials had cordoned off a path. "Why don't you give me a rundown, Inspector?"

"The missing woman is Carolee Grogan, tourist from Missouri, on board with her husband and two sons. Age forty-three. I've got her description and a photo taken aboard this afternoon. She and her youngest went to get drinks, hit the johns first. He went into the men's, and she was going into the women's. Told him to wait for her right outside if he got out first. He waited, and she didn't come out."

Warren paused outside the restroom area, nodded to another DOT official on the women's room door. "Nobody else went in or out either. After a few minutes, he called her on his 'link. She didn't answer. He called his father, and the father and the other son came over. The father, Steven Grogan, asked a woman—ah, Sara Hunning—if she'd go in and check on his wife."

Warren opened the door. "And this is what she found inside."

Eve stepped in behind Warren. She smelled the blood immediately. A Homicide cop gets a nose for it. It soured the citrusy/sterilized odor of the air in the black-and-white room with its steel sinks, and around the dividing wall, the white-doored stalls.

It washed over the floor, a spreading dark pool that snaked in trails across the white, slashed over the stall doors, the opposing wall, like abstract graffiti.

"If that's Grogan's," Eve said, "you're not looking for a missing passenger. You're looking for a dead one."

CHAPTER
TWO

"Record on, Peabody." Eve switched on her own. "Dallas, Lieutenant Eve; Peabody, Detective Delia; Warren, DOT Inspector . . ."

"Jake," he supplied.

"On scene aboard Staten Island Ferry."

"It's the *Hillary Rodham Clinton*," he added. "Second deck, port side, women's restroom."

She cocked a brow, nodded. "Responding to report of missing passenger, Grogan, Carolee, last seen entering this area. Peabody, get a sample of the blood. We'll need to make sure it's human, then type it."

She opened the field kit for Seal-It she hadn't fully believed she'd need. "How many people have been in and out of here since Grogan was missed?"

"Since I've been on board, just me. Prior, to the best of my knowledge, Sara Hunning, Steven Grogan and two ferry officers on board."

"There's an Out of Order sign on the door."

"Yeah."

"But she came in anyway."

"Nobody we've spoken to can absolutely confirm. She told the kid she was going in."

Sealed, Eve stepped into the first of the four stalls, waved a hand over the sensor. The toilet flushed efficiently. She repeated the gesture in the other three stalls, with the same results.

"Appears to be in order."

"It's human," Peabody told her, holding up her gauge. "Type A Negative."

"Some smears, but no drag marks," Eve murmured. She gestured toward a narrow utility closet. "Who opened that?"

"I did," Jake told her. "On the chance she—or her body— was in there. It was locked."

"There's only one way in and out." Peabody walked around to the sink area. "No windows. If that's Carolee Grogan's blood, she didn't stand up and walk out of here."

Eve stood at the edge of the blood pool. "How do you get a dead body out of a public restroom, on a ferry in the middle of the harbor, under the noses of more than three thousand people? And why the hell don't you leave it where it dropped in the first place?"

"It's not an answer to that," Jake began, "but this is a tourist boat. It doesn't carry any vehicles, has extra concession areas. People tend to hug the rails and look out, or hang in a concession and snack as they watch out the windows. Still, it'd take a lot of luck and enormous *cojones* to cart a bleeding body along the deck."

"Balls maybe, but nobody's got that kind of luck. I'll need this room sealed, Inspector. And I want to talk to the missing woman's family, and the witness. Peabody, let's get the sweepers out here. I want every inch of this room covered."

Eve considered Jake's foresight solid in having the Grogan family sequestered in one of the canteens. It kept them away from other passengers, gave them seats, and access to food and drink. That, she assumed, had kept the kids calm.

Calm enough, she noted, for the smaller of the two boys to curl on the narrow seat of the booth with his head in his father's lap.

The man continued to stroke the boy's hair, and his face was both pale and frightened when Eve crossed to him.

"Mr. Grogan, I'm Lieutenant Dallas, with the New York City Police and Security Department. This is Detective Peabody."

"You found her. You found Carolee. She's—"

"We haven't yet located your wife."

"She told me to wait." The boy with his head on Steve's lap opened his eyes. "I did. But she didn't come back."

"Did you see her go into the other bathroom?"

"Nuh-uh, but she said she was gonna, and then we were going to get dogs and drinks. And she gave me the routine."

"Routine?"

He sat up, but leaned against his father's side. "How I had to wait *right* there, and how if I needed anything, I was supposed to get one of the guys who work on the boat. The uniform guys."

"Okay. Then you went into the men's bathroom."

"It was only for a minute. I just had to . . . you know. Then I came out and waited like she said. It *always* takes girls longer. But it was really long, and I was thirsty. I used my 'link." He slid his eyes toward his father. "We're only allowed to use them if it's really important, but I was thirsty."

"It's okay, Pete. She didn't answer, so Pete tagged me, and Will and I headed back to where he was waiting. They'd been gone at least ten minutes by then. There was the Out of Order sign on the door, so I thought she might've used another restroom. Except she wouldn't. She wouldn't have left Pete. So I asked this woman if she'd just take a look inside. And then . . ."

He shook his head.

"She said there was blood." The older boy swallowed hard. "The lady came running out, yelling there was blood."

"I went in." Steve rubbed his eyes. "I thought maybe she fell, hit her head, or . . . But she wasn't in there."

"There was blood," Will said again.

"Your mom wasn't in there," Steve said firmly. "She's somewhere else."

"Where?" Pete demanded in a voice perilously close to weeping. "Where did she go?"

"That's what we're going to find out." Peabody spoke with easy confidence. "Pete, Will, why don't you help me get drinks for everybody? Inspector Warren, is it okay if we forage in here?"

"You bet. I'll give you a hand." He added a warm smile. "And make it Jake."

Eve slid into the booth. "I need to ask you some questions."

"It was too much blood," he said in a soft voice, a voice that wouldn't carry to his children. "A fatal loss of blood. I'm a doctor. I'm an ER doctor, and that much blood loss without immediate medical attention . . . For God's sake, what happened to Carolee?"

"Do you know her blood type, Dr. Grogan?"

"Yes, of course. She's O Positive."

"You're certain?"

"Yes, I'm certain. She and Pete are O Positive. I'm A Positive, so's Will."

"It wasn't her blood. The blood in the restroom wasn't hers."

"Not hers." He trembled, and she watched him struggle for composure, but his eyes teared. "Not her blood. Not Carolee's blood."

"Why were you going to Staten Island?"

"What? We weren't. I mean . . ." He pressed his hands to his face again, breathed, then lowered them. Steady nerves, Eve thought. She imagined an ER doc needed them. "We were taking the ride over, then we were going to ride

MISSING IN DEATH   213

back. Just for the experience. We're on vacation. It's our second day on vacation."

"Does she know anyone in New York?"

"No." He shook his head slowly. "She wasn't in there. But she wouldn't have left Pete. It doesn't make sense. She doesn't answer her 'link. I've tried it over and over." He pushed his across the table. "She doesn't answer."

He glanced toward the concession where Peabody and Jake kept the kids busy, then leaned closer to Eve. "She would never have left our boy, not willingly. Something happened in that room. Somebody died in that room. If she saw what happened—"

"Let's not get ahead of ourselves. We're still searching. I'm going to check on the status."

Rising, she signaled to Peabody. "It's not her blood. It's the wrong type."

"That's something. They're really nice kids. They're scared."

"They're on vacation. Don't know anyone in New York according to the husband, and he comes off straight to me. What doesn't come off is how a body could disappear, a woman who we'll presume for the moment is alive could disappear, and potentially a killer/abductor could disappear. They're here somewhere. Get the wit statement, though I don't think that's going to add anything. I'm calling in more officers, ours and DOT's. We're going to need to get data, statements and do a search on every person on this damn ferry before we let anyone off."

"I'll take care of our end before I talk to the woman. Ah, he's kind of flirting with me."

"What? Who?"

"The adorable inspector."

"Please."

"No, seriously. I am spoken for," Peabody added with a flutter of lashes, "but it's still flattering to have cute guys flirt."

"Do the job, Peabody."

Shaking her head as her partner went out to do just that, Eve gestured to Jake. "We're going to need more men. I can't let anyone off until we've confirmed IDs, interviewed and searched."

"Over three thousand people?" He let out a low whistle. "You're going to have a revolt."

"What I've got is a missing woman, and very likely a dead body somewhere on this vessel. I've also got a killer. I want somebody in here with them," she added. "I want a look at all security discs, cams, monitors."

"That's no problem."

"We need an e-man to try to triangulate the signal with Grogan's 'link. If she's still got it, we may be able to locate her. What time did she go missing?"

"As close as we can determine, right about one thirty."

Eve glanced at her wrist unit. "More than an hour now. I want to—"

She heard the boom, the gunfire crackle, the shouts. Before the next blast, she was rushing through the door and out on deck.

Passengers whistled, stomped, cheered, as an impressive shower of color exploded into the sky.

"Fireworks? For Christ's sake. It's still daylight."

"There's nothing scheduled," Jake told her.

"Diversion," she muttered, and began to push and shove her way in the opposite direction of the show. "Get somebody to find the source, stop it."

"I'm already on it," Jake said and shouted into his communicator. "Where are we going?"

"The scene of the crime."

"What? I can't hear a freaking thing. Say again," he yelled into his communicator. "Say again."

Eve broke through the celebrating crowd, ducked under the barricade.

She stopped as she saw the woman arguing frantically with the DOT officer guarding the door of the restroom.

"Carolee!" she called out, and the woman whirled. Her face was deathly pale with high spots of color on the cheeks, and a purpling knot on her forehead.

"What? What is this? I can't find my boy. I can't find my son."

The eyes were wrong, Eve thought. A little glassy, a little shocky. "It's okay. I know where he is. I'll take you to him."

"He's okay? You . . . Who are you?"

"Lieutenant Dallas." Eve watched Carolee's eyes as she took out her badge. "I'm the police."

"Okay. Okay. He's a good boy, but he knows better than this. He was supposed to wait right here. I'm sorry to be so much trouble."

"Where did you go, Carolee?"

"I just . . ." She trailed off. "I went into the restroom. Didn't I? I'm sorry. I have a headache. I was so worried about Pete. Wait, just wait until I—" She stepped into the snack bar when Eve opened the door. Then slapped her hands on her hips.

"Peter James Grogan! You are in so much trouble."

The boy, his brother, his father, moved like one unit, bolting across the room. "Didn't I specifically tell you not to—"

This time the words were knocked back as her three boys grabbed her in frantic embraces. "Well, for heaven's sake. If you think that's going to soften me up after you disobeyed me, it's not. Or only a little." She stroked the boy's hair as he clung to her legs. "Steve? Steve? You're shaking. What is it? What's wrong?"

He pulled back to kiss her, her mouth, her cheeks. "You— you're hurt. You've hit your head."

"I . . ." She lifted her fingers to touch the bump. "Ouch. How did I do that? I don't feel quite right."

"Sit down. Pete, Will, let your mother have some room. Sit down here, Carolee, let me take a look at you."

When she had, he took her hands, pressed them to his lips. "Everything's okay now. It's okay now."

But it wasn't, Eve thought, not for everyone.

Someone was dead. Someone had caused that death.

They were both missing.

CHAPTER
THREE

"Inspector, I need you to locate the source of those explosives, then I want that area secured. I want a complete list of DOT and ferry employees, including any independent contractors, aboard at this time. I want those security discs. When NYPSD officers arrive, they will support those assignments. Peabody, make that happen. Now."

She glanced toward the Grogan family. She could give their reunion one more minute. "There are lifeboats, emergency evacuation devices on this boat?"

"Sure."

"They need to be checked, and they need to be guarded. If any have been used, I need to know. Immediately. I want to talk to the guard Mrs. Grogan talked to when she . . . came back. For now, get his statement."

"No problem. Lieutenant, we're going to have to deal with getting these people, at least some of these people, off."

"I'm working on it. Explosives, employees, discs, emergency evac, secured areas. Let's get on it."

She turned away, moved to where Carolee still sat surrounded by her family.

"Mrs. Grogan, I need to speak with you."

"I'd like to treat her head wound." Steve kept his arm protectively around his wife. "And check her out more thoroughly. If there's a medical kit, I could use it."

"I'll find one," Peabody told him, then glanced at Eve. "Our guys will be on board in a couple of minutes."

"Okay. Find the kit. Organize the team. I want another search, every square inch of this ferry. I want the sweepers in that bathroom. I want it scoured. See if you can find out if anyone else has been reported missing."

"Yes, sir."

As Peabody left, Carolee shook her head. "I'm sorry, I'm a little confused. Who are you again?"

"Lieutenant Dallas, NYPSD."

"The police," Carolee said slowly. "You need to talk to me? I know I got a little upset with the security man, but I was worried about Pete. I couldn't find my boy."

"Understood. Mrs.—"

"If you're police, do you have a zapper?" Obviously content now that his mother was where she belonged, Pete gave Eve a curious squint.

"Don't interrupt," Carolee admonished.

"Mrs. Grogan," Eve began again, but lifted her jacket aside to reveal her sidearm—and the boy flashed her a grin. "Can you tell me what happened, after you and your son went to use the restrooms?"

"Actually, we were going to get drinks, then Pete needed to go, so we swung over that way. I told him to wait, to stay right there if he got out before I did."

"But, Mom—"

"We'll talk about *that* later," she said in a tone that warned of lecture, and the kid slumped down in his seat.

"And then," Eve prompted.

"Then, I waited a minute, watched Pete go in, and I . . ."

Her face went blank for a moment. "That's funny." She offered a puzzled smile. "I'm not quite sure. I must've hit my head. Maybe I slipped?"

"Inside the bathroom?"

"I—It's silly, but I just don't remember."

"Don't remember hitting your head, or going into the bathroom?"

"Either," she admitted. "I must've really knocked it." She tapped her fingers to the bump, winced. "I could use a blocker."

"I don't want to give you anything until I check you out a little more," Steve told her.

"You're the doctor."

Eve thought of a case, not so long before, where memories had been lost. Or stolen. "How bad's the headache?"

"Between crappy and lousy."

"If you try to remember, does the pain increase?"

"Remember hitting it?" Carolee closed her eyes, squeezed them in concentration. "No. It stays between crappy and lousy."

"Any nausea, baby, or blurred vision?" Steve shined a penlight in her eyes to check pupil reaction.

"No. I feel like I walked into a wall or something and smacked my head. That's it."

"There was an Out of Order sign on the door," Eve reminded her.

"There . . . That's right!" Carolee's eyes brightened. "I do remember that. So I . . . but I wouldn't—I *know* I didn't go off to one of the other restrooms. I wouldn't leave Pete. I must've gone in. I must've, because I had to come out again, right? He wasn't there waiting. I must've slipped and hit my head, and I'm just a little shaky on the details. I'm not sure I understand why it matters to the police."

"Mrs. Grogan, you were missing for over an hour."

"Me? Missing? That's crazy. I just—" But she glanced at her wrist unit, and went sheet white. "But that can't be.

That can't be the right time. We were only gone for a few minutes. The ferry ride takes less than a half hour, and we'd barely started. This can't be right."

"Nobody could find you. We couldn't find you," Steve said. "We were so scared."

"Well, God." She stared at her husband, shoved a hand through her hair as it started to sink in. "Did I wander off? Hit my head and wander off? Maybe I have a concussion. I wandered off." She looked down at Pete. "And then I yelled at you when I was the one. I'm sorry, kiddo. Really."

"We thought you were dead 'cause there was the blood." The boy pressed his face to Carolee's breast and started to cry.

"Blood?"

"Mrs. Grogan, the DOT officials notified the NYPSD not only because you were, apparently, missing, but because the facilities they believed you entered had a considerable amount of blood on the floor, as well as spatter on the walls and doors of the stalls."

"But . . ." Her breathing went shallow as Carolee stared at Eve. "It's not mine. I'm okay."

"It's not yours. You went into the bathroom," Eve prompted, "despite the Out of Order sign."

"I can't remember. It's just blank. Like it's been erased. I remember watching Pete go into the boys' room, and I . . . I remember seeing the sign, but then, I can't. I would've gone in," she murmured. "Yes, that's what I would've done, just to check, because it was right there and why not look? I couldn't leave Pete. But I don't remember going in, or . . . coming out. But I couldn't have gone in, or I would've come out. Probably screaming if I saw blood all over the place. It doesn't make sense."

"No," Eve agreed, "it doesn't."

"I didn't hurt anyone. I wouldn't."

"I don't think you hurt anyone."

"An hour. I lost an hour. How can that be?"

"Have you ever lost time before?"

"No. Never. I mean, I've lost track of time, you know? But this is different."

"Will, how about getting your mom a drink?" Steve sent his older son an easy smile. "I bet she's a little dehydrated."

"Actually—" Carolee laughed a little weakly. "I could really use the restroom."

"Okay." Eve watched Peabody come back in with a med kit. "Just a second." She walked over to waylay her partner. "Go ahead and give the kit to Grogan, and take the woman to the john. Stick with her."

"Sure. We're on board, and we've got a deck-by-deck search going. I have to say, the natives are getting a little restless."

"Right. They'll have to hang on a little longer."

"I wonder if maybe this whole thing isn't some stupid prank. Somebody dumps a bunch of blood in that bathroom, hangs the sign, sits back and waits for somebody to go in."

"Then why hang the sign?"

"Okay, a flaw in the scenario, but—"

"And how did they transport a couple quarts of human blood? And where did Mrs. Grogan go for an hour?"

"Several flaws."

"Stick with her," Eve repeated. "Get their New York address. Let's arrange for them to be taken back so she can get a full check at a health center, and I want a watch on them." She glanced back. "If she saw something, someone, maybe whoever's responsible for the blood will start to worry about her."

"I'll make sure she's covered. Nice family," Peabody added, studying the group.

"Yeah. Welcome to New York."

Eve tracked down Jake.

"All emergency evac devices are accounted for." He passed her a file of security discs. "Those are from all cams on board. The list of employees, DOT officials, is labeled."

"Good. Where the hell did those fireworks come from?"

"Well." He scratched his head. "It looks like they were set off starboard side, probably the stern. That's from figuring the basic trajectory from witnesses. But we haven't got any physical evidence. No ash, no mechanism. Nothing so far, so I'm not sure they were set off from the boat."

"Hmm." Eve pondered and glanced out at the wide harbor.

"The NYPSD is crawling all over the place, and your CI team's covering the crime scene. If it is one," he added. "We've accounted for every DOT employee on board, and between your people and mine, we've been interviewing passengers, concentrating on those who are in the areas of the scene. So far, none of them saw anything. And you have to admit, hauling a body around would attract some attention."

"You'd think."

"What do we do now?"

As far as Eve could determine, there were two options. The killer—if indeed a murder had taken place—had somehow gotten off the ferry. Or the killer still needed to get off.

"Looks like we're going to Staten Island. Here's how we'll handle it."

It was going to take time, and a great deal of patience, but nearly four thousand passengers would be ID'd, searched and questioned before they were allowed to disembark at St. George terminal. Fortunately a good chunk of that number was kids. Eve didn't think—though kids were strange and often violent entities to her mind—that the pool of blood was the work of some maniac toddler.

"It's actually moving along okay," Peabody reported, and got a grunt from Eve.

"The search is ongoing," Peabody continued. "So far, no weapon, no body, no evil killer hiding in a storage closet."

Eve continued to review the security disc on boarding on her PPC. "The body's dumped by now."

"How?"

"I don't know how, but it's dumped or transported. Two searches, and this one with corpse detectors. He, or an accomplice, used the fireworks as a distraction. Get everyone's attention in one direction, do what you need to do in the other. Has to be."

"It doesn't explain how he got the DB out of the bathroom."

"No."

"Well, if it wasn't a prank, maybe it's a vortex."

Eve shifted her gaze up, gave Peabody a five-second pitiable stare.

"Free-Ager here, remember. I grew up on vortexes. It's a better theory than abracadabra." On a sigh, Peabody studied the bright, tropical fish swimming behind the glass of an enormous aquarium.

"He didn't toss the body overboard, then dive in and swim away," Peabody pointed out. "Like a fish." Noting Eve's considering expression, Peabody threw up her hands. "Come on, Dallas. There's no way out of the bathroom, not without walking in front of dozens and dozens of people."

"In back mostly, since they'd be looking out at the water. If the blood currently being rushed to the lab proves to have come from a warm body—one we hope to identify through DNA matching—there has to be a way out and a way off, because he used it."

"Parallel universe. There are some scientific theories that support the possibility."

"The same ones, I bet, that support sparkly winged fairies skipping around the woods."

"A mocker." Peabody wagged a finger. "That's what you are, Dallas. A mocker."

"In my world, we call it sane."

Jake joined them. "We're about halfway through. Maybe a little more."

"Find any vortexes, parallel universes or sparkly winged fairies?" Eve asked him.

"Mocker," Peabody repeated.

"Ah . . . not so far." He offered them both a go-cup of coffee. "No weapons, no blood, no dead body either, and so far everyone who's gone through the ticker and the interview station is alive."

"I'm going back on board," Eve told him. "If we get a hit—any kind of hit—contact me. Peabody, with me."

"Hey." Jake tapped Peabody's arm when she started to move off with Eve. "We're probably going to put in a long one here. Maybe we could get a drink after we're clear. You know, decompress."

Flustered, she felt heat rise to her cheeks that was a giddy mix of pleasure and embarrassment. "Oh, well. Um. That's nice—it's nice, I mean, to ask and all that. I live with somebody. A guy. An e-guy. We're . . . you know. Together."

"Lucky him," Jake said, and had her blush deepening. "Maybe, sometime, we can grab a brew, just on the friendly side."

"Sure. Maybe. Ah . . ." She flashed a smile, then shot off after Eve.

"Did you forget what 'with' means?"

"No. In fact, I remembered exactly, in that I'm *with* McNab. I remembered even when Jake hit on me."

"Oh, that's different." Eve shot out a sunny smile that had Peabody's stomach curdling. "Let me apologize for interrupting. Maybe the two of you want to take a break, go get a drink, get to know each other better. We can always puzzle out whether or not we have a missing DB and killer later. We wouldn't want a potential murder investigation to get in the way of a potential romance, would we?"

"I speak sarcasm fluently. He did ask me out for a drink though."

"Should I note that in my memo book, on today's date?"

"Jeez." Sulk warred with smug as Peabody boarded the ferry with Eve. "I'm just saying. Plus I get double credits. First I get the satisfaction credit of being hit on by the sexy DOT inspector, and second I get loyal and true credit for turning him down because I have my personal sexy nerd. I hardly ever get hit on, unless you count McNab—which really doesn't since we cohab—so it *is* noteworthy."

"Fine, so noted. Can we move on?"

"I should get at least five minutes of *woo*. Okay," she mumbled under Eve's withering stare. "I'll put the rest of the *woo* time on my account."

With a shake of her head, Eve crossed the deck, now empty but for cops and sweepers, to speak to a crime-scene investigator.

"Schuman, what've you got?"

She knew him to be a hard-bitten, seen-it-all type, as comfortable in the lab as on scene. He'd shed his protective suit and booties and stood unfolding a piece of gum from its wrapper. "What we've got is about two quarts of blood and body fluids, plenty of spatter. Got some flesh and fibers, and a virtual shitload of prints. We're gonna want to get it in for a full workup and analysis, but with the on-scene exam, we got your blood type—A Neg, and spot samples indicate it's all from the same person. Whoever that is would be dead as my uncle Bob, whose demise went unlamented by all who knew him."

He popped the gum, chewed for a thoughtful moment. "I can tell you what we ain't got. That would be a body or a blood trail, or at this point one freaking notion how said body got the hell out of that john." He smiled. "It's interesting."

"How soon can you tell me if the blood came out of a warm body, or came out of a damn bucket?"

"We'll look at that. Wouldn't be as fun, but the bucket'd make more sense. Problem being, the spatter's consistent with on-scene injuries." Obviously intrigued, he chewed and smiled. "Looks like a damn slasher vid in there. Whoever walked in living got sliced and diced, stuck and gutted. Then, you gotta say it's interesting, went *poof*!"

"Interesting," Eve repeated. "Is it clear to go in?"

"All swept. Help yourself."

He went in with her where a couple of sweepers examined the sinks, the pipes.

"We're looking at everything," he told Eve. "But you'd have to have a magic shrinking pill to get out of here through the plumbing. We're gonna take the vents, the floors, walls, ceilings."

She tipped her face up, studied the ceiling herself. "The killer would have had to transport himself, the body, and a grown woman. Maybe more than one killer."

She shifted to study the spatter on the stalls, the walls. "The vic standing about there. Killer slices her throat first; that's what I'd do. She can't call out. We get that major spatter from the jugular wound, partially blocked by the killer's body."

Eve turned, slapped her hand to her throat. "She grabs her throat, the blood pumps through her fingers, more spatter there, but she doesn't go down, not yet. She falls toward the wall—we get the smears of blood—tries to turn around, more smears. He cuts her again, so we have the spatter on the next stall there, and lower on the wall here, so he probably stuck her, and she stumbled back this way." Eve eased back. "Maybe tries to make it to the door, but he's on her. Slice and dice, and down she goes. Bleeds out where she falls."

"We'll run it, like I said, but that's how I read it."

"He'd be covered in blood."

"If he washed up at any of the sinks," Schuman put in, "he didn't leave any trace, not in the bowls, not in the traps."

"Protective clothes? Gloves?" Peabody suggested.

"Maybe. Probably. But if he can get a DB out of here, I guess he could walk out covered in blood. No trail," Eve repeated. "No drag marks. Even if he just hauled it up and carried it out, there'd be a blood trail. He had to wrap it up. If we go with protective gear and a body bag or something along the line, he planned it out, came prepared, and he damn well had an exit plan. Carolee was a variable, but he didn't have too much trouble there either. He dealt with it."

"But he didn't kill her. He didn't really hurt her," Peabody pointed out.

"Yeah." That point was something Eve had puzzled over. "And he could have, easily enough. The door doesn't lock. Safety regs outlaw locks on public restroom doors with multiple stalls. He makes do with a sign, even though this had to take several minutes. The kill, the cleanup, the transport. And Carolee was missing for over an hour, so wherever he went, wherever he took her, he needed time."

"A lot of places on this boat. Vents, infrastructure, storage. You got big-ass ducts for heating and cooling the inside cabin deals," Schuman told her. "You got your sanitary tanks, your equipment storage, maintenance areas. We're going through here, but it doesn't show how the hell he got out of this room."

"So, let's find out where he went and work backward. And we need to find out who the vic was, and why she got sliced on the Staten Island Ferry. It had to be specific, or Carolee Grogan's blood would be all over this room, too."

For the moment, Eve thought, the best she could do was leave it to the sweepers.

CHAPTER

FOUR

"Why didn't he kill Carolee?" Peabody wondered when they were back on deck. "It would've been easier. Just cut her throat, and get back to business. It wasn't as if he worried about covering up a crime. All the blood was a pretty big clue one had been committed."

Eve walked toward the stern, trying to reconstruct a scene that made no sense. "I'm looking forward to asking him. I don't think it's just his good luck she can't remember. Let's see what the medical exam concludes after she's done there. But the bigger question is, yeah, why bother to suppress her memory? And why would the killer have something on him that could?"

"Hypnosis?"

"I'm not ruling it out." She leaned back against the rail, looked up at the twin smokestacks. "They're not real. They're show. Just to keep the ferry looking old-timey. Big. Way big enough for somebody to hide a body and an unconscious woman."

"Sure, if he had sparkly fairy wings and an invisibility shield."

Eve had to laugh. "Point. Regardless, let's make sure they get checked out." She turned when Jake walked toward them.

"We let the last of the passengers through the ticker. Two short. We've accounted for everyone, passengers, crew, concession. Two people who got on didn't get off."

"They just got off before we made port," Eve corrected. "This ferry is out of service until further notice. It's sealed by order of the NYPSD. Guards on twenty-four/seven. Crime Scene hasn't finished, and will continue until they've covered every inch, including those," she added, pointing at the smokestacks.

Jake lifted his gaze to follow the gesture. "Well. That should be fun."

"Something this size, with this layout? There are places to hide, to conceal. He had to know the boat, the layout, at least to some extent."

"Having a place to hide doesn't explain getting out of that bathroom without anyone seeing him. Unless he has the cloak of invisibility."

Jake's remark got a quick laugh from Peabody and a cool stare from Eve.

"We work the wit and the evidence. We'll be in touch, Inspector."

"You're leaving?"

"We'll be following up with the security discs, Carolee Grogan, and the lab. The sooner we identify the victim, if a victim there is, the sooner we can move on the killer. You may want some of your men backing up mine on guard duty. I don't want anyone on that ferry without authorization."

"All right."

"Let's move, Peabody."

"Ah, Detective? Should your situation change . . ."

Peabody felt the heat rise to her cheeks again. "It isn't likely to, but thanks." She scrambled to keep up with Eve's long strides. "He hit on me again."

"I'll mark it down, first chance."

"It's markable," Peabody mumbled. "Really." She risked a look over her shoulder before they boarded the turbo. "I figured we'd be staying, going over the boat again."

"We have enough people on that." Eve braced herself as the turbo shot across the water. "Here's a question—or a few. Why kill in a public restroom on a ferry in the middle of the water? No easy way off. Why not leave the body? Why, if interrupted by a bystander, spare that bystander's life? And go to the trouble, apparently, to secret her away for an hour?"

"Okay, but even if we find the answer to any of the whys, we don't answer the hows."

"Next column. How was the victim selected? How was the method of killing selected? How was Carolee Grogan moved from the crime scene to another location? And straddling columns, why doesn't she remember? How was the body—if there was one—removed? All of it comes back to one question. Who was the victim? That's the center. The rest rays out from there."

"The victim's probably female. Or the killer. One of them, at least, is probably female. It makes more sense, given the location of the murder."

"Agreed, and the computer agrees. I ran probability. Mid-eighties for female vic or killer." She pulled out her 'link when it signaled, saw Roarke's personal code on the readout. "Hey."

"Hey back." His face—that fallen-angel beauty—filled the screen as dark brows lifted over bold blue eyes. "You're out in the harbor? The ferry incident?"

"Shit. How much has leaked?"

"Not a great deal. Certainly nothing that speaks of murder." His voice, Irish whispering through, cruised over the words as she rocketed back toward Manhattan. "Who's dead, then?"

"That's a question. I'm hoping the lab can tell me. I'm heading there, and depending on the answer, I might be late getting home."

"As it happens I'm downtown, and was hoping to ask my wife out to dinner. Why don't I meet you at the lab, then depending on the answer you get, we'll go from there?"

She couldn't think of a reason against it, and, in fact, calculated the opportunity to run it all by him. A fresh perspective might give her some new angles. "Okay. It'll be handy to have you right there if I have to bribe Dickhead to push on the ID."

"Always happy to bribe local officials. I'll see you soon."

"It's nice, isn't it?" Peabody asked when Eve stuck her 'link back in her pocket. "Having a guy."

Eve started to shrug it off, then decided the turbo pilot couldn't hear them. Besides, there was no reason not to take a few minutes for nonsense. "It doesn't suck."

"It really doesn't. Having a really cute guy like Jake flirt with me has some frost, but knowing I'm going to be snuggled up with McNab tonight? That's the ice."

"Why do you always have to put you and McNab and sex in my head? It brings pain no blocker can cure."

"Snuggling isn't sex. It's before or after sex. I especially like the after-sex snuggle when you're all warm and loose like a couple of sleepy puppies." She cocked her head. "I'm getting horny."

"So glad you shared that with me. Let's try to get this pesky investigation out of the way so you can go get your puppy snuggles."

"You know, I've got this new outfit I've been saving for a night when—"

"Do not go there. Do not," Eve warned. "I swear by all that's holy, I'll chuck you overboard, then order the turbo to run over you while you sputter in the water."

"Harsh. Anyway, maybe that's what the killers did, just chucked the victim in the water, then jumped in after the body wearing SCUBA gear."

"If he was going to chuck the body in, why move it in the first place? He didn't just want the kill, he wanted the body."

"Ewww. I know, a police detective's not supposed to say 'ewww.' But why would he want the body?"

"A trophy." Eve narrowed her eyes.

"I'm not saying 'ewww.'"

"You're thinking it. Proof," she added, "which strikes me as more likely than trophy. A body's unassailable proof of death. Which, at this point, we don't have. He does. Which brings us to another why. Why would he need proof?"

"Payment?" At Eve's nod, Peabody lifted her hands. "But for a hit, it was messy and complicated. It doesn't smell like a pro."

"No, it doesn't. Unless you add in the rest. Missing body, public arena, two people vanishing like smoke. That strikes me as very professional."

It kept her mind occupied on the drive to the lab. And at least she was navigating on solid ground instead of water. New York appeared to have burst open for summer, and out of its nooks and crannies poured tourists and the street thieves who depended on them. Glida carts did brisk business with cold drinks and ice pops, while portable knockoff vendors raked it in with cheap souvenirs, wrist units that might function until the buyer got back to his hotel, colorful "silk" scarves, fashion shades and handbags that could be mistaken for their designer counterparts if you were a half block away and had one eye closed.

But it also brought out the sidewalk florists with their bounty of color and scent and the alfresco diners taking in the sun over glasses of wine or thimbles of espresso.

It added to the street and air traffic, jammed the glides and sidewalks, and yet, Eve thought, it all rushed and roared exactly as it was meant to.

She spotted Roarke before she parked, standing outside the drab edifice that housed the busy hive of the lab and forensics. The dark charcoal suit fit the lean length of him perfectly, and showed a subtle flare with a tie nearly as bold a blue as his eyes.

Black hair fell in a mane around that striking face, shades shielded those stunning eyes as he slipped the PPC he'd been working on into a pocket and started toward her.

She thought he looked like some elegantly urban vid star with just a hint of edge. And she supposed it suited him as one of the wealthiest and most powerful men in the world— and on its satellites—who'd pulled himself by hook or—ha-ha—crook out of the grime of the Dublin alleyways.

"Check on Carolee," she told Peabody. "See if they've finished the medical, have any results."

She watched Roarke's lips curve as they walked toward each other. She didn't need to see his eyes to know they mirrored that smile. And her heart gave a quick, giddy jump. She had to admit Peabody was right. It was nice to have a guy.

"Lieutenant." He took her hand and, though she lowered her eyebrows to discourage him, bent to brush those curved lips lightly over hers. "Hello, Peabody. You look fetchingly windblown."

"Yeah." She brushed ineffectually at her hair. "Boat ride."

"So I hear."

"Check on the wit, Peabody," Eve repeated as she led the way inside.

"What was witnessed?" Roarke wondered.

"Tell me what the media's saying. I haven't bothered to tune in."

"I caught bits and pieces on my way downtown to my meeting, then a bit more after. A woman apparently lost on the ferry, then found. Or not, depending on the report. A possibility someone was injured or fell overboard."

He continued as Eve led them through the maze, signed and badged them through security.

"The main thrust seems to be that DOT and NYPSD officials held up the ferry for over two hours, then additional time with a security search of passengers as they disembarked. A few of the passengers sent various media outlets some vids or statements. So, you can imagine, it's all over the board."

"Fine." Eve opted for a down glide rather than an elevator. "Better that way."

"Is someone missing? Or dead?"

"Someone was missing, but now she's not. Someone might be dead, but there's no body. Passenger count is off by two on disembarking."

"Which might equal victim and killer. How'd they get off the ferry?"

"That's another question." She stepped off the glide. "First, I've got a couple quarts of blood in a public restroom on the ferry. I need to find out who it belonged to."

CHAPTER

FIVE

She wound through the labyrinth bisected by glass walls. Behind them techs worked with scopes and holos, forensic droids, tiny vials and mysterious solutions.

The air hummed in a blend of machine and human into a single voice Eve found just slightly creepy. She would never understand how people worked, day after day, in a vast space without a single window.

She found the chief lab tech, Dick Berenski, sliding his stool soundlessly along his long white counter as he commanded various comps. Dickhead was an irritant, a pebble in the shoe on a personal level, but she couldn't deny his almost preternatural skill with evidence.

He looked up, cocking his egg-shaped head as she approached, and she didn't miss the light in his eyes when he recognized Roarke.

"Got yourself an entourage today, Dallas."

"Don't think about trying to hit up the civilian for liquor, tickets to sporting events or cash."

"Hey." Dickhead couldn't quite pull off offended.

"Let's talk blood."

"Got enough of it. I got the initial sample a couple hours ago, and they're bringing in the rest. We'll run tests on samples of that, too. Could be more than one source. Got my blood guy reconstructing the scene, pool and spatter, from the record. That's a fucking beaucoup of blood."

"Fresh or frozen?"

He honked out a little laugh. "Fresh." He tapped some keys and had squiggles and swirls in bold reds, yellows, blues, filling a comp screen. "No indication the sample had been stored, cold-boxed, flash-frozen, thawed or rehydrated."

He tapped again, brought up another screen of shapes and colors. "Coagulation rate and temp says it hit the air about two hours—maybe a little more—before I tested it. That's consistent with the time it took to get here."

"Concluding the sample came out of a live human, and came out of said human between one and two this afternoon."

"What I said. A Neg, human blood, healthy platelets, cholesterol, no STD. We filtered out trace portions of other body fluid and flesh. Double X chromosomes."

"Female."

"You bet. We'll keep separating other body fluids when we have the larger samples, and the sweepers tell me they've got some hair in there. We'll be able to tell you pretty much everything. Fluids, flesh and hair." He grinned widely. "I could freaking rebuild her with samples like that."

"Nice thought. DNA."

"I'm running it through. Takes some time, and there's no guarantee she's on the grid. Might get a relative. I programmed for full match and blood relations."

Thorough, Eve thought. When Dickhead got his weird little teeth into something, he was thorough. "There were fibers."

"Like I said, we'll separate and filter. I'll give hair and fiber to Harpo. She's the queen. But I can't pull the vic's ID

out of my ass. She's either on the grid or—Hey!" He swiv-
eled, scooted as the far comp beeped. "Son of a bitch, we got
a match. I am so freaking good."

Eve came around the counter to study the ID photo and
data herself. "Copy to my unit," she ordered. "And I want a
printout. Dana Buckley, age forty-one, born in Sioux City,
why are you dead?"

"Nice-looking skirt," Berenski commented, and Eve
ignored him.

Blue-eyed blonde, she thought, pale skin, pretty in a
corn-fed sort of way. Five-six, a hundred thirty-eight, parents deceased, no sibs, no offspring, no marriage or cohab
on record. "Current employment, freelance consultant. What
does this personal data tell us smart investigators, Detective?"

"That the deceased has no family ties, no employer to
verify identification or give further data on said deceased.
Which makes a smart investigator go *hmmm*."

"It does indeed. She lists a home and office address here
in New York. Park Avenue. Peabody, run this down."

"It's the Waldorf," Roarke said from behind her.

"As in Astoria?" Eve glanced back, caught his nod, and
the look in his eyes when they met hers.

She thought, *Crap*, but said nothing. Not yet.

"Check and see if they have her registered," she told
Peabody. "And get a copy of the ID print, show it to the desk
staff to see if they make her. Quick work, Berenski."

"After quick work, I like to relax with a good bottle or
two of wine."

She took the printout and walked away without a second
glance.

"Worth the shot," Berenski said at her back.

"There's nobody by the name of Dana Buckley registered
at the Waldorf," Peabody told her as she caught up to Eve.
"No make from the desk staff. This new data rates a second
hmmm."

"Go back to Central, do a full run on her. You can start on the security discs. Send copies to my home unit. I'm going to swing by, reinterview Carolee, show her the printout. Maybe she'll remember seeing the vic."

"We were lucky to get a DNA match that fast. I'll tag you if I dig up anything on her." She sent a quick smile to Roarke. "See you later."

Eve waited until she and Roarke were in her vehicle, with her taking the wheel. "You knew her."

"Not really. Of her, certainly. It's complicated."

"Is there any way you could be connected to this?"

"No. That is, I have no connection to her."

Eve felt the knot in her stomach begin to loosen. "How do you know her, or of her?"

"I first heard of her some years ago. We were working on a prototype for some—at the time—new holo technology. It was very nearly stolen, or would have been if we hadn't implemented multiple layers of security. As it was, she got through several before the red flag."

"Corporate and/or technological espionage."

"Yes. I didn't know her as Dana Buckley, but as Catherine Delauter. I expect you'll find any number of IDs before you're done."

"Who does she work for?"

He lifted a shoulder in a dismissive if elegant shrug. "The highest bidder. She thought I might be interested in her services, and arranged to meet me. That's seven or eight years ago."

"Did you hire her?"

He glanced at Eve with mild exasperation. "Why would I? I don't need to steal—and if I did, I could do it myself, after all. I wasn't interested in her services, and made it plain. Not only because I don't—never did—steal ideas. It's low and common."

Eve shook her head. "Your moral compass continues to baffle me."

"As yours does me. Aren't we a pair? But I warned her off not only for that, but because she was known—and my own research confirmed—not only as a spy but an assassin."

Eve glanced over quickly before she pushed through traffic. "A corporate assassin?"

"That would depend on the highest bidder, from what I learned. She's for hire, or apparently was, and didn't quibble at getting her hands bloody. Peabody won't find any of this in her run. A large percentage of her work, if rumor holds, has been for various governments. The pay's quite good, particularly if you don't mind a bit of throat slitting."

"A techno spy, heavy into wet work, takes a ride on the ferry. And ends up not just dead, but missing. A competitor? Another kill for hire? It struck me as a pro job, even—maybe because—it was so damn messy and complicated. It's going to get buckets of media when the rest of the data leaks. Who would want that?"

"A point proven?" He shrugged again. "I couldn't say. Was the body dumped off the ferry?"

"I don't think so." She filled him in as she wound and bullied her way to the East Side. "So, as far as I can tell, he moved the body and the wit, in full view of dozens, maybe hundreds of people. And nobody saw anything. The wit doesn't remember anything."

"I'll have to ask the obvious. You're sure there were no escape routes in the room?"

"Unless we've got a killer who can shrink to rat size and slither down a pipe, we didn't find any. Maybe he popped into a vortex."

Roarke turned, grinned. "Really?"

Eve waved it away. "Peabody's Free-Agey suggestion. Hell, maybe he waved his magic wand and said, 'Hocus-pocus.' What?" she said when Roarke frowned.

"Something . . . in the back of my mind. Let me think about it."

"Before you think too hard?" She veered into the health

center's lot. "Just let me point out there is no magic wand, or rabbit in the hat, or alternate reality."

"Well, in this reality, most people notice when a dead body's paraded around under their noses."

"Maybe it didn't look like one. They have a couple of maintenance hampers on board. The killer dumps the body in, wheels it out like it's just business as usual. And no, we haven't found any missing hampers, or any trace in the couple on board. But it's a logical angle."

"True enough." Once she'd parked, he got out of the car with her. "Then again, logic would say don't kill in a room with only one out, and a public one, don't take the body, and don't leave a witness. So, it may be hard to hold to one logical line when the others are badly frayed."

"They're only frayed logic until you find the reason and motive." Eve pulled out her badge as they walked into the health center.

The Grogans crowded into a tiny little room with Carolee sitting up in bed, a bouquet of cheerful flowers in her lap. She looked tired, Eve thought, and showed both strain and resignation when she saw Eve come in.

"Lieutenant. I've been poked and prodded, screened and scanned and scoped. All over a bump on the head. I know something bad happened, something awful, but it really doesn't have anything to do with me."

"You still don't remember anything?"

"No. Obviously I hit my head, and I must've been dazed for a while." Her hand snuck from under the flowers to reach for her husband's. "I'm fine now, really. I feel fine now. I don't want the boys to spend their vacation in a hospital room."

"It's just a few hours," Steve assured her. The youngest, whose name was Pete, Eve remembered, crawled onto the bed to sit at his mother's side.

"Still. I'm sorry someone was hurt. Someone must've

been hurt, from what Steve said. I wish I could help, I really do. But I don't know anything."

"How's the head?"

"It pounds a little."

"I have a photo I'd like to show you." Eve offered the printout of Dana Buckley. "Do you recognize her? Someone you might've seen on the ferry."

"I don't think . . ." She lifted her hand to worry at the bandage on her forehead. "I don't think . . ."

"There were a lot of people." Steve angled his head to look at the photo. "We were looking out at the water most of the time." He glanced with concern toward the monitor as his wife's pulse rate jumped. "Okay, honey, take it easy."

"I don't remember. It scares me. Why does it scare me?"

"Don't look at it anymore." Will snatched the photo away. "Don't look at it, Mom. Don't scare her anymore." He thrust the photo back at Eve. "She was in the picture."

"Sorry?"

"The lady. Here." He pulled a camera out of his pocket. "We took pictures. Dad let me take some. She's in the picture." He turned the camera on, scrolled back through the frames. "We took a lot. I looked through them when they had Mom away for tests. She's in the picture. See?"

Eve took the camera and looked at a crowd shot, poorly cropped, with Dana Buckley sitting on a bench sipping from a go-cup. With a briefcase in her lap.

"Yeah, I see. I need to keep this for a while, okay? I'll get it back to you."

"You can keep it, I don't care. Just don't scare my mom."

"I don't want to scare your mother. That's not why I'm here," Eve said, directly to Carolee.

"I know. I know. She—that's the one who was hurt?"

"Yes. It upsets you to see her photo."

"Terrifies me. I don't know why. There's a light," she said after a hesitation.

"A light?"

"A bright flash. White flash. After I see her picture, and I'm scared, so scared. There's a white flash, and I can't see anything. Blind, for a minute. I . . . It sounds crazy. I'm not crazy."

"Shh." Pete began to stroke her hair. "Shh."

"I'm going to speak to the doctor. If Carolee's clear, I want to get her and our boys back to the hotel. Away from this. We'll get room service." Steve winked over at Will. "In-room movies."

"God, yes," Carolee breathed. "I'll feel better once we're out of here."

"Let's go find the doctor," Eve suggested and sent a glance at Roarke. He nodded, and moved to the foot of the bed as Steve went out with Eve.

"So, Mrs. Grogan, where would you be staying here in New York?"

It took another thirty minutes, but Roarke asked no questions until they were out of the health center. "And so, how is the lady?"

"I had the doctor dumb it down for me. He was giving it to the husband—he's a doctor, too—in fancier terms."

"You can keep it dumbed down for me."

"She's good," Eve told him, "no serious or lasting damage. The contusion, mild concussion, and most interestingly what he dumbed down to a 'smudge' on her optic nerves— both eyes. He seemed to be pushing for another test, but he'd already done a recheck and as the smudge was already dissipating, I don't think Steve's going to go for it. Added to it, the brain scan showed something wonky in the memory section—a blip, but that's resolved, too, on retest. Her tox is clear," Eve added as she got back into the car. "No trace of anything, which is too damn bad, as that's where logic was leading me."

"A memory suppressor would've been logical. And maybe yet." He shook his head at her look. "We'll have some things to check into when we get home. You'll likely have to follow up with the Grogans?"

"Yeah."

"Then you'll find them at the Palace. They'll be moving there tonight."

"Your hotel?"

"It seems they're a bit squeezed into a room at the moment, and it struck me they could use a bit of an upgrade for their troubles. Plus the security's better there. Considerably."

"I'm putting a watch on them," Eve began, then shrugged. "It is better." She engaged the 'link to update her men on the change. "Let's go home and start 'checking into.'"

CHAPTER

SIX

Summerset, Roarke's man about everything, wasn't lurking in the grand foyer when Eve walked in. She spied the fat cat, Galahad, perched on the newel post like a furry gargoyle. He blinked his bicolored eyes twice, then leaped down with a thud to saunter over and rub against her legs.

"Where's Mr. Macabre?" Eve asked as she scratched the cat between the ears.

"Stop." Roarke didn't bother to sigh. The pinching and poking between his wife and his surrogate father were not likely to end anytime soon. "Summerset's setting things up in my private office. We need to use the unregistered equipment," he continued when she frowned. "Any serious digging on your victim is going to send up flags to certain parties. And there's more."

He took her hand to lead her up the steps.

"If I don't dig into the vic through proper channels, it's going to look very strange."

"You have Peabody on that," he reminded her. "And you can do some of your own, for form. But you won't find what you're after through legitimate channels. Set up your runs, on Buckley, the Grogans, the possible causes of this optic smudge. All the things you'd routinely do. Then come up and meet me."

He lifted her hand to kiss her fingers. "And we'll do the real excavating. She's a freelance spy and assassin, Eve, who works for the highest bidder or on a whim. That work would definitely include certain areas of the U.S. government. You won't get far your way."

"What's the 'more'?" She *hated* the cloak-and-dagger crap. "You said there's more?"

But he shook his head. "Start your runs. We'll go over what I've heard, know, suspect."

Since there was no point in wasting time, Eve walked into her home office to set up the multiple runs and searches. She sent an e-mail to Dr. Mira, the NYPSD's top profiler and psychiatrist, to ask about the validity of mass hypnosis. It made her feel foolish, but she wanted a solid opinion from a source she respected.

Before compiling and updating her notes, she checked in with Peabody, and read over all the initial lab and sweepers' reports. No witnesses had come forward to claim they'd seen anything unusual, including any individual transporting a dead body. Which was too bad, she mused. Also in the too-bad department was the report that the pipes and vents within the crime scene were just too damn small to have served as an escape route.

Solid walls, no windows, one door, she decided. And that meant, however improbably, both killer and victim had exited through the door.

He hadn't stepped into Peabody's vortex, hadn't employed an alien transporter beam or flourished a magic wand. He'd used the damn door. She just had to figure out how.

She made her way to Roarke's private office, used the

palm pad and voice recognition to enter. He sat behind the U-shaped console with the jewel-toned buttons and controls winking over the slick black surface. The privacy screens shielded the windows and let the evening sunlight filter into the room in a pale gold wash. A small table stood by those windows, set with silver domed plates, an open bottle of wine, the sparkle of crystal.

His idea of a working dinner, she mused.

He'd already tied his hair back—serious work mode—and commanded keyboard and touch screens with rapid movements.

"What are you hacking into?" she asked.

"Various agencies. CIA, Homeland Security, Interpol, MI5, Global, EuroCom, and that sort."

"Is that all?" She pressed her fingers to her eyes. "I was going to stick with coffee, but now I think I need a drink."

"Pour me one. And after I get these to auto-search, I'll tell you a story over dinner."

She poured two, pleased the wine was red, which lowered the chances of something healthy like fish with steamed vegetables on the plates. She peeked under the silver cover and was instantly cheered. "Hey, lasagna!" Then, on closer study. "What's this green stuff in there?"

"Good for you."

"Why is good for you mostly green? Why can't they make it taste like candy or at least pizza?"

"I'm going to get my R and D right on that. And we're going to speak of R and D, as it happens. There now." He sat back, nodded at his screens. "We'll see what we see." He rose, crossed to her. Taking up his glass, he tapped it to hers, then smiled. "I think I'll have another of these," he decided, and cupped her chin before taking her mouth with his.

"No distracting with wine and lip-locks," she ordered. "I want to get to the bottom of this. The whole thing is . . . irritating."

"I imagine it is, to someone of your logical bent." He gestured for her to sit, then settled across from her. "Your victim," he began, "was a dangerous woman. Not in an admirable way. Not like you, for instance. She fought for nothing, stood for nothing, save her own gain."

"You said you didn't really know her."

"This is what I know of her. It's not the first time I've looked into her, which will make tonight's work a bit easier on that score. Information on her is, naturally, sketchy, but I believe she was born in Albania, the result of a liaison between her American mother and an unknown father. Her mother served in the U.S. Diplomatic Corps. She traveled with her mother extensively, saw and learned quite a bit of the world. It seems she was recruited, at a young age, by a covert group, World Intelligence Network."

"WIN?"

"Which was exactly their goal. To win data, funds, territories, political positions—however it was most expedient. They only lasted a decade. But in that decade, they trained her, and as she apparently showed considerable ability and no particular conscience, used her in their Black Moon sector."

"Wet work."

"Yes." He broke a hunk of bread in two, passed her a share. "Somewhere along the line, she opted to freelance. It's more lucrative, and she'd have seen WIN was fragmenting. She tends to take high-dollar jobs, private or government. As I said, I had a brush with her several years ago. I believe, two years after that, she killed three of my people in an attempt to acquire the data and research to new fusion fuel we had under development."

Eve ate slowly. "Did she target you? Have you been a target?"

"No. It's generally believed I'm more useful alive than dead, even to competitors or . . . interested parties. I'm able to fund the R and D, the science, the manufacturing, and others may hope to steal it. Nothing to steal if you cut off the head."

"That's a comfort."

He reached across for her hand. "I watch out for myself, Lieutenant. Now, depending on the source, your victim is given credit, so to speak, for anywhere from fifty to two hundred and fifty deaths. Some were in the game, some were just in the way."

"You couldn't find her." Eve watched him as she ate. "You thought she killed three of your people, so you'd have tried."

"No, I couldn't find her. She went under, considerably under. I thought she might be dead, having failed to secure what she was hired for." He studied the wine in his glass. "Apparently I was wrong."

"Until now. It's unlikely she was on that ferry to sightsee."

"Very. It might've been a meet or a target, but odds are it was business."

"Double cross. But someone like this, experienced, how does she get caught off guard and taken out? Someone she knew? Someone she trusted or underestimated maybe? Another spook? Another assassin?" She felt the frustration rising again, like flood water behind a dam. "Why so freaking public?"

"I couldn't begin to guess. Tell me what you think about this smudge, this flash of light."

She blew out a breath. "I left a message for Mira, asking her about the possibility of mass hypnosis. And that sounds crazy when I hear myself say it out loud. Not as crazy as vortexes or invisibility cloaks, but in that mix of nuts. Still, we've dealt with mind manipulation before. The tiny burn in the cortex found in autopsy after suicides, manipulated by your pal Reeanna Ott."

"Hardly my pal, as it turned out." But he nodded to show they were on the same page. "Manipulation, in that case, done through audio."

"So, a possible manipulation done optically," Eve finished. "One that affects memory. But it has to do more. I can almost swallow people wouldn't remember seeing someone haul out a dead body, but I have to figure they wouldn't just let him by in the first place. And Carolee, whether she was conscious or unconscious, her kid wouldn't have just stood where he was, would he, if he saw her come out? So, maybe we're dealing with a device that can manipulate behavior, or sight, and memory? That's a big jump. Mass hypnosis suddenly doesn't sound so crazy."

"There have been rumors, underground and through the tech world, of a device in development. A kind of stunner."

"Ah. Got one of those." Eve tapped the weapon at her side she'd yet to take off.

"Not your conventional stunner, but one that renders the target incapacitated through an optical signal rather than the nervous system. It sends a signal, through light, that shuts down certain basic functions. Essentially, in a theory not that far from your mass hypnosis, it puts the target into a kind of trance. Hocus-pocus." He lifted his wineglass in half salute. "It's often referred to as that, which made me think of it when you used the term. The rumors are largely dismissed, but not entirely."

"We're talking dozens of people," Eve argued. "Potentially hundreds."

"And the idea this device exists, and has a possibility for that sort of range, is . . . fascinating. And used as a weapon? Devastating."

Eve pushed up from the table to pace. "I hate this kind of shit. Why can't it just be regular bad guy crap? You've got money, I want it, I kill you. You've been screwing my wife, it pisses me off, I cut out your heart. No, I've got to worry about disappearing bodies and weapons designed to turn the lights out on masses of people. Crap."

"It's an ever-changing world," Roarke said lightly.

She snorted. "How much credence do you and your R and D people put into this device?"

"Enough to be working on something similar—and a counterdevice. Though both are still in the theoretical stages. I'm getting the data for you," he added, gesturing toward the console.

She sat again, drummed her fingers on the table. "Okay, say this device exists, and was used today. Say its existence speaks to why Buckley was on that ferry, either with the device in her possession or with the hopes to make that so. It still doesn't explain why she was murdered in the way she was, or why her body was taken off the ferry. Stealing or obtaining the device, even killing Buckley to get it, that's business. Basically exsanguinating her and taking what's left? That's personal."

"I wouldn't argue, but business and personal often overlap."

"Okay." She lifted her hands and swiped them in the air as if clearing a board. "Why remove the body? Maybe to prove the hit, if it's hired. Maybe because you're a sick fuck. Or maybe to buy time. I like that one because it's weirdly logical. It stalls the identification process. We have to depend on a DNA search and match. And then, we get what appears to be an innocuous vic, corn-fed Iowa-born female consultant. Maybe, given some time, we'd dig under that, have some questions. But the bigger puzzler would remain, at least initially, *how* rather than *who*, since we had the who."

"But, because I wanted to spend a bit more time with my wife, I happened to be there when she was identified."

"Yeah. You recognized her, and that's a variable the killer couldn't have factored in."

"Logical enough," Roarke agreed. "But buy time for what?"

"To get away, to deliver the device and/or the body. To destroy the body, certainly to get the hell away from the scene. This spy stuff doesn't work like the job. It's convoluted, covered with gray areas and underlying motivations. But when you wipe away all of that, you've still got a killer, a victim, a motive. We cross off random, because no possible way. It wasn't impulse."

"Because?" He knew the answer, or thought he did, but he loved watching her work.

"The sign on the door, the getaway. It was vicious—all that spatter. A pro wouldn't have wasted time with that. Cut the throat, skewer the heart, hit the big artery in the thigh. Pick one and move on. But blood doesn't lie, and the spatter clearly says this was slice, hack, rip."

The light softened as they spoke, and he wondered how many couples might sit in the evening light over a meal and talk of blood spatter and exsanguination.

Precious few, he supposed.

"Are you sure none of the blood was the killer's?"

She nodded. It was a good question, she thought, and only one of the reasons she liked bouncing a case around with him. "Reports just in, taking samples of every area of spatter, and several from the pool, confirm it all belonged to Buckley."

"Then she was caught seriously off guard."

"I'll say. So, specific target, specific location and time, personal and professional connections. Add one more element, and I think it matters. Whoever killed Buckley didn't kill Carolee Grogan when it would've been easier, more expedient and even to his or her advantage to do so."

"Leaving her body behind. More confusion," Roarke agreed. "A longer identification time on the blood pool. A killer with a heart?"

She tossed back the rest of her wine. "It's more that a lot of people with a heart kill."

"My cynical darling."

She rolled her eyes. "Let's see what we've got so far." She jerked a thumb toward the console.

Roarke walked back behind the command center, sat. Then, smiling at Eve, patted his knee.

"Please."

"And thank you," he said, grabbing her and tugging her down. "There now, this is cozy."

"It's murder."

"Yes, yes, on a daily basis. Now, see here, we're through several levels on HSO, but then, I've been through that door before." He brushed his lips over her cheek. "And making some progress on the others. They'll have done some code shifting and housekeeping since my last visits, but see there, we're rerouting with them."

"I see a bunch of gibberish, numbers and symbols flashing by."

"Exactly. Let's see if we can nudge it along." He reached around her, began tapping keys. "There are all sorts of tricks," he continued as the codes zipped by on the screens. "Realignments, firewalls, fail-safes, trapdoors and back-doors. But we keep updating along with them."

"Why? Seriously, why do you need access to this stuff?"

"Everyone needs a hobby. What we want here are eyes-only personnel files, their black ops consultants. And verification if the device rumored to exist does indeed exist. Eyes-only again, but the trick would be to find where it might be tucked and by whom. Ah well, bugger it. Let's try this way."

Assuming from the oath and his increased tapping that he'd hit a snag, Eve wiggled away. "I'm getting coffee, and I'm going to run some data of my own."

When his answer was a grunt, she knew playtime was over. It was time for serious work.

CHAPTER

SEVEN

Using an auxiliary computer, Eve initiated her own search for any mention of a device such as Roarke had described. She found several articles on medical sites detailing the memory suppressive drugs and tools used during routine surgeries, others edging toward hypnotherapy in both medical studies and gaming.

She also found a scattering of fringe blogs raging about government mind control, enslaving of the masses and the ever-popular doomsday warnings. A nation of human droids, forced experimentation, personality theft and human breeding farms were on their top-ten list of predicted abominations. This led her to others claiming to have been abducted by aliens in league with the shadow forces of government.

"I'm surprised the government has time to, you know, govern, when they're so busy working with aliens and their anal probes or pursuing their mission to turn the global population into mindless sex droids."

"Hmm," Roarke said, "there's government, then there's government."

She glanced over to where he sat, fingers flying, eyes intent. "You don't actually believe this crap? Alien invasions, secret bunkers in Antarctica for experimentation on human guinea pigs."

He flicked his glance up. "Icove."

"That was . . . Okay." Hard to argue when they'd both nearly been killed when dismantling a subversive and illegal human cloning organization. "But aliens?"

"It's a big universe. You should get out in it more often."

"I like one planet just fine."

"In any case, I have your victim. No, don't get up." He waved her back. "I'll put it on-screen. Data, wall screen one. This is from HSO, but the data matches what I've got from the other sources."

"Dana Buckley," Eve read. "With her three most common aliases. Same age as her current ID. But with the biographical data you had."

"Now it lists her assets. The languages she spoke, her e-skill level, the weaponry she was cleared for. Included in her dossier is this list." He scrolled down. "Names, nationalities, ranks if applicable, dates."

"Her hit list," Eve mumbled. "They know or believe she's killed these people, but they let her walk around."

"Undoubtedly she killed some of those people for these agencies. They let her walk around until now because she's useful to them."

Eve dealt with murder every day, yet this offended and disturbed her on some core level she wasn't sure she could articulate.

"That's not how it's supposed to be. You can't just kill or order someone's death because it's expedient. We've managed to virtually outlaw torture and executions; if a cop terminates in the line, he has to go through testing to ensure it was ultimate force that was necessary. But there are still people, supposedly on *our* side, who would use someone like her to do their dirty work."

"People who use someone like her rarely, if ever, get their hands dirty."

"She was a psychopath. Look at her psych profile, for God's sake." Eve swung an arm at the screen. "She should've been put away, just like the person who did her needs to be put away."

He watched her as she read the data on-screen. "You have less gray area than most."

"You think this is acceptable? Jesus, read the list. Some of them are kids."

"Collateral damage, I expect. And no," he added as she swung around, her eyes firing. "I don't think it's acceptable to kill for money, for the thrill or for expedience. There may be more gray in my world than yours when it comes to killing for a cause, but that's not what she did. It was profit and, I believe, for fun. And I suspect, if it had been Buckley standing in that room when Carolee walked in, those boys would be grieving for their mother tonight instead of cuddled up with her watching in-room movies."

"Not all assassins are created equal?" Calmer, she angled her head as she studied the screen. "We need to look at this list, see if we can connect any of these names to someone in the same business. Someone skilled enough to get the drop on her."

"I'll set it up. Meanwhile, there's interesting data on the device. This memo was issued two days ago." Again, he ordered the data on-screen.

"'The Lost delayed. Owl to commence new series of tests in Sector Twelve. Owl request for seventy-two and blackout approved.'" Eve puzzled over it a moment. "She's not Owl. Who'd code-name a female assassin—a young, attractive one—Owl?"

"We can go over the earlier memos, but I'd say Owl would be in charge of the development of the device."

"The Lost. You lose time, yourself, your memory of what happened when you're . . . gone. So, if this Owl or someone under him/her had it, maybe it was an exchange. No, no, it was a setup. It was planned. He had to have a way off the damn ferry, so none of it was spontaneous. Delayed? But if it was used, it was complete."

"It wouldn't be the first time a member of the team decided to go free agent."

"Fake a delay so you could sell it, but you don't sell it. You walk away with whatever she had in that briefcase and the device. A twofer. If this is the last memo in the file, HSO isn't yet aware they have a problem."

"Still another reason to take the body," Roarke pointed out. "Buys that time you spoke of. Maybe he had another offer. Or wants to renegotiate the fee, from a safe location."

"It wasn't about money," Eve murmured. "Not just about money. Buying time, yeah, that plays. She won't be identified, officially, to the media until tomorrow."

"There's more. Photos of some of her work. Images on-screen, slide-show method," he ordered.

She'd seen death, in all its forms, too many times to count. She watched it now, roll over the wall screen. Rent flesh, spilled blood, charred hulks.

"Some of these, of course, were very bad people. Others, very bad people wanted out of the way. It appears she didn't discriminate. She followed the money. Some might argue whoever killed her did the world a favor."

"And what makes him any better than her?" Eve demanded.

He only shrugged, knowing on some points they would never agree. "Some would argue otherwise."

"Yeah, some would. Let's find Owl." She pushed her hands through her hair. "And I have to figure out a logical way to explain how I came by anything we get out of this tonight."

"The ever-popular anonymous source."

"Yeah, that'll fool everybody who knows us."

He initiated a series of searches, then studied her as she

stood still watching death scroll by. "It's harder when the victim is abhorrent to you."

Eve shook her head. "I'm not allowed to decide if a murder victim is worth standing for. I stand for them."

He rose, went to her. "But it's harder when that victim has so many victims. So much blood on her hands."

"It's harder," she admitted. "It can't always be an easy choice. It's just the only choice."

"For you." He kissed her brow, then cupped her face, lifted it and laid his lips gently, softly, over hers.

When she sighed and leaned into him, he hit the release on her weapon harness.

"Working," she said against his mouth.

"I certainly hope so."

She laughed when he tugged the harness off her shoulders. "No, I've got work."

"Searches will take a while." He circled her, reaching out to press a control on his console. The bed slid out of the panel in the wall.

"And you figure sex will cheer me up?"

"I'm hoping it's a side benefit to cheering me up."

He circled again, then launched them both toward the bed. She hit with a breathless thump, bounced and, what the hell, let herself be pinned under him.

"Rough stuff."

He grinned. "If you like."

He yanked her shirt over her head, let it fly as he lowered his mouth, with a hint of teeth, to her breast.

She arched, urging him on. The violence here, so full of heat and hope, helped erase all those images of blood and loss. And helped her remember that no matter how they might differ on an issue, even an ideology, there was, always, love.

And lust.

She could take—a handful of that black silk hair, a ripple of muscle as she dragged at his shirt in turn. She could feel the pound of her heart and his as they rolled over the bed in a battle they would both win.

He made her laugh, made her breath catch. He made her skin shimmer and her blood swim. And when she wrapped around him, found his mouth with hers again, she could taste the flood of love and lust and longing.

So strong, so sweet. Her body moved under his, over his, agile and quick. The hum of the work that would draw them both back drowned under the thrum of his own pulse when his hands swept over her. Curve and angle, soft and firm. Wet and warm.

She arched again, rising up where he drove her, to break, then to gather again. Open for more, for him.

When he filled her, when they rose and fell, rose and fell, to break together, it gave her not only pleasure. It gave her peace.

Curled against him, warm and naked and replete, it occurred to her Peabody had been right again. After-sex snuggles were very, very good.

"You should sleep." He spoke quietly, stroking her back. "It's late, and there's no urgency on this one."

"I don't know. Isn't there?" She thought how lovely it would be to just close her eyes, to drift away with the scent of him all over her. "Closing the case, maybe that's not so urgent on a technical level. But if the killer did have this thing, this weapon, and still has it, ready to sell it to God knows, doesn't that make finding him, stopping him, part of the job, too?"

"Close the case, save the world?"

She tipped up her head until their eyes met. "You said you had people trying to develop this thing. Why?"

"Better you do it before the other one does. Self-preservation."

"I get that. It's always going to be that way. Bad guy has a stick, you get a knife. He has a knife, you get a stunner. The ante keeps going up. It's the way it is. So, there have to be rules and laws, and even when the line blurs, we have to be able to know who the good guys are. If I have the chance to find this guy, stop him before he sells this thing, maybe we hold all of it back for another day."

"The comp will signal when we have extrapolated data. Sleep awhile, then we'll see about saving the world."

It sounded reasonable.

The next thing she knew, the comp was beeping and she was springing up in bed—alone.

"What? Morning?"

"Nearly." Roarke stood behind the command center, shirtless, his trousers riding low on his hips. "And your Owl's come out."

"You found him—her?"

"Him," Roarke said as she leaped out of bed. He glanced over, smiled. "Come over here and I'll show you."

"I bet." She snatched at her shirt, her pants.

"Killjoy. Well, at least get us both some coffee."

"Who is he?" she demanded as she dragged on her clothes.

"That depends. He, like his victim, has gone by more than one name. This data claims him as Ivan Draski, age sixty-two, born in the Ukraine. Other data, which on the surface appears just as valid, has him as Javis Drinkle, age sixty, born in Poland. As Draski, he worked for the Freedom Republic, the underground, at the end of the Urbans, in communications and technological development. He's a scientist."

She brought the coffee, gulping some down as she read the data.

"Recruited by European Watch Network, techno research and development," Eve continued. "A gadget guy."

"An inventor, yes. He makes the toys."

"An inside guy," Eve mused. "Sure there's some field time

clocked here, but primarily during the Urbans. It's primarily science during and after that era."

"Nanotech," Roarke began. "Hyperdimensional science, bionics, psionics and so on. He's worked on all this. It looks to me, according to this data, you owe your stunner to his work, among other things. And yet I've never heard of him. They've kept him tightly wrapped for decades."

"Maybe he decided it was time for a raise and some credit." She tried to make sense of it. "So, he's lured away from EWN to HSO nearly twenty years ago. And still, I'm not seeing wet work here. He's a techno geek."

"A brilliant one. No. No black ops or wet work listed. But look there, his wife and daughter were killed twenty years ago in a brutal slaying."

"That's interesting timing," Eve said.

"Isn't it? Officially a home invasion. Unofficially, a fringe wing of EWN who'd targeted him for his knowledge and accessibility to sensitive material."

"They eat their own." When he switched to the crime-scene photos, Eve hissed out a breath. "Jesus."

"Mutilated, hacked to pieces." Roarke's voice tightened in disgust. "The girl was just twelve. The wife was a low-level agent, hardly more than a clerk. You have higher clearance, I expect."

"The writing on the wall there. Did you translate?"

"The computer recognizes it as Ukrainian for 'traitor' and 'whore.' Neither EWN nor any other official file on the matter claims credit or responsibility for the killings."

"They were on her list. On Buckley's list of hits in HSO's data banks." She called for the computer to run the list on another screen to verify. "They're there, on her list, but no employer assigned. Nobody's taken credit."

"If there's data on that, it's in another area. If there's any more data on this hit, it's been wiped or boxed. Even I can't get at it from here, or certainly not quickly. You'd have to be inside to get at it."

"He's inside; he found it." There was motive, Eve thought. There was the personal. "Why the hell didn't they destroy the file if they continued to use her, and had him on the payroll?"

"Somebody fucked up, I'd say, but at the core HSO is a bureaucracy, and bureaucracies love their paperwork."

"Does he have a fixed address?"

"Right here in New York."

She looked back over her shoulder at him. "That's too fucking easy."

"Upper East Side, in a town house he owns under the name of Frank Plutz."

"Plutz? Seriously?"

"Frank J. Plutz, employed by HSO, who lists him as Supervisor, Tech R and D, U.S. Division, in their official file. Which of course is bollocks. He's a hell of a lot more."

Now Eve studied the ID shot of a middle-aged man with a thinning crop of gray hair, a round face, a bit heavy in the chin, and mild blue eyes who smiled soberly from the wall screen.

"God. He looks harmless."

"He survived the Urban Wars in the underground, has worked for at least two intelligence organizations, neither of which worries overmuch about spilled blood. I'd say appearances are deceiving."

"I need to put a team together and go visit the deceptively harmless Mr. Plutz."

"I want to play. And I very much want to meet this man."

"I guess you've earned it."

His eyes gleamed. "If you don't put him in a cage, I wonder what I can offer him to switch to the private sector."

EIGHT

As taking down a spy wasn't her usual job, Eve opted for a small, tight team. She had two officers in soft clothes stationed at the rear of the trim Upper East Side town house, McNab handling the com along with Roarke in the unmarked van. She, along with Peabody, would take the front.

It struck her as a bit of overkill for one man, but she had to factor in that one man had over forty years of espionage experience, and had managed to slip off a ferry of more than three thousand people with a dead body.

In the van, she cued up the security tape from the transpo station. "There he is, looking harmless. Computer, enhance segment six, thirty percent."

The man currently known as Frank J. Plutz enlarged on-screen as he shuffled his way through the ticker. "Anonymous businessman, complete with what looks like a battered briefcase and a small overnight bag. Slightly overweight, slightly balding, a little saggy in the jowls."

"And this is the guy who sliced up the high-level assassin, then poofed with her." McNab, his sunny hair slicked back in a sleek tail, his earlobes weighted with a half dozen colorful studs each, shook his head. "He looks a little like my uncle Jacko. He's famed in our family for growing enormous turnips."

"He does!" Peabody gave the love of her life a slap on the shoulder. "I met him last Thanksgiving when we went to Scotland. He's adorable."

"Yeah, I'm sure this one's just as adorable as Uncle Jacko. In a 'leaving a big, messy pool of blood behind' sort of way. He got a weapon—we assume—through the scanners without a hitch. Which, unfortunately, isn't as tough as it should be. More important, from my source, he's headed or been involved in the invention and development of all manner of high-tech gadgetry, weaponry and communications in particular."

"Love to meet him," McNab said and got a quick grin from Roarke.

"Right with you."

"Hopefully you geeks can have a real nice chat soon." Eve shifted her gaze to the other monitor. "I'm not seeing any heat source in there."

"That would be because there isn't." Roarke continued the scan of the house. "I've done three scans each on heat, on movement. There's no one in there."

"Takes the fun out of it. Well, we've got the warrant. Let's go, Peabody. McNab, keep your eye on the street. If he comes home, I want to know about it."

"Mind your back, Lieutenant," Roarke said as she climbed out. "They're called spooks for a reason."

"I don't believe in spooks."

"I bet they believe in you." Peabody jumped down beside her.

Scanning the building, Eve pulled out her master as they approached the door. "We go in the way we would if we had a suspect inside. And we clear the area, room by room."

Peabody nodded. "A guy who can disappear could probably beat a heat-and-motion sensor."

Eve only shook her head, then pounded a fist on the door. "This is the police." She used her master to unlock the door, noted the standard security went from locked red to open green. "He's got cams out here. I can't see them, but he's got them. Still, no backups set on the locks, and the palm plate's not activated."

"It's like an invitation."

"We're accepting. We're going in," Eve said to alert the rest of the team.

She pulled her weapon, nodded once to Peabody. They hit the door, Peabody high, Eve low. Swept the short foyer with its iron umbrella stand and coat tree, and the narrow hallway with its frayed blue runner. At Eve's gesture they peeled off, clearing the first floor, moving to the second, then the third.

"We're clear." Eve studied the data and communication equipment, the surveillance and security equipment ranged around the modest third-floor room. "Blue team, take the first floor. Roarke, McNab, we can use you on the third floor."

"Do you think he's coming back?" Peabody wondered.

"It's a lot to leave behind. I guarantee all this is unregistered, calibrated to duck under CompuGuard radar. But no, he's done here. He's finished."

"His wife and kid?" Peabody gestured to the framed photo on the console.

"Yeah." Eve moved over, opened a mini fridge. "Water and power drinks." She hit menu on the AutoChef. "Quick, easy meals." The sort, she thought, she'd have had in her own mini fridge—when she remembered to stock it—before she'd married Roarke. "Sofa, with a pillow, a blanket, wall screen, adjoining john. He spent most of his time up here. The rest of the house, it's just space."

"It all looks so tidy, kind of homey and neat."

Eve made a sound of agreement as she turned into the next room. "VirtualFit. It's a nice unit. He wanted to keep in shape. A weight machine, muscle balls, sparring droid. Female, and at a guess, just about the height and weight of Buckley."

Eve studied the attractive blond droid currently disengaged and propped in a corner. "He practiced here." She moved across the room, opened the doors on a built-in cabinet. "Wow, toy chest."

"Holy shit." Peabody gaped at the display of weapons. "Not so much like Uncle Jacko after all."

Knives, bats, stunners, blasters, clubs, short swords, guns, throwing discs all gleamed in tidy formation.

"A couple missing," Eve noted, tapping empty holders. "From the shape, he took a couple of knives and a stunner. In one of his carry-ons, on his person."

"This is a lot to leave behind, too," Peabody commented.

"He did what he set out to do. He doesn't need them anymore." She turned as Roarke came in with McNab, and caught the gleam in Roarke's eyes as he crossed toward the weapons chest. "Don't touch."

The faintest line of irritation marred his brow, but he slipped his hands into his pockets. "A nice little collection."

"Don't get any ideas," she muttered under her breath. "It's next door you might be useful." She led the way and heard both Roarke and McNab hum in pleasure as some men would at the sight of a pretty woman.

"Geek heaven," she supposed. "Seal up, then see what you can find on all this. Peabody, let's take the second floor."

"Do you want me to get someone in to take over street surveillance?" McNab asked.

"He's not coming back. He hasn't been back since he took those weapons out of the chest. He doesn't need this place anymore."

"There are still clothes in the closet," Peabody pointed out when they started down. "I saw them when we cleared the bedroom."

"I'll tell you what we won't find. We won't find any of

his IDs, any of his emergency cash, any credit cards, passports."

She moved into the bedroom where the decor managed to be spartan in neatness and homey in its fat pillows and frayed fabrics. She opened the closet.

"Three suits—black, gray, brown. See the way they're arranged, spaces between? Probably had three more. Same with the shirts, the spare trousers. He took what he needed." She crouched, picked up a pair of sturdy black shoes, turned them over to reveal the worn-down heels, scuffed soles. "Frugal. Lived carefully, comfortably, but without any excess. I bet the neighbors are going to say what a nice, pleasant man he was. Quiet, but friendly."

"He's got drawer dividers. Cubbies for socks, boxers, undershirts. And yeah," Peabody added, "it looks like several pair are missing. Second drawer's athletic wear. T-shirts, sweats, gym socks."

"Keep at it. I'll take the second bedroom."

Across the hall in a smaller room fashioned into a kind of den, Eve opened another cabinet. She found wigs, trays of makeup, facial putty, clear boxes holding various styles of facial hair, body forms.

She saw herself reflected, front and back, in the mirror-backed doors.

She began a systematic search of the room, then the bathroom. He'd left plenty behind, she thought. Ordinary pieces of the man. Hairbrush, toothbrush, clothes, book and music discs, a pair of well-tended houseplants.

Everything well used, she thought, well tended. Very clean, ordered without being obsessive.

Food in the AutoChef, slippers by the bed. It all gave the appearance of a home someone would return to shortly. Until you noticed there was nothing important. Nothing that couldn't be easily replaced.

Except the photo over his work area, she mused. But he'd have copies of that. Certainly he'd have copies of that image that drove him. She studied the wigs and other enhancements again.

He'd left all this, and the weapons, the electronics. Left what he'd been all these years? she wondered. He'd done what he'd set out to do, so none of it mattered to him now.

Peabody came in. "I found a lock box, open and empty."

"One in here, too."

"And bits of adhesive behind drawers, behind the headboard."

Eve nodded. "Under the bathroom sinks, behind the john. He's a careful guy. I'd say he kept weapons, escape documents, in several places around the house, in case he had to get out fast."

"We're not going to find him, Dallas. He's in the wind. It's what he does."

"What he *did*. I'd say he's finished, so it depends on what he's decided to do next. Check on the first floor, will you?"

Eve went upstairs to find both Roarke and McNab huddled with the electronics. On a quartet of small monitors she saw various spaces of the house—Peabody walking down the steps, her two men searching, an empty kitchen, the street view from the front of the house. Every ten seconds, the image changed to another location.

"Guy covered his ass double," McNab told her. "This place is hot-wired, not a trick missed. Motion, heat, light, weight. He's got bug sensors every fricking where. And check it."

He flipped a switch and a panel slid open in the wall beside her. She peered in, scanned the stairs and the weapon adhered to the wall. "Emergency evac."

"Icy. Plus, he could shut and bolt that door from right here."

"It's blast-proof," Roarke added. "He's got his C and D buried on here, but we're digging it out. I'd have to say it's not as well covered as I'd expect when you consider the rest of the security."

McNab shrugged. "Maybe he figured he didn't have to worry about anyone getting this far in."

"Or he didn't care particularly what they found at this point."

She glanced back up at the photo. "Possibly. It looks like he's finished, and with or without the cloak of invisibility, gone. No reason to stay in New York. He eliminated his target. We dig here, hoping we find some link to where he might go. If we don't find it, we're going to have to contact HSO."

Roarke gave her a long, cool look. "I don't see the value of that."

"It's not a matter of value. It's SOP. He's their operative. If he's gone rabbit or rogue, and has a device that's as dangerous as this one might be, we'll need their resources."

"Give us a moment, would you, Ian?"

McNab glanced over at Roarke, then at Eve. He didn't need a sensor to feel the blips of tension and trouble. "Ah, sure. I'll . . . ah, see if I can give She-Body a hand."

"This is my job," she began as soon as they were alone. "When I report in with what we have here, Whitney's going to order me to contact Homeland and give them what I have."

"You have nothing," he said evenly, "but the nebulous connection of one Frank Plutz, on the word of an 'anonymous source' connecting him to HSO and to Buckley."

"I have him getting on the ferry, and not getting off, which secured the warrant more than the source did. I have what we found here."

"And what have you found here that verifies he's an operative for HSO, or that he targeted and killed Buckley?"

She felt her stomach muscles quiver even as her spine stiffened. "We know he has a potentially dangerous weapon. He may intend to sell that weapon. In the wrong hands—"

"Homeland's aren't the wrong hands?" Roarke demanded. "Can you stand there and tell me they aren't every bit as ruth-

less and deadly as any foreign bogeyman you can name? After
what they did to you? What they allowed to be done to you
when you were a child? Standing by, listening, for Christ's
sake, while your father beat you and raped you, all in the
hopes they could use him to catch a bigger monster?"

The quivering in her gut became a roil. "One has nothing
to do with the other."

"Bollocks. You tried to 'work' with them before, not so
long ago. And when you found murder and corruption, they
tried to ruin you. To kill you."

"I know what they did. Damn it, that wasn't the organization, as much as I despise it, but individuals inside it. Ivan
Draski is probably thousands of miles away by now. I can't
chase him outside New York. I don't *know* where he might
try to sell this thing."

"I'll look into it."

"Roarke—"

"Goddamn it, Eve, you're not going to ask me to stand
by a second time. I did what you asked before. I let it go. I
let go the ones who'd had a part in letting you be abused and
tormented."

Now it was her heart, squeezing inside a fist of tension.
"I know what you did for me. I know what it cost you to do
it. I'm not going to have a choice. It's national security. For
God's sake, Roarke, I don't want to bring them in. I don't
want anything to do with them. It makes me sick. But it's
not about me, or you, or what happened when I was eight."

"You'll give me twenty-four hours. I'm not asking," he
said before she could speak. "Not this time. You'll give me
twenty-four hours to track him."

Here was the cold and the ruthless that lurked under the
civilized. She knew it, understood it, even accepted it. "I
can stall that long. At twenty-four and one minute, I have to
turn it over."

"Then I'll be in touch." He started to walk by her,

stopped, looked into her eyes. "I'll be sorry if we're at odds on this."

"Me, too."

But when he walked out she knew sorry was sometimes all you could be.

CHAPTER
NINE

When a trail went cold, Eve's rule of thumb was go back to the beginning. For a second time she stood on the deck of the ferry under a blue summer sky.

"According to the security discs, the victim boarded first." Eve studied the route from the transport station to the deck. "He was easily a hundred passengers behind her. Several minutes behind her."

"It doesn't seem like he could've kept her in view," Peabody commented. "And from the recording, it didn't look like he tried to."

"Two likely scenarios. He'd managed to get a tracker on her, or had set up this meet in advance. Since I can't think of any reason he'd take chances or play the odds, my money is he did both."

"We haven't turned up a thing that points to her meeting a third party on Staten Island."

Eve huffed out a breath. "I'd say we haven't turned up a lot of things. Yet." She started up to the second deck. "She went up here. We've got that from the Grogan kid's camera.

The ride over takes less than a half hour, so if she had a meet, and if she planned to make an exchange, she wouldn't have waited too long once they left port. The best we can gauge, Carolee went into the restroom less than halfway through the trip. About ten minutes in."

"But since she doesn't remember, and we've got no body to calculate TOD, we don't know if Buckley was already dead when Carolee went in."

"Odds are." Eve stood at the rail, imagining the roll and hum of the ferry, the crowds, the view. "Lots of excitement as people are boarding, right? Crowds, happy tourists off on an adventure. People would be securing their places at the rails, grabbing a snack, taking pictures. If I'm Buckley, I take my position, scope it out."

She took a seat on the bench. "Sitting here, and you can bet she sat here before or she'd never have picked or agreed to the location, she can judge the crowd, the traffic, the timing. If I'm Buckley, I move to the meet location as close as possible to leaving port."

Rising, Eve strolled off in the direction of the restroom. "That's around ten minutes before Grogan went in. Plenty of time for the kill. If Grogan had gone in before the attack, why not let her finish up, get out? If she'd gone in during, she should've been able to call out or get out and raise an alarm. She went down at the dividing point between stalls and sinks. That's where the sweepers found trace of her blood and skin from her head hitting the floor. She'd just turned at the wall. And got an eyeful."

"Do you think Mira can help her remember?"

"I think it's worth a shot. Meanwhile . . ." Eve detoured toward concession. "Before the eyeful, Carolee and the kid—"

"Pete."

"Right. They start toward the concession area, then swing to the restrooms." Eve followed the most logical route. "Stand here, discuss. Wait for me, blah blah. Carolee watches the kid go in, then notices the sign on the door. Debates, then decides to give it a try after all. And after that, doesn't remember. So we reconstruct. Going with the theory the meet was set in advance, and the murder was premeditated, Draski would go in first. It's a women's room; he's a guy."

"Right. Well, he might've slipped in when most people are focused on the view, but the Out of Order sign. He'd be smarter to go in looking like maintenance. A uniform."

"Which he could've slipped into right next door." Eve gestured toward the other restroom. "If we're dealing with premeditated, and a need to hide or transport the body, he'd need means. No one would question a maintenance guy going into an out-of-order bathroom pushing a hamper."

"None of the hampers were missing."

"He had an hour to put it back. He comes out of there"— Eve pointed toward the men's room—"goes in here. Who notices? Apparently nobody. Inside to wait for Buckley."

Eve pushed open the door. "I doubt he wasted much time once she came in."

"No way to lock the door from inside," Peabody began, "and no way to rig it shut because he needed Buckley to get in."

"Yeah, so he wouldn't waste much time. He'd want to make sure she had the payment, she'd want to make sure he had the device. Just business."

The congealed pool of blood, smeared now from several samplings, spoke to the nature of that business. As did the slight scent of chemicals, the faint layer of dust left by the sweepers spoke of the results of that business.

As did the long-bladed knife on the floor.

"Record on," Eve ordered, then, avoiding the blood still on the floor, approached the knife.

"But . . . how the hell did that get here?" Peabody demanded. "We've got the entire ferry covered with guards."

"Freaking invisibility cloak," Eve muttered, "answers that. So the first question is, why is it here?" She studied it where it lay. "Dagger style, about a six-inch blade. It looks like bone. That would explain how he got it through the security scanners. The natural material would pass, and it's likely he had a safe slot in that briefcase he carried on. Some protection against the scanner for shape, weight."

She coated her hands before lifting the knife. "Good weight. Good grip." Testing, she turned, swiped the air. "Good reach. You don't have to get close in. Arm's length plus six. Me, I'd use a wrist trigger. Click, it's in your hand, swipe, slice the throat."

Peabody rubbed her own. "Have you ever thought about going into the assassination game?"

"Killing for business, for profit, that was her line, not his. His was personal. Sure took him long enough though." She judged the spatter, the pool, swiped a second time, circled, jabbed, sliced.

"And now he goes to the trouble to put the weapon in our hand so we can see what and how."

"Bragging maybe."

Eve turned the blade, studied the blood smears. "It doesn't feel like bragging." She took out an evidence bag, sealed the weapon inside, tagged it. Holding it, she glanced toward the door. "If Carolee came in now, she'd see him, see the body as soon as she turned for the stalls. That puts, what, about ten feet between them, with her less than two from the door. What would most people do when they walk in on a murder?"

"Scream and run," Peabody provided. "And she should've made it, or at least gotten close. Plus, if he'd gone after her like that, you'd think he'd have stepped in some of the blood. She could've fainted. Just passed out cold. Smacked her head on the floor."

"Yeah, or he could've stunned her. Dropped her. A low setting. That would give him a little time to figure out how to handle the variable. He's got to get the body out, but he'd have prepped for that. Lined the hamper maybe, a body bag certainly. Load it up—along with the uniform. It had to be stained with blood."

"Then he'd use the memory blaster on Carolee as she came to."

Eve cocked her eyebrows at the term "memory blaster." "When she's under, he tells her she's going to give him a hand. He'd go out first."

"Mojo the people on this sector of the deck. He could do that as he made his way to wherever he wanted to go. It's one frosty toy."

"It's not a toy. It's lethal. If it does what it purports, it strips you of your will. You lose who and what you are." Worse than death to her mind was loss of self. "You're nothing but a droid until the effects wear off." She studied the knife again. "Sticks, stones, knives, guns, blasters, bombs. Some-body's always looking for something a little juicier. This." Through the evidence bag, she hefted the knife again. "It can take your life. This other thing, it takes your mind. I'd rather face the blade."

She glanced at her wrist unit. Roarke's twenty-four hours was down to twenty and counting. No matter what it cost her, she couldn't give him a minute more.

The little bakery with its sunny two-tops and displays of glossy pastries might have seemed an odd place to meet with a weapons runner, but Roarke knew Julian Chamain's proclivities.

He knew, too, that the bakery, run by Chamain's niece, was swept twice daily for listening devices, and the walls and windows shielded against electronic eyes and ears.

What was said there, stayed there.

Chamain, a big man whose wide face and wide belly proclaimed his affection for his niece's culinary skills, shook Roarke's hand warmly, then gestured to the seat across the table.

"It's been some time," Chamain said, with a hint of his native country in the words. "Four, five years now."

"Yes. You look well."

Chamain laughed, a big, basso bark, as he patted his generous belly. "Well fed, indeed. Ah, here, my niece's daughter, Marianna." Chamain gave the young woman a smile as she served coffee and a plate of small pastries. "This is an old friend."

"Pleased to meet you. Only two, Uncle Julian." She wagged her finger. "Mama said. Enjoy," she added to Roarke as she bustled away.

"Try the éclair," Chamain told Roarke. "Simple, but exquisite. So, marriage is good?"

"Very. And your wife, your children?"

"Thriving. I have six grandchildren now. The reward for growing old. You should start a family. Children are a man's truest legacy."

"Eventually." Understanding his role, Roarke sampled an éclair. "You're right. Excellent. It's a pretty space, Julian. Cheerful and well run. Another kind of legacy."

"It pleases me. The tangible, the every day, a bit of the sweet." Chamain popped a tiny cream puff in his mouth, closed his eyes in pleasure. "The love of a good woman. I think of retiring and enjoying it all more. You keep busy, I hear, but have also retired from some enterprises."

"The love of a good woman," Roarke repeated.

"So, we've both been lucky there. I wonder why you asked to meet me, and share pastries and coffee."

"We were occasionally associates, or friendly competitors. We dealt honestly with each other either way. We were always able to discuss business, and important commodities. I feel we've lost time."

He watched Chamain's eyebrows raise before the man lifted his coffee for a long, slow sip. "Time is a valuable commodity. If it could be bought and sold, the bidding would be very steep. Time wins wars as much as blood. What man wouldn't want his enemy to lose time?"

"If a weapon existed that could cause such a thing, it would be worth a great deal on the market."

"A very great deal. Such a weapon, and the technology to create others like it, would command billions. Blood would be shed as well as fortunes spent to possess it. Dangerous games played."

"How much might you be willing to pay, should such a thing exist?"

Chamain smiled, chose another pastry. "Me, I'm old-fashioned, and close to retirement. If I were younger, I would seek out partners, form alliances and enter the bidding. Perhaps a man of your age, of your position, has considered such a thing."

"No. It isn't a commodity that fits my current interests. In any case, I would think the bidding would be closed at this date."

"The window closes at midnight. Games, *mon ami*, dangerous games." He gave a long sigh. "It makes me wish I were younger, but some games are best watched from the sidelines, especially when the field is bloody."

"I wonder if the people at home are aware of the game, its current status."

"The people at home seem to have misjudged the game, and the players. Shortsighted, you could say, and their ears not as close to the ground as they might be. Women are ruthless creatures, and excellent in business. Persuasive."

Roarke said nothing for a moment. "If I were a betting man, and on the sidelines, I'd be interested to know a key player has been eliminated, and she's no longer on the field."

"Is that so?" Chamain pursed his lips at the information, then nodded. "Ah, well, as I said, a dangerous game. Try a napoleon."

Within the hour, armed with the cryptic pieces Chamain

offered, Roarke sat in his private office. Clearly Buckley intended to make an exchange for the device—or more likely to kill the delivery boy and walk away with it. It was greed and arrogance that killed as much as the blade. Had it been self-defense all along, or a setup for revenge?

That wasn't his problem, but Eve's, he thought. His would be to track down Ivan Draski and the device. She'd keep her word on the twenty-four hours, just as he had kept his in not seeking revenge on the operatives who'd been a part of allowing her to be tormented and raped as a child, who'd allowed that child to wander the streets, broken and dazed, after she'd killed to save herself.

He'd destroyed the data on those men, for her sake. But their names were etched in his mind. So, he began the process of hacking his way through the agency, and to those men. On a secondary search he began the hunt for Ivan Draski, and Lost Time.

Well into his tasks, he glanced at the display of his pocket 'link when it signaled.

"Yes, Ian."

"As promised, I'm tagging you first, and praying Dallas doesn't skin my ass for it."

"I wouldn't worry."

"Not your ass," McNab replied. "I got through the shields and fail-safes. This guy's mega—more mega because it barely shows that he took down some of those shields and fail-safes so somebody with solid skills could get through."

"Is that so?" Roarke commented.

"That's my take. I'm saying I've got serious skills, but it should've taken me a couple days to get through, not a couple hours."

"Which means he wanted the information to be found." Roarke scanned his own data, jumbled the information and the theories together. "Interesting. What did you find?"

"He's got megabytes on this Dana Buckley, a massive

file on her, complete with surveillance—eyes and ears. I did a skim, and if half this stuff is true, she was one bad bitch."

"And he was following her, and documenting."

"Keeping tabs for sure, back, it's looking like, around six months. The thing is, the data goes back years and from a variety of sources. But he didn't start to collect it here until about six months ago. A lot of high-level stuff. I probably don't have the security clearance to skim, but, hey, just doing my job. But here's what's really the frost on the ice."

"He's running an auction."

"Shit." On-screen, McNab's face fell. "Why have I worked my personal motherboard to the bone? But you only got it partly right. *She's* running the auction, which is a hell of a trick, seeing she's dead."

"Ah." Roarke sat back as it fell into place for him. "Yes, that's clever."

"It's running out of a remote location. It bounces all over hell and back, scrambling the signal. I wouldn't've found the source if I wasn't right at ground zero. And, well, gotta be on the straight, if he hadn't left the bread crumbs. Upper East Side address. Swank. When I run it, I get it's owned by Dolores Gregory. That's one of Buckley's aliases."

"So it is. That's good data. Now you'd better call your lieutenant."

CHAPTER

TEN

Using her master, Eve opened the locks and shut down the security on the Upper East Side apartment. "That was too easy," she told Peabody. "Just like the Plutz town house. We go in hot."

She drew her weapon, went through the door for a first sweep.

Quiet, she thought as she worked right and Peabody left. A lot of expensive space filled with expensive things. The wall of windows led to a terrace lofty enough to provide a river view. Inside, rich fabrics showcased gleaming wood, and art dominated the walls. The same held true in the master bedroom where the closet held a forest of clothes.

"Some digs," Peabody commented. "I think some of those paintings are originals. I guess assassins rate a high pay grade."

"It's the opposite of Draski. She lived high, he lived low. Easy to underestimate somebody who lives the quiet life."

"Easy to get cocky," Peabody added, "when you live the high."

"Yeah, it is." Eve gestured to the security pad on the second bedroom doorway. It blinked an open green.

"Boy, that was careless of her."

"Not her. He laid those bread crumbs, he lowered the security. We're exactly where he wants us to be." She pushed open the door, swept it, then holstered her weapon.

The room was cold, nearly frigid. A way to keep the body as fresh as possible, she thought as she studied Dana Buckley. He'd arranged the bloody shell of her in a chair angled to face a framed photo of his wife and daughter, and the single rose he'd placed by it.

"Well." Peabody hissed out a breath. "She's not lost anymore."

"Call it in. You'd better go get the field kits."

While she waited, Eve studied the room. Her lair, she thought. She expected they'd find the equipment unregistered, and much of the data on it illegally hacked. Not so different from her killer's, she thought, right down to the photograph.

On the wall screen the current status of the bidding was displayed. Up to four-point-four billion, she mused, with several hours yet to go.

He hadn't taken the body for proof. Not for a trophy, and only in part to gain that time. In the end he'd brought it here so while her greed ran behind her back she would stare sightlessly at the innocents she'd killed.

He'd taken the body, she thought, to pay homage to his family.

"We've got an e-team and sweepers on the way." Peabody opened a field kit, passed Eve the Seal-It.

Eve nodded and thought they'd find nothing he hadn't wanted them to find. "I want all the data found copied. We'll have to turn it over to whatever agency the commander orders, but we'll have backup." She turned to her partner. "I think we've just spearheaded a breakdown on a whole bunch of really bad guys. The sort of thing that leaks to the media."

"I don't know whether to be happy or scared."

"Be satisfied. Now let's do the job and deal with her. Record on."

Roarke sat back, absorbing the data he'd just uncovered. Odd, he thought, the world was a very odd and ironically small place. And the people in it were never completely predictable. He saved and copied the data, slipped the copy into his pocket.

He walked to the house monitor. "Where is Summerset?"

Summerset is in the parlor, main level.

"All right, then, a fine place for a chat."

As he came downstairs he heard voices, and the roll of Summerset's amused laughter. It wasn't unprecedented for Summerset to have company in the house, but it certainly wasn't usual.

Curious, he stepped in. Then stopped and shook his head. "Aye, unpredictable."

"Roarke, I'm glad you've come down. I didn't want to disturb you, but I'm happy to introduce you to an old friend. Ivan Draski."

As the man rose, Roarke crossed the room to shake hands with his wife's current quarry.

"Ivan and I worked together in very dark times. He was hardly more than a boy, but made himself indispensable. We haven't seen each other in years, so we've been catching up on old times, and new."

"Really?" Roarke slid his hands into his pocket where the disc bumped up against the gray button he carried for luck, and for love. "How new?"

"We haven't quite caught up to the present." Ivan smiled a little. "I thought that should wait until your wife comes home. I believe she'll have an interest."

"I'll fetch more cups for coffee." Summerset laid a hand briefly on Ivan's shoulder before leaving the room.

"Are you armed?" Roarke asked.

"No." Ivan lifted his arms, inviting a search. "I'm not here to bring harm to anyone."

"Have a seat, then, and maybe you should bring Summerset and myself up-to-date."

Ivan sat, and an instant later Galahad jumped into his lap. "He's a nice cat."

"We like him."

"I don't keep pets," Ivan continued as he stroked Galahad's length. "I couldn't handle the idea of having a living thing depending on me again. And droids, well, it's not the same, is it? I don't want to bring trouble into your home, or cause my old friend distress. If it had been anyone but your wife involved in this, I believe I would be somewhere else."

"Why my wife?"

"I'd like to tell her," Ivan said as Summerset came back.

"The lieutenant's come through the gate." He set the cup down to pour.

"This should be interesting," Roarke murmured. He waved off the coffee Summerset offered, deciding he might need both hands.

Eve walked into the house and frowned. It was rare not to find Summerset lurking in the foyer with the cat at his heels. She heard the rattle of china from the parlor, hesitated at the base of the stairs.

Roarke came to the doorway and said her name.

"Good, you're here. We need to talk. The situation's changed."

"Oh, it has, yes."

"We might as well have this out before I—" She broke off at the parlor doorway when she spotted the man she hunted sitting cozily in a chair with her cat on his lap. She drew her weapon. "Son of a bitch."

"Have you lost your mind!" Summerset exploded as she stormed across the room.

"Get out of the way or I'll stun you first."

He stood his ground while shock and fury radiated from him. "I won't have a guest, and a dear friend, threatened in our home."

"Friend?" She flicked a glance toward Roarke, a heated one.

"Don't waste your glares on me. I just got here myself." But he touched a hand to her arm. "You don't need that."

"My prime suspect is sitting in my house, petting my cat, and you're all having coffee? Move aside," she said coldly to Summerset, "or I swear to God—"

Ivan spoke in a language she didn't understand. Summerset turned sharply, stared. His answer was just as unintelligible, and with a tone of incredulity.

"I'm sorry, that's rude." Ivan kept his hands in plain sight. "I've just told my friend that I've killed a woman. He didn't know. I hope there's no trouble for him over this. I hope I can explain. Will you let me explain? Here, in an easy way, with a friend. After, I'll go with you if that's your decision."

Eve skirted around Summerset. She lowered her weapon, but kept it drawn. "What are you doing here?"

"Waiting for you."

"For me?"

"I feel you need an explanation. You need information. I won't try to harm you, any of you. This man?" He gestured to Summerset. "I owe him my life. What belongs to him is sacred to me."

"Brandy, I think." Roarke handed Summerset a snifter he'd filled. "Instead of coffee." And gave another to Ivan.

"Thank you. You're very kind. I killed the woman calling herself Dana Buckley. You know this already, and, I think, some of the how. I read a great deal about you in the night, Lieutenant. You're smart and clever, good at your work. But the why matters, it must, when it's life and death. You know this," he said, searching her face. "I think you believe this."

"She killed your wife and daughter."

His eyes widened in surprise. "You work quickly. They were beautiful and innocent. I didn't protect them. I loved my work in my own homeland." He glanced at Summerset. "The purpose, the challenge, the deep belief in making a difference."

"You were—are—a scientist," Eve interrupted. "I read your file."

"Then you're very good indeed. Did you find the rest?"

"Yes. Just shortly ago," Roarke answered. "I'm very sorry. Homeland wanted to recruit him," he told Eve, "possibly use him as a mole or simply bring him over."

"I was happy where I was. I believed in what I was doing."

"They considered various options," Roarke continued. "Abducting him, torture, abducting his child, discrediting him. The decision was, as time was of some essence, to strip him of his ties, and offer him not only asylum but revenge."

"They sent that woman to murder my wife, my child, to make it seem like my own people had ordered it. They showed me documentation, gave me the name of the assassins, the orders to terminate me and my family. I should have been home, you see, but I had car trouble that delayed me. They'd rigged it, of course, but I believed them. I of all people should have known how these things can be faked, but I was grieving, I was wild with grief, and I believed. I betrayed good men and women because I believed the lie and was happy to take my pound of flesh. And I became one of them. Everything I've done for these twenty years has been on the blood of my wife and child. They killed them to use me."

"Why now?" Eve demanded. "Why execute her now, and with such theatrics?"

"Six months ago I found the file. I was searching for some

old data, and found it. The man who'd ordered the murders is long dead, so perhaps there was carelessness. Or perhaps someone wanted me to find it. It's a slippery world we live in."

He stroked the cat methodically. "I thought of many ways to kill her." He sighed. "I've been one for the laboratory for a very long time, but I began to train. My body, with weapons. I trained every day, like the old days," he said with a smile for Summerset. "I had purpose again. I found my way with Lost Time. So apt, isn't it? All the time I'd lost. Time she'd cost me, had stolen from my wife, my baby."

"I'm sorry, Ivan." Summerset laid a comforting hand on his friend's arm. "I know what it is to lose a child."

"She was so bright, the light . . . the proof of light after all those dark times. And this woman snuffed her out, for money. If you've read her files, you know what she was."

He paused, sipped brandy, settled himself again. "I formed the plan. I was always good at tactics and strategy, you remember."

"Yes, I remember," Summerset concurred.

"I had to move quickly, to leak the data to her, to paint the picture that I was dissatisfied with my position, my pay, and might be willing to bargain for better."

"You let her make the approach, let her pick the time and the place so she believed she had the advantage."

Now he smiled at Eve. "She wasn't as smart as you. Once, perhaps, but she was arrogant and greedy. She never intended to pay me for the device and the files I'd stolen. She would kill me, have the device and all the records on it, while others competed. She had no allegiance, you see, to any person, agency, any cause. She liked to kill. It's in her psych file."

Eve nodded. "I've read it."

Again his eyes widened before he glanced toward Roarke. "I think you may be better even than the rumors. How I'd enjoy talking with you."

"I've thought the same."

"In my business there's no law, as in yours," Ivan said to Eve. "No police, so to speak, where I could go and say this woman murdered my family. She was paid to do so. It's . . . business, so there's no punishment, no justice. I planned, I researched and I accessed her computers. I'm very good at my work, too. I knew before she arranged the meet what she intended. To take the money, disable or kill me, then—" He gestured to the case beside his chair. "May I?"

"No. She was carrying this," Eve said as she rose to retrieve the case, "when she got on the ferry."

"It's a bomb. Disabled," he said quickly. "It's configured inside the computer. It's rather small, but powerful. It would have done considerable damage to that section of the ferry. There were so many people there. Children. Their lives meant nothing to her. They would be a distraction."

"Like fireworks?"

"Harmless." He smiled again.

"Let me have that." Roarke glanced at Summerset, got a nod, as he took the case from Eve. And opened it.

"Wait. Jesus!"

"Disabled," he assured Eve after a glance. "I've seen this system before.

"You know, I think how we came to meet. The location was her choice," Ivan added. "She thought of me as old, harmless, someone who creates gadgets, we'll say, rather than one who would use them. But old skills can come back."

"Six months to refine your skills," Eve said, "and set the trap."

"Maybe there was a cold madness in the planning, in my dedication to it. Even so, I don't regret. I thought to do it quickly. Slit her throat. Put her in the hamper. I'd use the device to get away."

"How?" Eve demanded. "How did you get off the damn ferry?"

"Oh. I had with me a motorized inflatable." He shifted to Roarke as he spoke now, and his face became animated. "It's much smaller than anything used, as yet, in the military or private sectors. Inactivated, it's the size of a toiletry kit you might use for travel. And the motor itself—"

"Okay." Eve cut him off. "I get it."

"Yes, well." Ivan drew in a long breath. "I had thought I'd do what I'd set out to do quickly, then I'd disappear. But I . . . I can't even remember, not clearly, after I looked in her eyes, saw her shock, saw her death. I can't remember. I think I will someday, and it will be very hard."

Tears glinted in his eyes, and his hand trembled slightly as he drank more brandy. "But I looked down at what I'd done. So much blood. The way I'd found my wife and daughter, in so much blood. There was a stunner on the floor. She must have tried to stop me, I'm not sure. I picked it up. Then the woman came in."

"You didn't kill her when you had the chance."

He shot Eve a shocked stare. "No. No, of course not. She'd done nothing. Still, I couldn't let her just . . . It happened so quickly. I used the weapon on her, and she fell. I remember thinking, this is very unfortunate, a very unfortunate turn of events. In the old days, you thought on your feet or died. Or someone else did."

"You used the device on her when she came around, and took her with you," Eve supplied.

"Yes. I told her to hide. You can influence people when they're under. She was to hide until she heard the alarm. I set it on her wrist unit. Then she was to go back where she came from. She wouldn't remember. She looked so frightened when she came in and saw what I'd done. I didn't want her to remember. I saw her with her children when we boarded. A lovely family. I hope she's all right."

"She's fine. Why the fireworks?"

"A good distraction. You'd think I used them to get away, and I'd already be away. And my little girl loved fireworks.

You know the rest, I think. You've hacked into my system at home, and into hers. You have a very good e-team."

"Why did you come here?" Eve asked. "You could be thousands of miles away."

"To see an old friend." He glanced at Summerset. "Because you were involved."

"What difference does it make who led the investigation?"

"All," he said simply. "It was a kind of sign, a connection I couldn't ignore." He looked at Eve then with both understanding and sorrow. "I know what they did to you. They ignored the cries of a child being brutalized. They killed my child, who must have cried out for me in fear and pain. The same man ordered both. The slaughter of my family, and some years before the sacrifice of a child's body and mind."

He sighed when Eve said nothing. "I couldn't ignore that. It seemed too important. You and Mylia would be of an age now, had she lived. You lived, and you're part of the family of my old friend. How could I ignore that?"

"How did you come by that information?" Eve asked, her voice flat.

"I . . . accessed it when you married. Because of my friend. I couldn't contact you," he said to Summerset. "It might cause you trouble, but I wanted to know your family. So I looked, and I found. I'm sorry for what was done to you. He's dead, the one who ordered the listening post to do nothing to interfere. Years ago," Ivan added. "I don't know if that comforts you. It comforts me because I believe I would have killed him, killed again if he wasn't dead."

"It doesn't matter. It's done."

He nodded. "So is this. There are dirty pockets in the well of the organization. She, this woman, was one of the things that crawled around inside those pockets. But still, I took her life, and it doesn't, as I thought it would, balance the scales. Nothing can. These people shaped our lives, pieces of our lives, without giving us a choice. They took something deeply personal from us. So, when I learned it was you looking for me, I had to come. If I may?"

He held up two fingers, pointed them at his jacket pocket. At her nod, he reached in carefully and slid out what looked like an oversized 'link.

"It's only the casing," he said when both Eve and Roarke lunged for it. "I dismantled and destroyed the rest. And all the data pertaining to it."

Roarke let out a breath. "Well, bugger it."

Ivan laughed, then blinked in surprise at the sound. "It needed to be done, though I admit it was difficult. So much work." He sighed over it. "If I'm arrested, they'll come for me. Or others like them will come. I have knowledge and skill. Your law, your rules, even your diligence won't stop them. I don't say this to save myself," he said gently. "But because I know they'll find a way to make me use my knowledge and skill for them."

"He saved lives, innocent lives, on that ferry," Summerset said. "He's certainly saved others, perhaps scores of others, by destroying that thing."

"That's not why I went there. I went to kill. The lieutenant knows that. The rest is circumstance. I'm content to leave this in her hands. Content to face justice."

"Justice?" Summerset snarled at the word. "How is this justice?" He rose, rounded on Eve. "How can you even consider—"

"Shut it down. Don't," she added to Roarke before he could speak. She paced away to stand at the window and wait for the war inside her to claim a victor.

"I saw her files, as I'm sure you wanted me to when we found her body. She kept reports and photos of her kills like a scrapbook. She's what I work against every day. So is what you did on that ferry."

"Yes," Ivan said quietly. "I know."

"They will come for you, and whatever obstacles I put in their way so you can face justice won't be enough to stop them. I consider this matter out of my jurisdiction, and will certainly be told the same when I contact HSO to report what I've learned up to the time I walked into this house."

She turned back, spoke briskly. "This is an internal HSO matter, involving one of their people and a freelance assassin they have previously employed. It's possible this is a matter of national security, and I'd be derelict in my duty if I didn't report what my investigation has turned up. I'm going to go up to my office, inform my commander of my findings and follow his directive. You'd better say good-bye to your friend," she told Summerset.

She turned to Ivan, his pleasant face and mild eyes. "Disappear. You've probably got an hour, two at the outside, to get lost. Don't come back here."

"Lieutenant," Ivan began, but she turned her back and walked out of the room.

EPILOGUE

Roarke found her in her office, pacing like a caged cat. "Eve."

"I don't want any damn coffee. I want a damn drink."

"I'll get us both one." He touched the wall panel and chose a bottle of wine from inside. "He was telling the truth. I got deep enough to find considerable data on him, on his work prior to Homeland, on the decision to kill his family and plant evidence that led to his own organization."

He drew the disc from his pocket. "I made you a copy." He handed her the wine, set the disc on her desk. "And he was telling the truth when he said they, or others like them, would come for him. He would have self-terminated before he worked for anyone like them again."

"I know that. I saw that."

"I know a decision like this is difficult for you. Painfully. Just as you know I stand across the line so it wouldn't be difficult for me. I'm sorry."

"It shouldn't be for me to decide. It's not my place, it's

not my job. It's why there's a system, and mostly the system works."

"This isn't your system, Eve. These things have their own laws, their own system, and too many of those pockets inside them don't quibble about letting a child be tortured, don't lose sleep over ordering the death of a child to reach the goal of the moment."

She took a long sip. "I can justify it. I can justify what I just did because I know that's true. It's not my system. I can justify it by knowing if Buckley had gotten the upper hand yesterday, Carolee Grogan would be dead, and that kid waiting for his mother outside the door would be blown to pieces along with dozens of others. I can justify it knowing if I arrested him, I would be killing him."

She picked up the disc from her desk, and remembering what he'd once done for her, snapped it in two. "Don't let him come here again."

He shook his head, then framed her face and kissed her. "It takes more than skill and duty to make a good cop, to my way of thinking. It takes an unfailing sense of right and wrong."

"It's a hell of a lot easier when they don't overlap. I have to get my report together and contact the commander. And for God's sake, get that boomer out of the house. I don't care if it is defused."

"I'll take care of it."

Alone, she sat down to organize her notes into a cohesive report. She glanced over when the cat padded in, with Summerset behind him.

"Working," she said briefly, then frowned when he set a plate with an enormous chocolate chip cookie on her desk. "What's this?"

"A cookie, as any fool could see. It'll spoil your dinner, but . . ." He shrugged, started out. He paused at the door without turning around. "He was a hero at a time when the world desperately needed them. He would be dead before the night was over if you'd taken him in. I want you to know that. To know you saved a life today."

She sat back, staring at the empty doorway, when he'd left her. Then she scanned her notes, the report on-screen, the photographs of the dead. They were the lost, weren't they? All those lives taken. Maybe, in a way that nudged up against that line between right and wrong, she was standing for the lost.

She had to hope so.

Breaking off a hunk of cookie, she got back to work.

M995T1011